AN IMPOSSIBLE DILEMMA

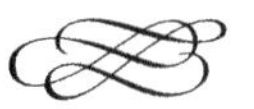

NETTA NEWBOUND

Junction Publishing

United Kingdom - New Zealand

Junctionpublishing@outlook.com

www.junction-publishing.com

Ordering Information:

Quantity sales. Special discounts are available on quantity purchases by corporations, associations, and others. For details, contact the "Special Sales Department" at the email address above.

An Impossible Dilemma/Netta Newbound -- 2nd ed.

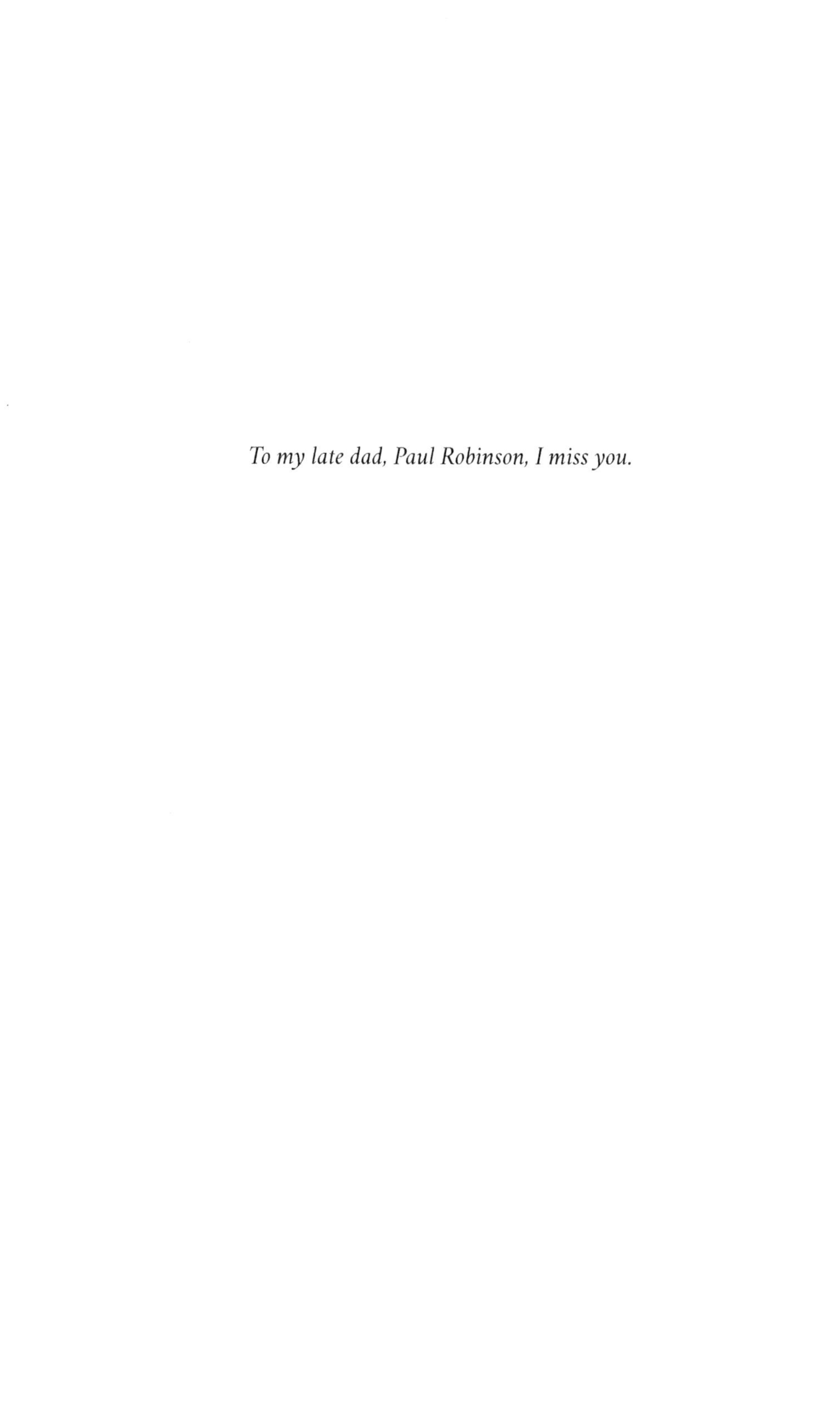

To my late dad, Paul Robinson, I miss you.

CHAPTER 1

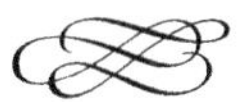

"She looks terrible, Jon. We should have taken her straight to the hospital."

The shrill peal of the surgery phone made my stomach twirl. I spun around as Stacey, the pretty, young blonde receptionist lifted the receiver, her voice all sickly sweetness.

I glanced around the room. Apart from an elderly gentleman dozing in the corner, we were the only people waiting to see the doctor. The clinic had had a makeover since my last visit—the pale cream walls, glossy magazines, and plush maroon covers on the chairs presented the image of an upmarket clinic instead of the laid-back, sleepy practice we knew it to be.

"Stop being a fusspot, Victoria. We're here now." Jonathan stroked Emily's forehead. She lay half on his knee with her legs sprawled out on the bench seat beside him. He pinched her chin and smiled down at her. "Mummy's being a fusspot, isn't she, Miss Em?"

Emily nodded, her large grey eyes rolling as he stroked her golden brown curls.

"You know he's going to say she has a virus or some other

rubbish. The hospital would at least do tests," I said, stopping mid-pace in front of them.

Jon reached for my hand and pulled me down beside him. "I get that you're worried, Vic. We both are. And if things are no clearer after we've seen the doc, we'll go straight to the hospital."

"You promise?"

"I promise."

I bent to kiss the top of my daughter's head. Her eyelids fluttered and closed again.

As I sat up, I noticed Stacey gazing at us with interest. The village nosy parker was probably looking for a story to keep her friends entertained. Our eyes met, and she quickly turned away.

I chewed at the inside of my cheek, a habit I'd formed when in stressful situations as a child. It would be sore later.

At the sound of a buzzer, we both turned towards Stacey, who got to her feet and nodded at the old man. "You can go through now, Mr Delaney."

All of a sudden, I thought I was going to vomit. I needed to get out. "I'm going for some fresh air. Give me a shout when it's our turn," I said, kissing Emily once more before heading for the double doors.

Outside, the chilly afternoon wind took my breath. I sat on the cold, stone surgery steps, pulled my orange woollen jumper over my knees, and hugged my legs. Daffodils filled the two garden squares on either side of the steps.

I sighed as the familiar hollow ache resurfaced between my ribs. Memories of my mother's daffodil-laden casket brought tears to my eyes. I missed her so much. My fingers closed around her gold locket that I wore on a chain around my neck.

My legs began to bounce with irritation; the long wait had my nerves at screaming point. One of the problems with living in the country was the slow pace of village life. We'd been here almost six years, and I was still trying to acclimatise.

I was used to large surgeries with umpteen doctors to choose from. Here you got who were given, like it or lump it.

We'd sold our veterinary clinic in Manchester after Frank, Jon's father, had suffered a stroke. Jon was an only child, and the responsibilities of the farm fell solely at his size nines.

Jonathan had been born on the farm, and Doctor Taylor, our family doctor, had even delivered him—as he had most of the children in the area. But Doctor Taylor had gone to New Zealand for a year, leaving a locum in his place.

A hammering on the window behind me jolted me from my daydream. Jonathan was standing behind the glass, waving at me to hurry.

Doctor Davies seemed too young to be fully qualified. He had a large moon-shaped face with a helmet of floppy, fine blond hair atop a head that looked too big for his weedy body.

"Hello—this must be Emily," the doctor said with an overused, insincere smile.

"Hello," Emily whispered.

"Are you feeling poorly, sweetheart?"

I inhaled noisily and raised my eyes to the wooden panelled ceiling before refocusing on Jon.

Jonathan's eyes flashed at me as he gave his head a tight shake.

I shrugged and turned away, fiddling with the locket at my throat.

Emily nodded and closed her eyes, leaning against Jon's shoulder again.

"She's not been right for a while, doctor. She's lethargic and clumsy. I don't know—just off, somehow," Jonathan said.

The doctor nodded, raised his eyebrows and began typing on a keyboard in front of him.

"I've been doing some research and I'm positive she has some kind of neurological disorder," I said.

Doctor Davies stopped typing and took off his frameless

glasses. His beady brown eyes locked on mine. "Are you a doctor, Mrs—," he glanced at the computer screen, "—Lyons?"

"A vet. I'm a vet—we're vets," I wiggled a finger between Jon and myself. "And although I'm not a doctor—doctor, I know my stuff, *and* I know my daughter."

The doctor cleared his throat and sighed. His hands were in a praying position in front of his face, the index fingers touching the tip of his nose, contemplating me.

"I'm sure you do, Mrs Lyons, but let's go through this from the beginning for my benefit, shall we? Then I will try to make my own diagnosis, and we can compare notes later. Is that okay with you?" he said.

His patronizing attitude was starting to get my back up. I bit my lip and stifled a sigh, trying to eyeball Jonathan, who did his best to avoid my stare. Of course the doctor needed to make his own diagnosis, but I didn't want him poo-pooing Em's symptoms and just throwing a course of antibiotics at her.

"It started a few months ago," I said.

"Months?" the doctor's eyebrows furrowed.

"Yeah, but nothing bad. Just subtle changes at first. Jonathan blamed the clumsiness on her age."

"Typical five-year-old, doc," Jon said. "Too impatient to get where she wants to go. She climbs over anything in her path. I thought her falls were nothing more than that."

The doctor nodded. "So what changed?"

"This weekend, her coordination deteriorated. She struggled to feed herself and she was so clumsy she could fall over her own feet from standing still." I bent forward and stroked Emily's face.

"That's why we made an appointment first thing this morning." Jon said.

I nodded. "She slept most of the day, but by this afternoon, when I tried to wake her up, her speech had become slurred. She sounded drunk. Obviously I panicked and rang Jonathan, insisting he come home immediately. I wanted to take her straight to the hospital, but he said we should keep the appointment."

"Do you want to pop Emily onto the table and let me have a quick look at her?" He indicated the examination table in a curtained-off area at the side of the room.

Jonathan carried Emily to the table and tried to lie her down, but she held her body stiff and refused to cooperate.

"Filly, I want Filly," she cried.

"Shit," I said, looking around. "Where's Filly, Jon?"

"At home?" He shrugged.

"No, she had her in the truck."

"She must still be in the truck, then."

"I'll check," I said. "Emily, let the nice doctor have a look at you and I'll go and get Filly for you. Okay?"

She nodded, her eyes closing again as Jonathan managed to lie her down.

I suddenly noticed Jon's face had lost all colour and his normally vibrant grey eyes were dark with black smudges beneath them.

As I stepped through the double doors, a loud crash rang out from the back of the surgery, immediately followed by a car alarm.

I raced down the steps and along the side of the old brick building.

The door to Jonathan's truck stood open, and a man was leaning inside.

I stopped mid-stride. My insides dropped as my hand flew to my mouth. The outrage of this person stealing our belongings propelled me forward.

I grabbed the collar of his red and black checked lumberjack shirt and yanked him backwards.

"Hey!" he yelled, as he found himself flat on his back on the concrete.

I recognized him immediately.

"Well, well. Why am I not surprised? Shane Logan," I said.

He and his family were well known in the area. None of them had had any education, and probably had never done an honest day's work in their lives.

"Fuck off, bitch," he said. His lip lifted in a sneer, and hatred filled his eyes.

"You cheeky little—" Adrenalin coursed through me, exacerbated by all the pent-up anxiety of the past few weeks. A guttural roar escaped me as I smacked him around the head with the flat of my hand.

"Victoria. Stop!" Jonathan yelled as he appeared around the corner. Emily was wrapped around his neck, her pathetic little arms holding on for dear life as Jon ran across the car park towards us.

"Yes, Victoria. Stop," the scumbag mimicked like a child. He was still on the ground, one arm raised above his head as he cowered beneath it, trying to scuttle away from me.

Emily began to cry.

"Call the police, Jon. This piece of shit smashed your window and dismantled your stereo," I said, trying to control the urge to punch the cocky waste of space on his scruffy, ginger goatee. I dug my nails into my palms.

Emily sobbed. "Filly, I want Filly."

I reached into the back seat and plucked out the scruffy rag doll Emily carried everywhere. I threw it to Jonathan, and Emily snatched it from him and held it to her chest. Jonathan continued to bounce her on his hip and stroke her hair, trying to calm her down.

I turned back to the nasty creature at my feet. "Stand up!"

"Fuck off," he said with a sneer—or maybe it was his pathetic attempt at a smile.

"Watch your mouth, boy," Jonathan said, pulling Emily's head into his chest and covering her exposed ear.

"You fuck off too, dick'ead." Shane stood up and spun away from us.

"Come back here, Shane," I said.

"Up yours, MILF. You know—Mum I'd like to ..." He thrust his disgusting pelvis in my direction, his tongue sticking out of the corner of his mouth and his eyes rolling in mock ecstasy.

"Enough!" Jonathan stepped towards him. "Shift yourself now, Shane, before I kick your arse myself."

"OOO-ooh." Shane's eyebrows rose as he sneered at Jonathan. He sniffed noisily, then hoicked a large glob of spit on the ground at Jonathan's feet before sauntering off.

My stomach churned. "You dirty little ... Jonathan, call the police!" I said, approaching Shane.

Shane rounded the end of the truck then ran, pausing briefly to flip us the finger.

"Why would you just let him go?" I turned on my husband, fuming.

Jonathan had opened the boot of the car and threw a towel at me.

"Clear the glass from the seat while I fasten Emily in," he said, as though nothing had occurred.

His serious no-nonsense tone worried me. I stared at him, completely lost for words.

"I'll tell you when we get home."

"What did the doc ... ?"

He tipped his head towards our daughter, his eyebrows raised. "When we get home."

Once Emily was snuggled up on the sofa with her favourite fleecy pink blanket, watching a DVD, Jonathan nodded his head towards the kitchen.

I got up and followed him.

"Now can you tell me why you did that?" I was stalling, not yet ready for him to tell me what the doctor said that got him so worked up.

"Did what?" A puzzled expression crossed his face.

"Did what? Are you serious? He smashed your window, for Christ's sake. He'd have had your stereo and anything else he could get his thieving little mitts on if I hadn't stopped him." I couldn't believe he didn't seem to care. I shook my head, bewildered.

"Oh, that." He rubbed a hand over his chiselled, bristly jaw.

"Yes, that!" I said, exasperated.

"To be honest, Shane Logan is the least of our worries right now, Vic," he said, his eyes filled with concern.

"Why? What did the doctor say?" I braced myself for bad news. Spine-tingling dread began spreading through my entire body.

The kitchen door opened and Frank, Jonathan's father, shuffled in. He froze as he realised we were deep in conversation.

"Sorry, am I interrupting?" Frank said, and turned to leave.

"No, Dad, come in. You need to hear this too."

"Hear what?" I shivered as each tiny hair on the back of my neck stood to attention.

Frank closed the door and, leaning heavily on his stick, limped over to stand beside his only son.

Jon cleared his throat.

"Doctor Davies agrees with you, Vic. He's going to refer Emily to a specialist for tests." His eyebrows furrowed, and a pained expression filled his eyes.

"Oh my God. Oh my God," I cried, grabbing Jon's arm to steady myself.

I'd been saying she was sick for weeks, and Jon insisted I was overprotective, but I knew. Call it mother's intuition— call it what the hell you like—but I knew.

"Hey, come here, Vic. It still might be nothing." Jonathan pulled me into his arms.

I buried my head into his chest, trying to seek comfort from the familiar scent of him. But I could hear his heart hammering, and I knew he too was terrified.

"I'm confused," Frank said. "What does this mean?"

"Let's not speculate, Dad. Best to wait for the specialist's verdict."

After putting Emily to bed, I ran a bath. Then I lay immersed in coconut-scented bubbles until I was shivering cold and my skin was in danger of becoming as wrinkled as a walnut.

Wrapped in a fleecy dressing gown with my long brown hair twisted in a towel, I popped my head into Emily's room. She was asleep. I crept to her side and bent to kiss the top of her head and my stomach contracted.

As I turned to leave, a little voice whispered, "Goodnight, Mummy."

"Goodnight, my precious girl. I love you."

"How much?"

"To the moon and back."

Emily's tinkling laughter filled my ears and broke my heart.

I closed the door behind me, and then turned, pressing my back against it and sighing noisily.

A movement down the hallway made me turn with a start.

Frank stood half-in, half-out of his bedroom door, eyeing me, tentatively.

Frank was over six feet tall with broad shoulders, a rugged complexion and a head of thick greying hair. He was still a handsome and distinguished looking man despite the ravages of the stroke. Always very capable and powerful, he'd run the farm single-handed for years, only employing casual staff at the busiest times.

He'd also had a homekill butchery business that he'd operated from a converted old stone barn at the back of the property.

Finding himself bed-bound and helpless had almost been enough to kill him in itself, but between us, we'd managed. Now he was slowly regaining some independence.

"Hi, Frank."

"Sorry to disturb you. I keep intruding on your private moments."

"Don't be silly. You're as much a part of this as anyone." I pulled the towel from my head and threw it over my shoulder, running my fingers through my wet hair.

"She'll be fine, lass. Jon's right. We should wait and see what they say at the hospital."

I nodded, my lips trembling. "I've got a bad feeling about this, Frank."

"Come here." He walked towards me, his walking stick supporting his weak right side. I met him halfway, drawing strength from his calm, controlled, all-encompassing hug.

Frank was the closest thing I had to a parent.

Both of mine had died years ago, leaving me feeling alone and abandoned at an early age. I had no other family, none that I knew of anyway. Maybe there were some distant cousins knocking about in Puerto Rico, where I was born, but nobody significant.

Frank cleared his throat. "You okay now?"

"Yes, thanks. I needed that," I said.

"There are plenty more where that came from, you know."

I smiled at him. "Come on. I'll race you downstairs. Last one down makes a cuppa."

I sped off, listening to him rant and curse, and then chuckle.

CHAPTER 2

Emily looked washed out propped in the back seat of the car as we drove to the hospital for her tests. Her chestnut brown curls hung lifeless and dull, her complexion sallow. She fell asleep with her head lolling in an unnatural position. She'd have a stiff neck later.

Doctor Desmond Wilson, was a white haired man in his fifties, who, according to Google, had a fantastic reputation as a neurologist. He was average height and build, not good-looking in the typical sense, but the glint in his eye made me trust him.

We sat around his huge oak desk, explaining Em's symptoms. He listened without rushing us at all, which I was glad about. Afterwards, he examined Emily who, once again, lolled in Jon's arms.

"We'll be doing a series of tests—blood and urine tests initially to rule out infection or autoimmune conditions such as lupus. Do any of you have a history of any neurological disorders in the family?" he asked.

I shrugged. "I'm not too sure. My parents brought me here

from Puerto Rico in the eighties. I never met any extended family. My parents are both dead."

"What caused their deaths?" he raised one bushy grey eyebrow.

"Nothing related to this. Mum died of liver cancer and Dad a car accident."

It sounded so matter of fact to my ears. Oh, Mum *just* had liver cancer and Dad a tussle with a car. Both are dead. The doctor must have thought me cold and unfeeling, but he couldn't be further from the truth.

My mum died when I was eleven years old. We had no warning or time to prepare.

It started as a twenty-four hour bug. But a whole week went by, then two. Dad forced her to go to the doctors in the end. The doctor sent her straight to the hospital where she died two days later. We never knew if she'd had any symptoms prior, but if she had, she kept them to herself.

Dad died just as suddenly. I was seventeen years old and away from home training to be a vet. One Friday night, on his way home from the pub, he stepped in front of a car. He never felt a thing, according to witnesses.

The police never charged the elderly driver. I didn't blame her. I'd seen him walk into the road hundreds of times after a skin-full.

But I couldn't go into this amount of detail, not here, not now. We were here for Emily. I'd dealt with enough tragedy to last a lifetime; I couldn't bear any more.

"How about you, Mr Lyons?" the doctor said.

"I don't think so. My mum also died a number of years ago—but she had a bad heart. My dad's still with us although he suffered a stroke. We're not sure about his family though—he was adopted."

"Okay, we'll be doing some tests to check for this. Some brain scans—an MRI and CT, to get a clear visual image of what's happening inside."

I know he meant search for tumours and the like and my stomach did a twirl.

"We'll also do a lumbar puncture, which means taking fluid from the base of her spine so we can test for any infections or abnormalities," the doctor continued.

I nodded and glanced at Jon, who reached for my hand. We'd discussed this earlier, and both dreaded this procedure the most. We'd heard they could sometimes be very painful, and the patient needs to lie perfectly still.

"And we'll perform a series of nerve conduction studies. We'll admit Emily first. It will be a long day, but you should be able to take her home afterwards," he said. "The lumbar puncture sometimes causes headaches, and she will need to rest, so we'll make that the last test. Do you have any questions?" he said.

The pocket of his tweed jacket began trilling like a cricket. Doctor Wilson seemed surprised as he plucked a phone out, hit a button and placed it on the desk before him.

"Sorry about that." He smiled, his cheeks flushing. "Now where were we? Oh yes, any questions?"

"Will we get the results today?" Jonathan asked.

"Not all of them. The lumbar puncture results might take a week or two, but we'll be in touch." He looked from Jonathan to me and then back again. "Okay then. If that's all, let's get cracking."

The rest of the day flew by. No sooner had they found Emily a bed then they began taking blood. They were on the ball at this hospital.

I remembered going to the hospital in Manchester with my mum and waiting around for ages. It was the same when I was pregnant with Emily, hour upon wasted hour flicking through magazines.

They allowed us in the room with Emily during the MRI scan.

The radiologist was a slim, dark-haired Liverpudlian called Tim. He wore a white gown over a green polo shirt and jeans. He wanted to show us the equipment, but Emily whimpered and held onto Jonathan's neck as if her life depended on it.

"Ya not scared, are ya?" Tim asked.

She nodded, her face still buried into Jon's neck.

"There's nothing to be scared of. We have children queuing up for a turn in our spaceship."

Emily stiffened and stopped whimpering.

"We borrowed it from NASA. Have you heard of NASA?" he said, winking at me.

Emily shook her head and peeked at Tim.

"Well, NASA is a special place in America where astronauts live. Do you know what an astronaut is?"

She shook her head again.

"Oh, now that won't do. I'm sure there are some pictures here somewhere."

Tim produced a large board covered with images of astronauts and spaceships, as well as photographs of children inside the scanner.

I marvelled at how, within minutes, Tim had Emily and Filly inside the large metallic dome, thinking she was in a spaceship. He even played "space music" for her on the headphones.

After that, getting her into the CT scan was a doddle and Emily held her tiny body perfectly still. My heart contracted, and tears stung my eyes as she lay there, hardly breathing.

Afterwards, she struggled with a series of physical tests to check her reflexes, but she was exhausted by then.

Back on the ward, they brought Emily a bowl of macaroni cheese—normally her favourite, but she just picked at it, uninterested.

After lunch, she had an hour's rest.

Jonathan stepped into the corridor and asked a pretty young nurse where he could buy a sandwich for us. I watched through the window as she batted her huge eyelashes at him and gazed into his gorgeous grey eyes.

I laughed.

The poor girl couldn't be more obvious if she tried, but Jonathan seemed oblivious to her attention.

After directing him to the hospital canteen, she and another nurse checked him out from behind as he left the ward.

He returned a short while later with a couple of sandwiches and coffee.

Sometimes I forgot how damn attractive he was. Nowadays I only got to see him in his farming overalls and stinking of dung. But he looked delicious when he made an effort. Today he wore a tight white t-shirt and stonewashed jeans that showcased his backside to perfection. He always had his dark hair cropped short and was usually clean-shaven, but today he had a bit of sexy stubble happening.

I kissed his lips, long and hard.

"What was that for?" he asked.

"Do I need a reason?"

Jonathan licked his lips and then chewed at them, his eyes twinkling and a cheeky smile playing on his face.

"Behave yourself, Mister. It was just a kiss." I laughed.

By the time the nurse came back for us, we were all refreshed and ready for the next round of tests.

The lumbar puncture was as bad as we'd imagined. Emily screamed as they inserted the needle into the base of her spine. It took two nurses, Jonathan, and me to hold her still.

Afterwards, Doctor Wilson came to speak to us briefly.

"That all went well," he said. "Some of the results are back but we won't get a full picture of what's happening until the rest are in. We'll send for you in approximately two weeks."

"Can't you tell us anything, Doctor?" I asked.

"Anything I told you now would be complete nonsense without the other results. I understand how difficult this is, but please, try to be patient."

"But …"

Jonathan placed his hand on my arm. "Thank you, Doctor," he said.

"It makes sense, Vic. With you tied up looking after Emily and Dad, I'm struggling to manage the farm and the clinic. A farm-hand will free you up and give us someone to rely on," Jonathan said.

We were sitting on the dated beige velour sofa in our open-plan lounge. The sun streamed in the large bay window, creating hazy patches throughout the room.

"Can we afford to pay a full-time wage?" I asked, chewing at the inside of my cheek.

"We'll have to. All right, it might mean no holiday this year, but that's the least of our worries right now." He put his arm around my shoulders and pulled me to him. "I think you need to ring Steph too."

"I don't think ..."

"She'll be here in a shot. I can only do so much in the clinic. We need her."

"How will we pay all these extra people?" I clasped at my locket as I mentally tried to tot up the extra cash we'd need to find every week.

"Steph will more than pay for herself, especially if we can take on more clients, but at this rate, we'll have no choice but to close the clinic." Jonathan sat back on the sofa and crossed one foot over his knee.

I knew he was right, and with two extra pairs of hands the running of the farm and the clinic would be a breeze.

"So what now? Shall we advertise?" I held my palms upward in a half shrug.

Jon shook his head. "Sam's recommended a young guy he's

been using on a casual basis. His name's Alex—he's from Idaho, America."

Sam was one of our neighbours, a hard-working old school farmer. If this lad had got the thumbs up from Sam, he must be good.

"Where's he staying?" I asked.

"That's the thing—he'll have to stay here."

My stomach dropped. "Can't he stay at Sam's farm? They have plenty of room, and ..."

"We've got plenty of room. Dad always let the casual workers stay here," he cut in.

"I dunno, Jon. Not with Emily so sick," I said, shaking my head.

"He can stay in the flat above the garage. Don't worry—it'll be fine. Now go and ring Steph."

He pushed me in the direction of the telephone in the hallway, giving my bottom a cheeky pat as he did so.

Stephanie, my best friend from school, had seen me through every traumatic experience in my life. Her Mum took me under her wing when I needed a mother's advice. Dad had never been any good with womanly things.

Steph shared my love of animals and we decided while still in primary school that we'd go to Veterinary College together. She met Jonathan first and did a bit of matchmaking to get us together.

Once we'd graduated, Jonathan and I were inseparable and married soon after. Using my inheritance, we opened our own practice in Manchester. Steph worked for us for a while, until six years ago, when we'd sold up and moved to Cumbria.

I begged her to come with us, mainly for my own sanity—being stuck in the middle of the countryside with no friends was hard. I told her about our plans to turn one of the stone outhouses into a veterinary clinic. With Jon taking on most of the farm work, I needed a back-up vet to help me and also someone to help care for Frank. But she had graciously declined.

She stayed on in Manchester, working for the new owners. Then she met a man whilst holidaying in Spain. After a whirlwind romance, and against everybody's advice, she packed up and moved to Spain to live where she'd stayed for two years.

However, three weeks ago, she split with her boyfriend and returned from Spain and was currently staying with her parents in Manchester.

I reached for the phone and dialled the number I knew by heart.

My stomach muscles clenched as she answered on the first ring.

"Hi, Steph, it's me."

"Hello, stranger, how are you?"

The familiar sound of her voice almost choked me. "Oh, you know—things are pretty full on here at the moment."

Her breath hitched. "Is it Frank?"

"No—actually, he's doing well to be honest. It's Em." My voice finally cracked.

"What's wrong with her?" she asked, her bubbly voice suddenly serious.

"I dunno, Steph. She's sick—really sick. She's had lots of tests, and we're waiting for the results." Tears began streaming down my face, and my chest compressed.

"Oh no, poor baby. Can I do anything to help?"

"That's why I rang. I need a massive favour. I wondered if you can come to stay for a few weeks? I'm struggling with everything."

"Oh, Vic, don't cry, of course I will. To be honest, my mum's driving me potty, and I need to get away—you'll be doing me a favour."

"I thought she would be," I said, laughing through my tears and wiping my eyes on the sleeve of my blouse. I cleared my throat. "How is she?"

"Oh, you know Mum. She never changes. Still keeping herself busy with her art groups."

"Say hi to her from me."

"Will do. So when do you want me?"

"The problem is I won't be able to pay you much. Not right away, anyway."

"Do you have wine?"

"Some. I'll get more."

"Fab. When do you want me?"

"Yesterday."

"Oh," she giggled. "Okay, give me till tomorrow and you're on."

"Thanks, Steph. You're a diamond."

So it was settled. Stephanie and Alex would both be joining us. The farmhouse had plenty of bedrooms, and I made one up for Steph. We'd always classed her as family anyway.

Jon offered Alex the self-contained studio above the garage, and he was thrilled to have his own front door. He didn't mind the fact it hadn't been lived in for years and needed a lick of paint. At least he could come and go as he pleased without disturbing anyone.

I warmed to Alex immediately. He had a mass of tight brown curls, green eyes and lean, wiry body, and seemed too young to be travelling the world alone. I figured his parents must be beside themselves.

I felt the familiar protectiveness that always gripped me when presented with a stray or sick and injured animal. Not that I thought of Alex as an animal, but I did think he needed someone to care for him—if only to give another mother, living thousands of miles away, some peace of mind.

In Manchester, we'd had a house full of strays. But we'd had to re-home them when we moved here. Frank didn't agree with house pets. Animals had to have a purpose in his eyes. The semi-wild cats in the barn and the two farm dogs that were kept in kennels, all earned their keep.

The following day, Steph bustled in as I was about to dish out the dinner.

She gave a little scream when she saw me, and I almost dropped the dish I'd just taken out of the oven.

She was always the same, like a tornado wherever she went. Her bubbly personality filled any room, which made up for her teeny five-foot-two stature. Her normally wild, bleached blonde hair had been scraped back into an elastic band, and her trademark black makeup surrounded her lovely pale blue eyes.

"Sorry, I'm so late, Vic. I tried to get away, but Mum had hundreds of extra jobs that just couldn't wait. I think she's worried I won't be going back." She laughed.

"Oh, don't be silly. You're not late." I placed the dish on top of the stove and threw the oven gloves down beside it.

I hugged her tightly, inhaling the familiar perfume she always wore.

"Where's Em?" She dropped two canvas holdalls onto the tiled floor and looked around the room.

I released her and took a step backwards. "Upstairs in bed. She doesn't want anything to eat, although she did have a bit of soup earlier," I said.

Stephanie dropped to the floor and began rummaging around in one of her bags.

"Can I pop up and say hi? I have something for her," she said, pulling a pair of maracas and a colourful Spanish fan from the huge holdall. She danced a little jig—the maracas in one hand and the fan in the other—and finished it off with, 'Ole'," and a double stamp of her heels.

I laughed. "Oh Steph, I'm so glad you're here. Of course you can go up—she'll be so excited. I didn't tell her you were coming; I wanted to surprise her."

Steph ran up the stairs in search of her god-daughter.

I continued dishing up the food, adding an extra plate to the already laid table.

Steph walked down the stairs much more subdued than when she'd bounced up a few moment's ago. "Gosh, Vic, she's really sick, isn't she?"

I nodded. "Yeah. I'm really worried. She's got no energy at all and absolutely no appetite." I shook my head and placed one hand over my mouth, taking a deep breath, trying hard not to break down.

"I couldn't understand her. I had to make her repeat herself over and over," Steph said.

"I'm sorry, I should have warned you. She sounds like she's drunk, doesn't she?"

Stephanie nodded. "I didn't want to say, but yes, she does, and she's so frail. She was never a big girl, but there's nothing left of her now."

Tears filled my eyes, and I buried my face in the tea towel, unable to hold them back any longer.

"I'm sorry, Vic. I didn't mean to upset you."

"No. It's not you. Tears are never very far from the surface lately."

Stephanie hugged me and stroked my hair as uncontrollable sobs escaped me.

"What did the doctor say?"

"We go for the results on Monday." I hiccupped.

Steph nodded. "Okay."

"Come on, the food'll be cold. I made your favourite, lasagne," I said, wiping my eyes on the towel once more.

"Yum. Come on then, what are we waiting for?" The mood suddenly lifted again.

I was so pleased to have her here. Not just for the extra help around the place, but because of the emotional support she would provide. And for the laughs that followed her around everywhere —God knows we needed more laughs around the place.

Monday loomed. I needed to know what was wrong with my baby, but I knew from the bottom of my heart that it wasn't going to be good news.

CHAPTER 3

Doctor Wilson shuffled the papers on the desk in front of him. He seemed to be avoiding our gaze.

Jonathan's jaw clenched and unclenched over and over, he had dark smudges under his eyes. Neither of us had slept properly in weeks.

He gave me a tight, half smile and reached for my hand, pulling it onto his lap. He stroked along the top of my knuckles with his thumb.

Emily sat on the floor to the side of us, leafing through a book we'd found in reception.

Unable to sit still, my legs twitched uncontrollably to match my erratic heartbeat. My breath struggled to reach my lungs.

I scanned the room in an attempt to calm myself.

A bookcase held lots of clues to the private Doctor Wilson. The numerous dead fish he'd held up to be photographed over the years indicated he was a keen fisherman. I could tell they spanned a period of time, simply due to the varying degrees of grey in his hair.

A large hunk of driftwood commanded one whole shelf, and I couldn't figure out why it was important—it didn't look like anything in particular. Several photo frames showed a pretty dark-haired woman and two teenage boys—his wife and sons?

"Okay then, as you know, the reason you're here today is for the results of the tests," the doctor said.

I almost leapt out of my skin as his booming voice broke the silence of the room. "I'm sorry, I was miles away."

He took a deep breath before continuing. "We have all the results back, but I'm afraid I don't have good news." He paused, as if waiting for his words to sink in.

Neither of us said a word. Jonathan gripped my hand tighter. I held my breath.

"The scan shows Emily's cerebellum is shrinking. The cerebellum is also known as 'the little brain' an area of the hindbrain that controls motor movement, coordination, balance, equilibrium and muscle tone. It contains hundreds of millions of neurons for processing data, and relays information between body muscles and areas of the cerebral cortex that are involved in motor control."

"Why is it shrinking?" I shrieked, unable to comprehend his words.

Emily snapped her head around to look at me.

"There could be a number of reasons. Nine times out of ten we never know the cause, but in this instance we do—Emily is not producing an essential hormone called Proteum that's normally produced in a tiny gland at the base of the skull."

"Can she be treated?" Jonathan whispered.

The room was spinning. How could this be happening to our gorgeous girl?

Emily, no longer interested in the book, glanced from me to her dad and back to the doctor. I realized she was listening to everything, and although I didn't think she'd understand, I didn't want her to ask questions.

"Is there any chance Emily can go and play in reception? She doesn't want to listen to all this boring grown-up talk do you, Em?" My voice sounded much brighter than I felt.

"Of course. I'll get Diane to watch her." He stood up and walked into the reception, returning with a middle-aged woman with spiky grey hair, laughing blue eyes and a smile to match.

"How about I show you where we hide the best toys, sweetie?" she said to Emily, who had climbed onto Jon's knee.

She turned her face into his chest.

"Come on, Em, we won't be long. We need to talk to the doctor for a few minutes, and then we'll go home to see Steph," I whispered.

"I've got a pretty dolly out here and her name's Steph. She has lots of different dresses. Shall I show you?" Diane urged.

Emily lifted her head.

"Come on, sweetie."

Emily took Diane's hand and followed her outside.

"Thanks, Doctor. I don't want her to hear what's coming next."

"I understand."

I gripped Jonathan's hand and braced myself.

"Now, where were we?" Doctor Wilson said.

"Can she be treated, Doctor?" Jonathan asked again.

He shook his head. "This hormone is essential for her development. Without it, she'll continue to deteriorate. I'm so sorry."

"I don't understand. There's nothing at all you can do?" I asked, my mind in a whirl. This was much worse than anything I'd imagined over the past weeks. My whole body shook. I couldn't absorb what he was telling us.

"No. It's incredibly rare. There were a number of trials conducted a few years ago. Attempts were made to transplant from a living donor, a similar procedure to a bone-marrow transplant, but on each occasion the donor died within twenty-four hours. The trials were stopped."

"What if I donated mine?" I said, grasping at any possibility, my mind racing.

"Even if you could donate yours, it wouldn't work because, although you do still produce Proteum, you no longer produce the quantities needed for the development of a young girl. Anybody over the age of twenty-five won't produce nearly enough."

"Do the donors have to be a match, like with a bone marrow transplant?"

"No—but we're getting way off track here, Mrs Lyons. The trials were stopped."

"What about someone who's already dead, or dying?"

"No. The Proteum needs to come from a living brain to be viable. I'm being purely hypothetical now as I know you're trying to understand. If a potential donor is brain-dead, the Proteum won't be viable either."

"So in other words, my daughter is going to die," Jonathan said, in a flat, matter-of-fact voice.

"I'm afraid so, Mr Lyons—and I'm sorry."

Hearing the words spoken out loud made my head spin. "How long?" I asked, my teeth chattered, I was shaking so much.

"I'm sorry?"

"How long until she dies? How long do we have?"

"It's hard to say, as the symptoms vary from person to person. I suggest we do some more tests in two months. It will enable us to see how quickly she's deteriorating and give us some idea of what to expect."

I wanted to scream at him—for his pompous, no-nonsense answers—for his calm manner—for his rotten lying mouth. But instead I felt my shoulders sag. An empty hole in the very centre of my being grew larger and more painful by the second. This couldn't be happening.

The posters on the wall were jumping out at me. One was entitled "Brain Jokes". I didn't read any further. Some fucking joke this was.

I looked at Jonathan and noticed he hadn't moved a muscle, except huge tears ran down his face and dripped off his chin.

"Jon. Jon? Are you okay?" I pulled him to me and held his head to my chest as loud sobs escaped him.

I couldn't cry. I was numb. My mind raced—there must be a way. We couldn't just allow our beautiful precious girl to die. There must be something we could do.

"I need a second opinion, Doctor," I said.

"Of course you do, and all the test results will go to my colleague for a second opinion automatically. However, I can assure you, the diagnosis will remain the same."

"It's not that I don't trust you," I gulped, "but this is our baby—we've got to try everything. We can't allow her to die without a fight."

"I understand."

"So what do we do now? Does she need medication to help with the symptoms?" I said.

"Not at the moment, but once her symptoms progress we can suggest a number of treatments that might help. A speech or language therapist will probably be needed, as she's already showing signs of this being a problem. She may have swallowing difficulties, but it's hard to say what Emily's symptoms will be. No two cases are identical."

I shook my head in confusion. How could this be true? My insides were churning, and I thought I might unload the contents of my stomach all over the pristine oak desk.

"What causes it?" Jonathan said.

"It's not clear, but studies show that it's probably caused by a defective gene passed down from both parents. It often turns out that siblings will also have the same condition."

"So we gave it to her?" I asked, horrified.

"We think so."

"If we have more children, they could be the same?" I asked, the room spinning wildly.

"If you have more children together, then yes, they will certainly have this condition." He shrugged.

"So what now?" My voice sounded flat and alien to my ears.

"There is nothing else, I'm afraid. Diana will give you some leaflets on your way out. If you have any questions, please contact me or my team, and we'll assist you in any way we can."

We all got to our feet.

"One last thing, doctor."

He nodded, "Of course."

"In the trials—how did the patients react to the treatment?"

"The results were immediate and it was around six months before the symptoms returned. Obviously the trials had ended by then, and no more treatment was available."

I couldn't believe what he was telling me. There was a possible chance to cure my daughter but instead they'd stopped all the tests. And although six months wasn't a long time in the grand scheme of things, I'd gladly give her my Proteum if it would help to buy her more time.

After all, a lot can happen in six months.

CHAPTER 4

Emily seemed lost in the hugeness of the red leather armchair. She appeared even smaller than she had yesterday, as though she was shrinking before my very eyes.

The concentration on her face was priceless as she tried to pull a pair of blue trousers onto a doll. Her trusty companion, Filly, had been propped up beside her in the corner of the chair.

"You ready to go, sweetheart?" I said. My heart breaking as she glanced up at me. Her large grey eyes, too big for her face, were wide with surprise. She'd been so engrossed in what she was doing that she hadn't noticed us come out of Doctor Wilson's office.

She looked at Diana and back at the doll.

"I'll finish dressing her for you, sweetie." Diana came around from the desk and took the doll from Emily and smiled. "Did you like the clothes I made for her?"

Emily nodded and also smiled.

"You can dress her next time. It's just our secret though, okay?"

"Okay." Emily smiled again as she stood up. Becoming embarrassed at us all staring at her, she grasped my hand and hid behind my leg.

"Come on, my baby—let's go. Shall we get something to eat?"

"Happy Meal," she squealed, and lifted her clenched fists up to her chin and held her breath, smiling.

"I think we can manage that, can't we, Daddy?" I glanced at Jonathan. He'd not said a word since leaving the doctor's office.

"Course we can. Anything you want, Em."

"McDonalds, here we come," I said.

I rarely let her eat junk food, but what good had that done her? My baby was dying, and I was damned if I would stop her from having anything she wanted now.

We found a restaurant on the roundabout just before the motorway entrance. The place was full. It always surprised me how children would choose McDonalds above anywhere else when given a choice.

After nibbling at a burger, Emily walked over to the climbing frame. She stood to the side, watching the other children charging up the steps and launching themselves down the slide.

Jonathan turned to me and reached for my hand. "How are we going to get through this, Vic? I feel like we're in a nightmare."

I grasped at his fingers, staring into his eyes. I couldn't tell whose hands were shaking the most. Words were too difficult without crying and I was adamant Emily wouldn't see any tears. I turned back to watch her.

Emily took tentative steps to the bottom of the ladder, looking at the slide with longing. I knew she wanted to race up them, but she hadn't the energy.

I sidled out from behind the table. "Do you want a turn on the slide, Em?"

She nodded.

I lifted her onto the platform at the top of the ladder, and she slid down the red plastic slide.

"Do you want to do it again, baby?" I held my arms out as she walked towards me.

"No thanks, Mummy," she said, then stuck her thumb in her mouth.

"Do you want anything else? Some dessert, an ice cream sundae?"

Her eyes lit up as she thought about it and then she shook her head, thumb still firmly in place. I could have kicked myself for all the times she asked us for ice cream or to go to McDonalds and we'd refused. Now we were going to allow her whatever her heart desired and the poor girl couldn't face anything.

I turned back to Jonathan, and he looked away, before hurrying to the bathroom.

This awful situation had hit him hard.

I'd prepared myself for bad news, although I'd not imagined the results to be this bad. But Jon had refused to think about it. He'd convinced himself she would be okay.

I dreaded going home, having to explain everything to Frank and Stephanie. I would be happy to stall the whole thing as long as possible, but Emily's energy was flagging, and she needed to go.

"Don't forget your Pinky Pie, Em." I rescued her My Little Pony toy from underneath the table. She'd been thrilled when she pulled it out of her Happy Meal carton earlier, discarding poor Filly to the top of my handbag.

"Oh!" she gasped, snatching the pink plastic horse from me and holding it to her chest dramatically.

I laughed. An immense sadness gripped my heart and I choked, almost bursting into tears but I controlled myself in time.

Jonathan returned. His face had paled even more, but other than that, he was smiling at Emily, covering his feelings perfectly. "Where to next, my dear?" he said, in a posh accent.

Emily laughed. "Daddy—we're going home."

"Home, James, and don't spare the horses!" He twirled Emily onto his shoulders and galloped out of the restaurant. Her tinkling laughter accompanied us to the car.

She slept all the way home.

"What are you thinking?" Jon asked after several minutes of silence.

"About my mum. For the first time in my life, I wish I'd inherited her gift."

"You want to be a medium, get visited by spirits of dead people while you're sitting on the toilet or taking a shower?"

I laughed. "No, you twit. She wasn't just a medium. She was a psychic. People queued around the block for a reading when I was a kid. There were always women sitting in our lounge waiting for their turn. I don't remember even one of those women leaving with dry eyes."

"I don't know, Vic. Imagine, if on the day you gave birth to Emily, we'd been told this would happen to her. How the knowledge would have tainted every single thing we've done over the past five years. Ignorance is bliss, I say."

"I guess you're right. What confused me the most growing up is if Mum was such a great psychic, why didn't she predict her own illness?"

Jonathan shrugged one shoulder. "Maybe you can't see the future of yourself or close family."

"Yeah, and like you say, it would drive you demented waiting for things to happen."

"Anyway, I don't believe in paranormal stuff. Choose not to believe it. I'd die of fright if a ghost appeared in front of me." Jonathan shuddered.

I laughed. "I know. That's why I'll never watch a scary movie with you *ever* again. Your screaming frightens me more than the movie does. You big wuss!"

Jonathan grabbed my knee, squeezing it playfully.

"I'm sorry, I'm sorry," I giggled until he let go.

I felt guilty to be behaving like this while still trying to absorb the awful news. However, our whole relationship had been built on laughter and torment and vast amounts of teasing, making it difficult for us to communicate any other way.

"Besides," he continued, "if it was true, why has she never come back for a visit? You'd think your mum would move mountains to visit her only daughter. To prove that there is life after death."

"I guess." I shrugged. "Dad always said she was with us. He said he could sense her and strange things happened around the house that had to be her doing. But I never saw anything."

"Yeah, but he did hit the bottle quite heavily after she died, didn't he?"

"He had to get drunk so he could sleep. He never got over her." I turned away and gazed through the window, my fingers automatically finding the locket at my throat.

"I'll make you a deal," Jon said. "If I go first, I promise to haunt you. So long as you promise if you go first, you won't even think about haunting me."

I laughed again, the sadness gone for a few seconds as I imagined myself as a ghost visiting Jon. "I'd make sure I came while you were on the toilet, seeing as that's your worst fear."

"Bitch!" Jonathan also laughed briefly.

We reached the farm and sat staring through the windscreen for several minutes. Both lost in our own thoughts, until Emily stirred in the back seat.

"Hey—there you are, Miss Emily. I was about to send out a search party to the land of nod."

"Daddy, you're silly," Emily whispered.

I smiled. "He certainly is, Pumpkin. Shall we go and show Stephy your Pinky Pie?"

She nodded and unbuckled her seatbelt.

I stepped out of the car and met Jonathan in front of the house.

"Ready?" he whispered, holding his hand, palm up.

I nodded. "Ready?" I placed my hand in his.

Emily had gone ahead of us and marched up the hall. She seemed livelier than she had been in a while.

Jonathan kissed my hand and we gazed at each other for a few seconds, then, each taking a deep breath, we followed her in.

Frank was sitting on the sofa, his bad leg propped up with a cushion on the coffee table in front of him. Steph stood in the open plan kitchen, wiping her hands on a tea towel. They both looked at us expectantly as we entered.

I envied them their ignorance—wished I didn't know what I did—wished I wasn't about to break their hearts as Doctor Wilson had broken mine.

Emily stood in front of Steph holding up her bright pink pony.

"What do you have there, beautiful?" Steph said, bending down to Emily's level.

"It's Pinky Pie."

"Well, hello, Pinky Pie. Don't you have a pretty name? And she's just the right colour for your bedroom isn't she, Em?"

Emily nodded. "I'm going to put her on my dressing table."

"Okay, Em—what do you want to do for an hour or so? I'm going to do a couple of hours on the farm," Jonathan said.

"Can I watch Mary Poppins?"

"You can—how about I go and put it on for you?" he said.

Emily nodded. "Do you want to watch it with me, Stephy?"

"You try and stop me—that's my all-time favourite movie. I'll finish off here, and then I'll be through."

"Okay." She followed Jonathan into the snug.

Steph turned to face me again and shrugged. "So?"

"Can we wait for Jon?" I smiled an apology, slumping down into the armchair opposite Frank.

The silence was deafening.

I felt certain they could hear the ba-bum—ba-bum—ba-bum sounds coming from my chest.

Frank took his foot off the table and placed the cushion on the carpet by his feet. Then he rubbed his eyes with his good hand.

Stephanie came over and sat next to him. Her eyebrows drawn together tightly over her heavily made up pale blue eyes. I noticed that her roots needed retouching. I knew this was a strange thing to be thinking about considering the circumstances, but my mind seemed to be all over the place.

I glanced behind me looking for Jonathan—needing Jonathan. I couldn't do this alone. I could hear him talking to Emily in the snug.

We had two lounges in the huge farmhouse. A large kitchen-dining-lounge, and a separate lounge we called the snug. There was also a separate dining room, seven bedrooms and three bathrooms. We mainly watched TV in the snug as it was quieter and had the biggest screen.

"Can I get you a cup of tea or coffee, Vic?"

"I'm okay, thanks, Steph." I played with my locket, pulling it backwards and forwards along the chain, making a sawing sound.

Jonathan came round the side of my chair and sat on the arm, bending to kiss me.

"Have you told them?"

"No!" we all said in unison.

"I was waiting for you," I said.

"Oh—sorry."

"Well—are you gonna tell us? I can't stand this much longer," Steph said.

I looked at Jonathan and he nodded.

"She has a rare condition. A form of Cerebellar Ataxia."

"What does that mean?" Frank said.

My mouth was suddenly dry and I licked my lips several times. "It means her cerebellum is shrinking. Her balance, speech, motor skills, toileting, in fact, everything will eventually become impossible and she ..." I couldn't continue. Suddenly freezing cold, I wrapped my arms around myself, looking at Jon.

He pulled me into his arms as he cleared his throat. "There's nothing they can do for her."

"Bullshit!" Steph blurted out. "She's a five-year-old girl, for Christ's sake. Surely they must be able to do something."

"I know—it's so cruel." Jonathan turned away and focused on

the photograph of the three of us on the far wall above the sideboard.

I was shaking uncontrollably now. I glanced at Frank, his face unreadable. He'd placed his good hand across his forehead and his fingers trembled.

"Are you okay, Frank?" I said.

He turned to me; his eyes brimmed with unshed tears. His mouth moved as though to say something and changed his mind instead. As he shook his head, the first tears fell.

I wanted to go to him—to comfort him, but I couldn't. I was barely managing to keep myself together.

Steph wiped her eyes on the tea towel, rubbing black mascara down her face. "I don't understand."

"She's not producing an essential hormone which is causing her cerebellum to shrink." I reached for my handbag by my feet and produced the information the doctor gave us. "We have some leaflets here to explain." I dropped them onto the coffee table.

"What's the cause?" she said.

"Nobody knows for sure. The condition is very rare, but they think we both may have a defective gene," Jonathan said.

"Oh my God. This is terrible." Steph stood up and began pacing the floor behind the sofa.

"This is so unfair. She's a child, with all her life ahead of her. I'm an old man—I've lived mine," Frank said.

"Your life is just as important to us, Frank, so don't you be thinking like that. What's happening to Emily is one of those tragic illnesses you read about all the time." I was amazed how together my voice sounded.

"They can't do anything at all for her?" Frank said shaking his head.

"No. There were some trials, apparently. They took the hormone from a live donor and transplanted it."

"So—what? It didn't work?" Steph stopped pacing and looked at me.

"No, the opposite. It worked, but the donors died. So the trials were stopped and ..." I shrugged.

Jonathan got to his feet. "I'm going to look in on Alex and try to clear my head a bit. Are you all right, Vic?"

I nodded. "Yes, I think so. How do you feel?"

"I'm okay—we have to be, don't we? Emily needs us both to be strong, so strong is what we'll be." He placed his hand on my neck and kissed me before leaving.

Stephanie came back around the sofa and began flicking through the leaflets. She passed them to Frank, who glanced at them briefly before placing them on top of the cushion on the floor.

The phone rang. I raced into the hallway, praying it was the hospital calling to tell me they'd made a terrible mistake.

"Hello?"

"C-helo."

"Hello. Can I help you?" I said louder.

"I-a speka do step."

"Sorry?"

"Step. Step-hanee."

"Steph—hold on a minute."

"Steph, phone," I called through to the kitchen.

As she approached me, I whispered, "A foreign man."

Her face screwed up as she took the phone from me.

"Hello, Hector?"

I returned to the lounge. Hector was the toy boy she'd lived with in Spain for the past two years. I didn't know the underlying cause of what went wrong. One minute she was blissfully happy and the next she'd packed up and moved home to her parents.

She'd been vague when I asked her what happened. But to be fair, I never pushed her. I'd been much too absorbed in my own problems.

Some friend I was.

I sat beside Frank on the sofa and stroked his arm.

He shrugged. "This can't be happening, lass. Our girl. Our sweet little girl."

"I know. I wish I could take her place, donate what she needs. I'd do so gladly, but I can't. I'm too old even if they'd agree to it." I felt so deflated. It was like a dream, a terrible, terrifying dream.

"Too old? Why, how old is too old?" His dark bushy eyebrows, that had several white hairs sticking straight out, were now knitted tightly together.

"Twenty-five was the cut-off age."

"Rules me out, too." He smiled sadly, and rubbed his unshaven chin causing a rasping sound.

"It won't sink in. I haven't cried yet, a few wobbly moments, but that's all. I just can't believe it."

"I know, lass. I don't need to tell you how cruel life can be. All the good ones go too soon." He patted my leg.

"No—I don't mean that. I mean—I can't believe it because it can't be true. I've got to fight for her, Frank. Find a way to stop this happening to my baby girl."

CHAPTER 5

The next few days flew by in a blur. I sat at the computer in the upstairs bedroom we'd converted to our home office from morning until night, trawling the Internet for a light bulb moment.

I'd found out all about the proteus, a tiny gland in the brain that produces the Proteum hormone. I read how they removed the hormone before injecting it directly into the patient who, within hours, showed signs of recovery. However, just as the doctor said, within hours the donor was dead.

I found many scientific explanations. Some I could decipher, having a 'sort of' medical background, but some were completely beyond me.

Then, by chance, I came across another site. Something the doctor hadn't mentioned but I had heard a little bit about in the past. Stem cell research in China. They were still very early on in the trials, but they'd had amazing results.

Jonathan walked into the office behind me. "Hey, babe, how's it going?" He kissed the back of my neck, his hands having a quick grope of my little boobs.

I laughed and slapped his hands away. “Look at this, Jon, I was about to call you,” I said, excited.

“Emily’s tucked up in bed and she’s waiting for you to kiss her goodnight.”

I nodded and indicated the website on the screen.

"Vic, I don't want you to wear yourself out on something you can't change." He sighed, deeply.

"Please read this before you say any more. I'll go in to Em and then make a cuppa. Do you want one?"

"Go on.” He winked, and swivelled the chair around so he faced the computer.

I left him reading, and popped my head in the room next door. "Hey, my baby, are you awake?"

Emily pulled her Barbie Princess quilt down and peeped over the top.

"There you are. I thought you’d vanished.” I laughed. “Can I have a big kiss off my bestest girl?" I kicked off my fluffy black slippers, lifted the duvet and climbed in beside her.

She puckered up and I kissed her worn out little face.

"I love you, baby,” I said, putting my arms around her. She laid her head on my shoulder as I stroked her hair.

"How much?" She smiled cheekily.

We’d played the same game every night for weeks now.

"Well now, let me see,” I said. “Take a rocket trip around the moon and the stars and then all the way back—that's how much."

She giggled. "Is that all?"

“Is that all! You cheeky little madam.”

She giggled again.

"Okay. Now, are you ready for this?”

“Ready,” she laughed.

“Right, take an express train four times around the world. Hop on the rocketship around the moon and stars and back again. Then take a submarine voyage to the bottom of the sea and ten times around Atlantis—that's how much."

More giggling. "Is that all?"

"All right, greedy guts." I tickled her tummy, bringing on another bout of giggles. "I think you've had more than enough. Now close those pretty eyes and get to sleep." I eased myself out of the bed and tucked the duvet under her chin.

"Goodnight, Mummy."

"Goodnight, my baby."

I felt blessed to have these moments with my daughter, when she almost seemed her normal self. But they were becoming few and far between.

I slowly walked down the stairs to the kitchen.

Frank was rummaging around in the fridge as I entered and emerged with a slice of ham.

"Gotcha!" I said, stamping my foot and laughed as he almost jumped out of his skin. "Are you still hungry?"

He glanced around before answering. "I miss your cooking, lass. Steph's a star for doing all she does, but her cooking's not a patch on yours."

"I'm sorry, Frank. Maybe tomorrow."

"Oh, pay no attention to a selfish old sod like me. Have you seen the size of this?" He wobbled his paunch. "Not like I'll starve anytime soon, with this. I know you're busy, love. How's the research going?"

"Yeah, good. I found some information on stem cell research in China." I took two cups out of the cupboard. "Do you want a cup of tea?"

"I'd love one." He nodded. "What's the research?"

"One sec, let me check on Steph."

I found Steph sprawled out on the sofa in the snug.

"You look shattered, missus," I said. "I'm making a brew, do you want one?"

"Yes, please. Then I think I'll have an early night," she said. "I'm barely able to keep my eyes open."

Back in the kitchen, Frank was waiting.

"Okay, where was I?" I said as I got another cup from the cupboard. "I found some info on stem cell treatment in China. It's apparently proving positive—although controversial as they use the stem cells from umbilical cords of newborn babies—but all that aside. If it works ..." I shrugged and sucked my teeth.

"Well done, lass. Let's hope they can do something for our Em," he said.

I placed his cup in front of him on the breakfast bar. "There you go. Do you want a couple of biscuits?"

"Ooh, go on then, I won't say no." His stomach growled as he spoke. "Excuse me!" he said, clearly embarrassed.

I laughed and reached for a packet of custard creams from the top shelf of the pantry, and put the full packet beside his cup. I smiled at him and rubbed his shoulder. "Fill your boots."

"Thanks, love," he smiled.

I took Steph's drink through to her before going back up to the office.

"There you go, Jon," I said, placing the mugs on the desk. "I caught your dad raiding the fridge, because he's still hungry—have I been neglecting everyone?"

He reached for my hand and pulled me onto his lap. "We all miss the normality we're used to, but things can't be normal at the moment, can they? It's all we can do to get through each day."

"What do you think of this?" I pointed to the screen.

He shrugged. "Seems too good to be true, but I'd be interested to learn more."

"Me too. Apparently the ex-Lord Mayor of Manchester had it done. I'm going to try and contact her tomorrow."

"Was hers the same as Emily's?" he said, surprised.

"Not exactly, no. She has Idiopathic Ataxia, meaning they don't know what caused hers." I was smiling. I felt lighter than I had in days. The future suddenly didn't seem so bleak.

I reached for the computer mouse. "Let me show you this." I brought up the before and after video footage from the stem cells China website. "It says they do a combination of umbilical cord stem cell transplants, cord serum and nerve growth factor, combined with acupuncture and rehabilitation therapy."

We spent the rest of the evening watching videos that showed the amazing recovery of a lot of patients, all with similar illnesses to Emily.

"Do you think we may have found a way through this, Jon?" I asked, clutching at the spot in between my ribcage, as I held my breath.

Jonathan licked his lips slowly, then nodded. "Maybe," he whispered, he eyes not leaving mine.

After weeks of not allowing myself to feel a thing, huge tears began to fall followed by deep gut-wrenching sobs.

Jon pulled me into his arms and hugged me to his chest.

My tears made two large spots on his pale blue cotton shirt. "I'm sorry," I said, when I eventually calmed down. I looked up into his eyes. His lovely grey eyes—so like Emily's.

I kissed him.

Light kisses at first that turned into deep, urgent ones. I realised how shut off from my emotions I'd become since all of this started. And how, in the process, I'd shut out this wonderful man who meant the world to me.

I pulled away, grabbed his hand and almost ran down the hallway to our bedroom.

As we made it in the door, I pushed him against the wall and pulled his shirt out of the waistband of his black Levis. I bent and pulled off my jeans, in desperate need of the comfort that only he could give me.

Jonathan took my hands. "Hey, hey. What's the rush?" he whispered. He looked into my eyes before kissing me deeply, making my heart dance. Then he led me to the unmade bed and laid me down tenderly.

Removing his clothes, he climbed onto the bed beside me and

pulled my t-shirt off over my head, placing light kisses all over my neck and shoulders as he travelled down my body.

Taking my nipple into his mouth, he grazed it with his teeth causing a loud groan. His hands kneaded at my breasts as his mouth went from one to the other.

I urged him down further—running my hands through his short, dark brown hair.

He hooked his thumbs under the flimsy elastic of my not-so-sexy purple cotton panties. He took his time as he pulled them down my legs and off each foot—teasing me until I was ready to scream.

Then he kissed his way back up my body, pausing at my most intimate spot, tantalising me with his lips and tongue. He was driving me into a wild, wanton woman.

I couldn't bear it a moment longer. I pulled him towards me, and our eyes met once again. Sex was no longer the main issue. A deeper, more meaningful connection was our goal.

He lay on top of me—our eyes fused—our breathing in sync.

As he entered me, my breath caught in my throat and escaped in a cry. Tears streamed down my face as we rocked together—deeply fused into each other—easing each other's pain, allaying each other's fears. The desire beyond physical—our contact beyond flesh.

Our minds merged and locked as we did the ageless carnal dance.

I awoke to an empty bed, surprised I hadn't heard Jonathan get up. But I'd slept better than I had in weeks.

Going downstairs, the sound of Emily's giggles lightened my step as I entered the kitchen. She sat at the table playing 'snap' with Frank. Steph stood at the stove, cooking bacon and eggs.

"You seem bright-eyed, my baby." I bent to kiss Emily's cheek before patting Frank on the shoulder. "Where's Jon?" I asked, glancing around the room.

"Already gone," Frank said.

"Aw, he didn't say goodbye, the bugger. He knows I hate it when he does that." I poured myself a glass of orange juice before sitting down opposite Emily.

"They were in a hurry. I made him and Alex some sandwiches to take. They said some walls are down on the other side of the farm or something. And they've got to dig out an awful pit," Steph said.

I'd just taken a swig of juice and almost spurted it out over the table. I began to cough and laugh, wiping my mouth on my sleeve.

It was lovely to see Frank also laughing. His pot belly bounced with every deep, chocolate coated chuckle and his laughter made me laugh even harder. Emily also joined in.

Stephanie stared at us as though we'd gone mad.

"What? What did I say?" she said, looking at each of us in turn.

Her confused expression made me laugh even harder.

"An offal pit you mean—not an awful pit—although your name is probably more fitting," I managed to say eventually.

"Oh, I wondered what they meant," she said and laughed with us.

I ate a full English breakfast, the first meal I'd enjoyed since this nightmare began.

Afterwards, I left them all playing cards while I went into the office. Business at the clinic had been slowly picking up again, but the appointments were mainly the ones already booked in. So we diverted the calls to the house.

I searched the Internet and found a couple of contacts regarding stem cell research. I dialled the main number, but there was no answer, so I sent an email instead.

Then I got onto some household chores I'd been putting off for ages. I stripped the bedclothes and opened the bedroom window. Taking a breath of fresh air, I admired the way the sunshine made the landscape appear more lush and green.

When the phone rang, I raced down the stairs to answer it, praying for a response to my email.

"Hello."

"I speka wid step."

"What? Oh, hold on, please," I said, sighing deeply. “Steph—phone,” I yelled.

After loading the washing machine, I began sorting through the massive pile of ironing that had been stuffed into the laundry cupboard. The phone rang, and I charged down the hallway once again.

"Hello?"

"Mrs Lyons—am—can—ad." The signal was poor and I couldn’t recognise the voice or understand what he was trying to say.

"I'm sorry, who is this? I didn't hear a word you said."

"Accident. I've called an ambulance, but he's bad."

"What's happened? Who is this?"

"This is Alex. It’s Jonathan. He's hurt. Badly."

The phone went dead in my ear.

CHAPTER 6

My legs felt as though they'd been hollowed out and concrete poured into each void. Every step was harder than the last. I eventually made it down the hallway, through the front door, across the path, through the gate and into the field.

"Victoria?"

I ignored Stephanie's calls and continued walking.

"Victoria—what the hell are you doing?"

Stephanie appeared beside me and grabbed my arm.

I shrugged her off. No words would form.

"Where are your shoes? Are you all right? VIC!" she shouted.

I stopped and glanced down at my bare feet, shaking my head I turned to face her, numb with shock. Palpitations in my chest were making me breathless. The sunshine I'd admired just a couple of moments ago now blinded me as I stared at Stephanie. Still no words would form at all.

The sound of sirens rang out from the road at the back of the farm, and the situation suddenly seemed to register with Stephanie.

"Who was on the phone, Vic?"

Stephanie's high-pitched voice sounded urgent, making my head snap in her direction.

I stared at her.

"Who was it? Was it Jonathan?" Her eyes bored into my face.

I shook my head.

"Was it Alex?"

I hesitated before nodding numbly.

"Oh, my God. Right, Victoria—we're going back inside and I'll go to see what's happening, okay? Okay, Vic?"

I nodded again and allowed myself to be turned back towards the house. My mind raced, causing massive confusion. I couldn't concentrate on any one thing, unable to think why I felt so devastated.

Back in the house Stephanie yelled something to Frank and shoved me towards him, before bolting from the house.

In his odd, shuffling way, Frank got me to the sofa and sat down next to me. He pulled me close to him with his good arm.

Emily came into the room. She'd been having a lie down in the snug and came to investigate what all the commotion was about. She sat at the other side of me.

"Are you okay, Mummy?" she whispered.

"I think we should leave her alone, Em. She's not feeling too well." Frank said.

"Shall I get her a blanket?"

"Not right now—why don't you go back into the snug and I'll come to see you shortly," Frank said.

"I don't want to. I want to stay with Mummy."

"Please, Em. Do it for me and stay there until someone comes for you."

"But why?"

"Do it, please."

I watched and listened to the whole exchange as though a spectator to a stage show. Once Emily had left, Frank got up and shuffled to the window.

"I wonder what's happening out there. Do you have any idea, lass?"

I shook my head and lay down on the empty seat Frank had vacated.

"Who called, Victoria? Before you went outside—who called on the phone?"

I looked at him slowly. I couldn't remember who called. I closed my eyes.

I needed to shut out his questions. They made my head hurt.

I needed to shut out the sound of the sirens.

I needed to shut out the world. Just for a minute or two.

The next thing I knew, Stephanie was on the sofa beside me, stroking my hair.

A memory, just beyond my grasp, kept coming close and then scurrying away before I could pin it down.

Stephanie was crying.

I sat up slowly. Frank was now perched on the edge of the armchair opposite.

"What happened?" I said, fine hair was standing on end all over my body.

She stared at me, a deep furrow between her eyebrows, before turning to face Frank. "There's been an accident. The digger rolled, trapping Jon underneath."

"Is he in the hospital?" I made to get up, but she placed her hand on my arm.

"No—Vic—I don't know how to tell you this ..." She took a deep breath. "Jonathan's dead."

CHAPTER 7

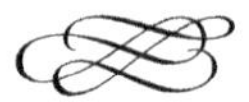

How could this be? She must be joking. I waited for her to laugh. For Jonathan to walk in with a cheeky grin on his face saying, "Gotcha!"

I glanced at Frank. He was smiling. Oh, no—not smiling. His face had twisted into something far from a smile. I turned back to Steph. Tears continued down her cheeks and dropped off the end of her chin.

"Oh my God! This can't be true—he didn't say goodbye." The deep pain between my ribs seemed to push all the air out of me. I began to think I'd never breathe again. My lungs felt as though they were turning inside out. I eventually sucked in enough air to enable the cycle to happen all over again.

This couldn't be. I needed him more than ever right now. He couldn't be dead. I was no stranger to this limbo-like disbelief, being somewhat experienced with death. First, my mum. I didn't think I'd recover from the shock of her death. At only eleven years old, I'd needed her more than ever before.

The death of my dad didn't hit me as hard. Of course, I was devastated, but being older and no longer living at home helped. My everyday stuff had been easier to deal with. Nobody knew my dad except Steph, and I'd sworn her to secrecy. So I was spared their sympathy and pitying glances. I had managed to forget about it until I got back to my room each night, where I acknowledged the truth and grieved alone. The reality didn't hit me until three months later when I eventually returned home.

Now Jonathan. My sweet, caring and considerate husband. My soul mate. Best friend. What had I done to make the universe punish me like this? I had a gnawing emptiness where my stomach should be.

"Emily!" I said, standing up on wobbly legs and rushing to the snug. Stephanie followed.

Emily had fallen asleep on the sofa. Her green fleecy blanket pulled up high under her chin.

Standing over her, I froze. This poor darling was already going through hell. Shit, we all were. But she was only five years old and very sick. And now, on top of all that, she would have the heartbreak of losing her dad. Just when I'd been thinking this nightmare couldn't possibly get any worse.

I walked back through to the kitchen, leaving her to sleep a while longer. I needed to figure out how I would explain where her daddy had gone.

The phone rang, and I automatically doubled back to the hallway.

"Shall I?" Stephanie said, appearing in the snug doorway.

"It's okay." I picked up the receiver. "Hello, Victoria speaking."

"Mrs Lyons?"

"Yes."

"Brian here, from stem cells Research. I got your email, and I've replied but I thought I should follow my email up with a phone call to explain. I'm afraid we're not able to accept any applications until after the first of July next year. The Chinese government are trying to—"

I didn't hear any more as I zoned out. One more kick in the teeth, just as I'd finished telling myself life couldn't get any worse.

I would never say that again. Someone up there was having a good fucking laugh at our expense. I had an overpowering urge to laugh.

Stephanie hovered to the side of me. As I glanced at her, I felt giggles bubbling up from my stomach until I could control it no longer. I dropped the phone. The handset dangled and swung, banging into the hall table. The laughter that belted from me sounded hysterical to my own ears, hysterical until it turned into choking sobs, and then I screamed.

Stephanie jumped forward and grabbed the phone. "Hello—I'm sorry—this isn't a good time right now—could you call back?"

Frank hadn't moved a muscle. He'd been in the same position for the past hour or so. Sitting bolt upright, one arm on the arm of the chair, the other looked as though it was twisted uncomfortably to the side of him. He was staring at an invisible spot in front of his face, not seeming to notice me at all.

I turned to a sound in the hall. Alex stood in the doorway. He removed his cap as he stepped into the living room.

"I'm so sorry, Mrs Lyons," he said, his face twisted with grief, as though having a huge battle with himself not to cry.

I knew that feeling well. I nodded at him. "What happened?" I said with an unrecognizable flatness to my voice, mirroring the way I felt inside.

"I'm not sure. I left Jon digging the pit and went to get us both a drink from the truck. When I got back the digger had rolled off the bank, and Jonathan had been thrown from the cab. He was trapped underneath," his voice cracked as he buried his head in his hands. "He was already dead."

Steph jumped forward and put her arms around him.

I couldn't say much. A strange numbness enveloped me once again. Jonathan had died, and my baby would follow him. The stem cell treatment had been her only hope. And now that was no longer an option.

I was tired of this rotten fucking life. Maybe it would be kinder all round if I injected Emily and myself with a sedative, and just go to sleep. At least we would avoid the pain of Emily's illness and we'd all be together again.

How could I live without Jon?

Why would I want to?

Nothing made sense without him.

I got to my feet. "I'm sorry, Alex. I need to go for a lie down."

I left Stephanie comforting Alex and went upstairs to my bedroom. Our dirty sheets covered the floor where I'd thrown them after stripping the bed earlier. I picked them up. They still smelled of Jonathan and our lovemaking. Wrapping them around me, I climbed onto the bed.

The breeze from the open window blew the curtains into the room, and something fluttering caught my eye.

A piece of paper had been wedged between the mirror and the frame of the dressing table.

I quickly got off the bed, sheets still wrapped tightly around me. My heart pounded so hard I could hear it.

It was a note from Jonathan.

I kissed you goodbye, but couldn't bear to wake you.

Thanks for a wonderful night—you are my world.

I love you.

Jon xxx

CHAPTER 8

"The cars are here, Vic." Steph called through the bedroom door.

"Won't be a minute." I glanced at my reflection. I wanted to do my beautiful man justice, but there was no denying the fact: I looked like shit.

My chestnut curls were scraped into a tight bun, which did nothing but accentuate the gaunt, widow look I'd perfected over the last few days.

Dark shadows surrounded my hazel eyes, making them appear sunken in my face. My thirty-one-year-old face resembled someone at least twenty years older today.

My black trouser suit hung off me. I've never been what you could call fat, but I normally had more curves than I did now. I rummaged through my drawers for a belt. Otherwise, as soon as I dropped my guard, I was sure to drop my trousers.

I smeared some tinted moisturiser onto my cheeks and applied a light coat of mascara. I had no doubt it would be running down my face before too long. Finally, I touched my lips with some strawberry lip-gloss. I would have to do.

I paused at the top of the stairs, held my breath and exhaled in several controlled blows.

"I can do this. I *can* do this," I whispered. Then closing my eyes, my fingers fiddling with my locket, I said a silent prayer for the strength to get me through the day. A lot of chatter came from downstairs, and I braced myself for the rush of sympathy.

Emily and Steph came out of the bathroom behind me.

"Oh, there you are, my baby." I held out my hand, and Emily ran towards me. I'd always hated seeing children dressed in black, and today was no exception. Steph had bought Emily an outfit for the funeral. A little black velour dress that finished mid-thigh, white tights and black patent leather shoes.

I had arranged a babysitter to start with. But Emily had begged to come, so I agreed in the end if she felt well enough.

"You ready, sweetheart? We'll give your daddy a fabulous goodbye, okay?" I flashed Stephanie a grateful smile, and she placed her hand on my shoulder briefly.

"Okay, Mummy. Will he see us?"

"You bet he'll see us." My voice sounded much brighter than I expected.

"I don't want to cry. Grandad said that Daddy wouldn't like to see me cry."

I sat down on the stairs and pulled her onto my knee. "Today's different. I'm quite certain we're all going to cry today, but hopefully, afterwards, we'll laugh, as well. It's okay to be sad. We loved him."

She was struggling to blink back huge, unshed tears. "I'm very sad, Mummy."

I thought my heart might stop. I had to force myself to breathe and keep my face as straight as possible. I swallowed down a huge lump in my throat before continuing. "So am I, sweetheart. Come on, let's do this."

We held hands as we walked into the kitchen. Everybody stopped talking, as though somebody had pressed the mute button. Then, one by one, they began chatting again.

A steady stream of friends and neighbours stepped forward to pay their respects. Jonathan had been well known and well liked.

I glanced out of the window at the funeral cars and my breath caught in my throat. Frank had chosen the coffin, and it was beautiful, pale pine with stainless steel fittings.

He'd also chosen a simple arrangement of spring flowers for the top. Mainly daffodils, and the sight of them brought back memories of my mother's funeral. I thought it ironic that I was burying my husband almost twenty years to the day after my mum was buried. Life could be so cruel.

We'd asked for donations to be made to Ronald McDonald House instead of hundreds of flowers.

I had a pet hate about flowers.

I loved them in their natural environment, but I hated seeing mountains of rotting flowers after funerals. They always set my mind racing, imagining what else was rotting.

I hated receiving flowers in everyday life, hated arranging vases and having to remember to change the water. Not to mention the cloying, sickly stench as they decomposed into slimy stems in the vase. I'd much prefer a box of chocolates to say thank you or sorry.

However, I'd left the final decision to Frank. Today was not all about me; he'd lost his only son. I searched the sea of tea-swilling bodies and spotted him standing next to the dining table, looking out of place.

I caught his eye and nodded at the door. He was beside me a few moments later, and I left the house on his arm. Emily held my other hand with Steph close behind. The four of us got into the only funeral car. Everyone else would follow in their own vehicles.

As we set off, Emily asked what the box in the other car was for. It hadn't occurred to me she wouldn't know, but why would she? She'd never had anything to do with death in her short life.

My eyes darted to Stephanie and Frank, who looked as horrified as I felt.

"Remember what we were talking about the other day? About what happens when a person dies?"

Her eyebrows furrowed. "Yes. They go up to heaven."

I nodded. "Yes, that's right. But not every part of them goes to heaven, just their spirit."

"What's the spirit?"

Her little screwed up face tore at my heart as she clearly tried her best to understand what I meant.

"The spirit is what everybody has inside their body, and when a person dies, it's because their body is broken or old. Which is why their spirit leaves the body and goes to heaven."

Emily didn't say anything, her gaze fixed on the car in front.

I continued, "So Daddy's body is in the casket. That's what a funeral is for, to say goodbye to his body."

"Daddy's inside the box?" Her face turned white and her little eyes bulged from her head.

"His *body* is in the box, baby. Daddy's in heaven."

"I want to see Daddy." She began to cry.

"You can't, my baby." I thought my heart would break as I listened to her sobs.

I hadn't gone to see Jonathan, myself. I couldn't bear the thought of seeing the damage he'd suffered to his lovely body. The inquest would no doubt fill in all the gruesome details for us. In the meantime, I chose to remember the way he'd been that last beautiful night.

Frank held his hands out towards Emily, and she scrambled onto his lap.

"I want to see my Daddy, Grandad," she cried.

"I know you do, lass, but Daddy is in heaven. He's not in the box, I promise. Like Mummy said, that's just an empty body, like an overcoat left behind."

Emily sobbed the rest of the way.

The service had been touching and beautiful. Several people got up to share stories about my wonderful husband, tales from before we'd even met. I didn't get up, but I'd written a poem and Jon's best friend, Pete, read it out for me.

There wasn't a dry eye in the place.

Afterwards, we went to the local pub for a bite to eat and a few drinks.

Stephanie seemed distracted, but insisted she was okay. When we arrived home later on, I realised why. A handsome young Spaniard sat on the doorstep.

"I think you have a visitor, Steph."

"Oh, my God. I thought he was joking when he said he was on his way."

"Looks serious to me—how about you, Frank?"

"Er—yeah he does." Frank nodded.

"I'm sorry, Vic. Today of all days."

"Don't be silly, life goes on. Plus Jon would have loved to see the look on your face right now." We all laughed, including Frank.

Steph climbed out of the taxi.

"Are you feeling okay, Frank?" I asked.

"Aye, lass, as good as can be expected."

"Come on then. I don't know about you but I'm dying for a nice cup of tea."

"Me too?" Emily chirped.

"You can indeed and I'll even put a spoonful of sugar in it for you."

"Like Mary Poppins?"

"Exactly like Mary Poppins," I said.

Emily had recovered from her earlier upset. She'd had a short nap on the sofa in the foyer of the pub, but considering her condition, she'd done well.

We passed Stephanie and Hector still standing on the front lawn. I smiled at Steph, and her eyes flashed with amusement.

Hector was extremely good looking, with dark brooding eyes and a shock of black hair, a complete contrast to Steph's pale freckly skin and bleached blonde hair.

The house seemed empty.

Now the funeral was over, we needed to get on with everyday life and develop new routines. At least my past meant I knew what to expect.

Emily was pale and exhausted and after our cup of tea I said, "Bath and then bed for you, Miss Em." That was Jonathan's special name for her, and it was out of my mouth before I realised what I was saying. "I'm sorry, my baby."

"It's okay. Do you think Daddy had a nice time today?"

"I do indeed. Did you see how many people came to say goodbye?"

She nodded. "When I die I'll only have two friends, Edward and Kaylie."

Her words tore a hole in my already tattered heart. My eyes filled; I couldn't believe I had any more tears left to cry.

"You will have many, many friends when your time comes, my baby. But that's a long way off yet."

Talk of Emily dying gave me physical pains in my head and my chest, all my nerve ending seemed on high alert. I'd faced enough tragedy in my life; Jon's death had been the last straw for me and I absolutely refused to allow another member of my family to die without a damn good fight. I made a vow to myself right then to do everything in my power to help Emily beat this, no matter what I had to do.

“Come on, let's both have a bubbly bath.”

“Together?” Her eyes lit up.

I nodded. “Why not?”

We squished into the smaller-than-average bathtub. I'd over-filled it, and the water gushed over the sides every time either of us moved. But I didn't care. For the first time in ages, Emily was giggling as we blew bubbles at each other.

Steph knocked on the bathroom door.

"Vic, can I have a word?"

"The door's open, Steph. Come on in."

She opened the door, taking in the mass of bubbles surrounding the bathroom and laughed. "Must be a tight squeeze in that bath, Em. There's no room left for the bubbles—they're all over the floor."

Emily laughed and blew a handful of bubbles at Steph.

"Hey, cheeky!" Steph said, trying to catch the bubbles in mid-air. Then she sat on the toilet lid and turned to me. "How are you doing?"

"I'm fine. Where's Hector?" I raised and wiggled my eyebrows and smiled.

"Downstairs. Which is what I wanted to talk to you about. He's asked me to go out for a drink but I wanted to check with you first."

"Of course you should go with him. You don't need my permission, silly," I said, shaking my head.

Emily giggled, and I plonked a handful of bubbles on the top of her head.

"I know I don't, but tonight of all nights, I thought you might need me here."

"No, you're fine. Emmie and I are going to bed soon. We're shattered, aren't we, baby?"

Emily nodded and continued piling bubbles around her face like Santa's beard.

"I bet you are. It's been a long day. Frank's gone to bed too. I'm worried about him, Vic."

"Now the funeral's over he'll probably begin to feel a bit better."

"You're amazing, Vic. I've wanted to say that to you all day."

"I'm no more amazing than you. You've kept us all going this week. Now go, before he changes his mind. He looks nice, by the way. Young, but nice." I smiled.

"He can be nice when he wants to be, but looks aren't everything."

I cocked my head to one side. "You still need to tell me what went on with you two."

"I will, over a glug of wine one night. I promise," she said.

"Sounds like a plan. Oh, by the way, you'll need a key to get back in. Take mine off the key-hook. I won't be going anywhere tonight," I said.

"Okay, my darlings. See you in the morning."

Once I'd tucked Emily up in bed, I went back downstairs to the kitchen and poured myself a glass of milk. The house seemed eerily quiet, and I wandered around for several minutes before ending up in the snug. After flicking through all the channels, I switched the TV off again, unable to concentrate on anything.

I prayed for the next few weeks and months to pass quickly. This rawness wouldn't last forever, no matter how hard that was to believe right now.

I turned the lights off, leaving only the hall light on for Stephanie, and climbed the stairs to bed.

Emily was asleep as I peered in her room. I considered getting into bed with her, but didn't want to create bad habits. I forced myself into my own bedroom, instead.

Last week's dirty sheets were back on the bed. I didn't know when I'd be able to wash them, but I wasn't ready yet. I switched my bedside lamp on and crawled under the duvet, burying my head into Jonathan's pillow and inhaling his rapidly fading scent.

An extreme rush of emptiness gripped my core, followed by an overwhelming urge to pack a bag, bundle Emily into the car and escape this hellhole. But I couldn't escape it, no matter how far or how fast I ran.

An intense loneliness like nothing I'd ever experienced before engulfed me. I missed Jon with every fibre of my being. I wanted, more than anything, to lock myself in my room, shutting everything and everybody out until I could make some sense of life without him. However, that wasn't an option. I needed to maintain a front for Emily's sake. She was all I had right now.

After a few minutes, I reached for the corny paperback I'd been using to switch my brain off all week. The turned down page corner indicated I was more than halfway through, yet I couldn't remember one word of it.

"Shove up fatty, you're on my side," Jonathan said, as he climbed in beside me.

"You're cold." I rolled across the bed.

"Will you let me warm my feet on you?"

I laughed. "Don't start that again." Cold feet at bedtime had started more play fights than I could possibly begin to count.

He pulled me back across the bed to him and we snuggled, my head on his shoulder.

"I've missed this," I buried my face into his chest and inhaled deeply.

"Me too. I told you I'd come back."

"Come back?" My stomach clenched. "Come back from where?"

"From the other side."

Realisation dawned, and I sat up with a start. My eyes fixed on the empty mattress beside me.

Where had he gone? He'd been here. Jonathan had just been here; I would stake my life on it.

I touched the mattress; it was still warm.

"Jonathan?" I called in a hushed voice, tinged with hysteria. "Jonathan. Please, come back."

My pulse thundered in my ears, and as I moved, the paperback slid to the floor making my heart leap once again. I glanced at the clock—almost eleven.

A bang rang out from downstairs, and I shot out of bed.

"Jonathan," I called again. My rational mind told me Steph must have arrived home, although it was unlike her to go banging and crashing through the house knowing everyone would be sleeping.

I passed Emily's room and checked on her again. Her soft snores told me she was sound asleep. I closed her door so she wouldn't be disturbed.

The bang came again, and prickles formed at the nape of my neck, spreading down my spine. The sound of my pulse mixed with the sawing sound of my locket as I pulled it side to side on the chain.

Maybe I had inherited my mother's gift after all? Jon promised he'd come back for me if he could. I'm sure I hadn't imagined him in my bed—no dream could be so vivid. But what made him vanish like that? Unless he wanted me downstairs for some reason.

I crept down the stairs, preparing to crap myself if I came face to face with Steph or Frank. They'd probably scream the house down too.

At the bottom of the stairs, I realised that, apart from the hall light I'd left on for Steph, the house stood in darkness. Steph would have turned at least the kitchen light on.

I crept into the kitchen, holding my breath and unsure of what I would find, but certain it wouldn't be Frank or Steph. I heard the sound again as the back door swung open and banged against the rubbish bin.

How odd. I didn't remember checking the door earlier, but sure I would have noticed it swinging open like this.

I shut the door and locked it with the key, relieved I'd found the cause of the noise.

Suddenly I sensed someone behind me, at the same moment I felt warm breath on the back of my neck.

I shuddered. "I knew you were here," I said.

Cold hands caressed my shoulders and down my back, sliding under my arms to fondle my small breasts.

The breath hitched in my throat. I was terrified to turn and face him in case he vanished once again.

"Oh, Jon," I whispered.

I slowly turned. My smile froze as I came face to face with Shane Logan.

CHAPTER 9

I stifled a scream as I staggered backwards, knocking the rubbish bin sideways. A half-eaten tray of fish, chips and mushy peas landed face down on the tiled floor beside me. Along with an array of empty tin cans, newspaper and spaghetti hoops.

"Well, if it isn't the merry widow herself." Shane smiled, showing his crooked yellow teeth. "You took your time. I was just coming to find you."

"Wh—what the hell are you doing in my house?" I managed to utter, my heart and head hammering in unison.

"That's not a very nice welcome is it? I merely came to pay my respects." The smile turned into a scowl and his eyes flashed menacingly. A large, yellow headed pimple quivered on his top lip.

"Get out. Get out of here now or so help me ..." I shook my head, terrified. My stomach twirled and I could barely breathe. I scratched at the back of my neck, trying to erase the memory of his warm breath.

"I've been dreaming about your fiery temper since you tried to stick the boot in outside the surgery that day. I love my ladies with a bit of push back." He made a grotesque hip thrusting motion towards me.

"What are you doing here, Shane?" My thoughts were in a riot. I needed to keep my cool.

"I came to ask if you need anything—" he paused and leered, "—now your hubby's gone and bit the dust."

"You're disgusting, do you know that?" I sneered at him, edging my way into the hallway.

"I like your sexy nightdress." His eyes ran down my body, making me shudder with dread.

I glanced down and was horrified as I realised I was wearing nothing but a skinny cotton slip that barely covered a thing.

"Don't be shy—your mother wasn't," Shane laughed at his own stupid joke.

"Just get out before I call the police, Shane. How do you think you'll get away with breaking and entering?" I prayed he wouldn't hear the quiver in my voice.

"No breaking in needed. You invited me over, today at the pub. Told me you'd leave the back door open," he raised his eyebrows, a smile still playing on his pockmarked face.

"You talk utter crap. Nobody will believe a word of out of your mouth," I said, shaking my head once again.

"You're not the first respectable woman to fancy a bit of rough and you won't be the last."

Reaching the hallway, I backed up to the telephone table. Shane still had a smile on his face and I could tell he was playing games with me.

I twirled round and fumbled for the phone. My hands could have been stumps for all the use they were and I dropped the handset. Shane jumped forwards and swiped the unit off the table. It made a loud crash as it hit the floor.

He shoved me towards the snug doorway.

"Just go, Shane. If you leave now, I promise I won't call the police. In fact, I won't tell a soul you were even here." My heart pounded in my chest.

"I'm going nowhere until I've paid my respects. I've been

dreaming about this for weeks." He shoved me backwards once again.

Although he wasn't that big, he was strong, much stronger than me.

"Shane! This isn't funny. Do you have no compassion at all? I buried my husband today." My back hit the snug door.

He leaned past me, twisted the knob and pushed me into the room.

I was terrified. If he continued like this, God only knows what he would be capable of once he passed the point of no return.

My heart hammered against my ribcage. "I'm tired, Shane. Please, just go. I appreciate you paying your respects but can we leave it at that? You don't want to get into trouble, I'm sure."

"One kiss." He licked his lips, his tongue stroking the top of the yellow pus filled mound.

My stomach lurched. "I beg your pardon?" I shook my head.

"One kiss and I'll go." He shrugged.

"I'm tired. I can't cope with this right now." I reached the sofa and could go no further. Although my voice sounded calm, silent screams exploded in my head.

He continued toward me until we were nose to nose. A broad, sickly smile spread across his spotty face as his putrid breath hit my nostrils, making my stomach lurch.

I considered slamming my knee into his crotch, but thoughts of Emily stopped me. I wanted the situation to stay calm. I'd have more of a chance of talking him round that way.

He licked my face. The stench of tooth decay, alcohol and rotten food almost knocked me over.

I yelped, recoiled and wiped my face with my arm. The smell wouldn't go away. I was bending backwards in an arc over the front of the sofa, the backs of my legs and my shoulders touching, but my bottom still raised.

As he pressed his crotch towards me, I gave up and collapsed backwards.

He straddled me.

I was shaking uncontrollably, petrified now, and strange whimpering sounds escaped me.

He lifted my hair and began kissing and licking my neck.

"Stop!" My voice a high-pitched squeal.

"I've not even started yet. Now be quiet. Think yourself lucky you've not had to wait too long to get your pussy stroked." He laughed. "What's the acceptable time-frame for a widow to abstain?"

"This isn't funny anymore, Shane. My friend will be back any minute now and her boyfriend will kick your arse."

"If you're talking about the bleached blonde pygmy who lives here, she doesn't even *have* a boyfriend. I've been watching. I know exactly who comes and goes, right down to the namby-pamby prick living over the garage."

The seriousness of the situation suddenly struck me. I wasn't going to be able to talk my way out of this.

He pinched my nipple through my slip.

I squealed, taken by surprise.

He repeated it with my other nipple.

"Hmmm, a matching pair, look at that," he said, staring at my chest. "I've dreamed of your little titties and I can't wait to slurp on those juicy big tit-ends. All I had to do was get rid of that dick-head husband of yours."

"What the hell are you talking about, Shane? I'm begging you, stop this before things go too far." The blood gushed in my ears. I was distraught, couldn't believe this was happening to me. His mention of Jon horrified me. Could he be responsible for the accident? My whole body sagged and succumbed to the tremors I'd managed to hold at bay up to now.

"No can do, I'm sorry, look at this," he leaned backwards, giving me an eyeful of the bulge filling the crotch of his jeans. "He has a mind of his own and there's no arguing with him." Once again he chuckled at his own words.

He undid his top button and holding onto the front of the waistband, he pulled each side of the denim apart. The zip slid down.

The tip of his angry penis poked above the waistband of his boxer shorts. But even worse than that—I could smell the dirty, cheesy thing.

It felt surreal, as though time had stopped. My raspy breath and thudding heartbeat filled my ears.

He pushed his underwear down further and his penis sprang free and hit my chest with a wet thud.

I squealed again, tears pouring from my eyes.

He laughed. "Kiss it."

"Please, Shane ..." My hands pushed at his bony hips.

"Kiss it, bitch!" he grabbed a handful of my hair and yanked my head towards the glistening, purple tip.

My tightly shut lips brushed against the disgusting, sticky head of his penis.

"Again," he said, thrusting towards my mouth.

I pushed at his hips with all my might, yet my strength had gone. My arms shook with sheer effort. I considered biting his dick, but the thought made me gag.

Tears streamed down my cheeks. My eyes squeezed tight shut, trying to block out what was happening.

"Suck it—suck it!" his voice came out in short gasps. I thought he was close to ejaculating. "Suck it!" He pulled my hair so hard I heard it snapping out at the roots. "Suck!"

My lips parted and he thrust himself into my mouth. My garbled cries seemed to excite him all the more as he bucked his pelvis towards my face. I retched at every thrust.

Suddenly he pulled himself away, grabbing me by the hair again he dragged me into a horizontal position on the sofa, tearing the flimsy straps of my slip. He ripped the rest away in one tug.

"Shane!" My voice close to hysterical.

"Delicious," he said as he glanced at my naked body. "A bit skinny, but fucking delicious."

He put one leg up on the seat and stared down at me. Gripping the shaft of his penis, he yanked at it several times, his testicles bouncing obscenely above my face.

I thought I might pass out. The room spun and sounds echoed reminding me of the swimming baths I went to as a kid in Manchester.

He put his leg down. His jeans were bunched around the other ankle and he kicked them off. Then he grabbed at my breast and squeezed it roughly before climbing on top of me, shoving his knee in between my legs.

I could feel him pushing his penis at the top of my thighs.

He re-positioned himself and found his target.

I cried out loud, biting my bottom lip as he thrust himself into me.

Hardly breathing, eyes shut tight. I couldn't escape, so I would have to let him finish, which by the sound of his grunts, shouldn't be too far off.

His thrusts became more frenzied and erratic. He ejaculated half inside me and the rest in a puddle on my stomach.

A white hot pain tore through me as Shane sank his teeth into my breast. I couldn't hold back any longer, the intense pain was too much to bear and a scream belted from me.

All of a sudden the snug door burst open and Frank stood in the doorway with his walking stick raised above his head. He moved faster than I'd seen him do in years. The stick connected with Shane's head with a deafening crack.

Shane didn't seem at all fazed by the attack.

He pushed himself off me in one fluid movement and back-handed Frank, sending him flying to the ground.

Frank didn't move. He lay on his back with half of his broken walking stick still in his hand.

I looked for the other half and found it on the floor at my feet.

Shane jumped on top of Frank blocking my view. All I could see was Shane's bony, bare arse in the air, thin legs ending with grimy white socks and grubby trainers. But the sound was unmistakable as Shane's fists made sickening contact with Frank's face.

Without thinking, I snatched up the jagged, wooden stick and launched myself towards them, thrusting the tip into the middle of Shane's back with all my might.

Shane let out a blood-curdling scream.

He tried to reach behind his back as he writhed around on the floor, but to no avail. His dark grey t-shirt had an even darker stain surrounding the protruding stick.

I grabbed hold of his hair and pulled him backwards. The stick thrust even deeper into him as he hit the polished wooden floor.

On automatic pilot now, I ran to the kitchen and got a packet of cable ties from under the sink, a towel and a dining chair.

When I returned, both Frank and Shane were as I'd left them.

Tapping into an energy source I didn't know I possessed, I had Shane tied like a trussed chicken and fastened to the chair within minutes. The wet gurgling sounds coming from him were terrible—it was obvious to me the stick had punctured his lung. Blood dripped noisily, landing in a puddle on the floorboards.

I stuffed the towel around the wound as much as I could, but he was losing a lot of blood.

I rolled the hand-knotted wool rug to the side of the room before the blood could reach it.

Satisfied I'd tied Shane properly, I ran to Frank's side.

"Frank?"

His eyes flickered but stayed shut.

"Frank, can you hear me? I'm going to call an ambulance."

"No, lass, no ambulance," he said in a whisper. His eyes flickering open. A small trickle of blood ran from his mouth.

"Are you all right? Where are you hurt?" I said, my teeth chattering.

He shook his head and tried to lift himself up onto his good elbow.

"Help me up, lass," he said, seeming a little more with it.

"Here you go, after three. "One—two—three." I'd forgotten how solid he was. We managed to get him up and sitting on the sofa.

"Get dressed, lass," Frank said softly.

I looked down and crossed my arms about my nakedness before I sped from the room to the laundry where I threw on a sweatshirt and a pair of jogging bottoms. I winced as the fabric touched the bite mark on my chest.

When I got back Shane's mouth was moving, as if having a full on conversation without sound. I couldn't understand a word of it.

"I'd better call an ambulance, Frank. Not that I want to. The bastard doesn't deserve anyone saving him." I couldn't stand still my legs shook so much and my voice warbled. "If you hadn't come in, God knows what he'd have gone on to do." I turned to leave. "I'll call the police too."

"Wait," Frank said. He was lying back on the sofa, trying to catch his breath. "How old is he?"

"I dunno, nineteen, twenty, but he won't see twenty-one if I don't do something quick."

"Can you fix him?"

I paused in the doorway. "Eh?"

"Can you fix his wound, temporarily?"

"Yes, but he still needs a doctor."

"No, you don't get me. If you can fix him for now, he's the right age … You know … to be a donor."

His intention hit home. I considered what he was saying for a split second. "We can't do that, Frank. It'll kill him. We'll be locked up for life."

"Who would know? We could feed him to the pigs, or even make use of Jon's offal pit."

"Although I'm tempted at the prospect of turning this sack of shit into pig chow, I'm not a murderer, and neither are you," I said, my voice sharp and to the point.

"What's our alternative?"

"Call the ambulance and the police. Like I was going to." I shrugged.

"Think about it for a second, lass. What will happen if you call the police?"

I shook my head.

"I'll tell you, shall I? They'll get him fixed up and he'll claim damages, probably bankrupt you if this country's law system is anything to go by. You'll be charged with attempted murder and he'll get off scot free with a pocket full of *your* cash. And Emily will still die."

His last sentence hit me like a smack in the face. I plonked down beside him on the sofa, my eyes glued to Shane. Gurgling noises came from his chest, and although he looked unconscious with his head lolling backwards, his mouth still moved.

"Can you do the transplant?" Frank grasped my wrist with both of his hands, his eyes large and hopeful.

"If we got him to the clinic, perhaps, but I'd struggle alone," I said quietly.

"You're not alone, I can help. What about putting it into Emily safely?"

I nodded, "That's the easy part. It's just an injection."

I couldn't believe we were really discussing this.

Shane's breathing was becoming even shallower.

"He needs help now or he'll be dead."

I tipped Shane's chair back onto two legs and dragged him down the hallway to the front door, leaving a trail of blood behind me. I searched for my car keys, remembering Stephanie had taken them.

"Fuck!" I snatched the keys to Jon's truck from the key-hook beside the front door but realised the truck was jammed in behind my car. "Fuck! Fuck! Fuckity, fucking fuck!"

Frank came down the hallway towards me. He seemed more unsteady on his feet than normal. "Calm down, lass. What's wrong?"

"I need to get him to the clinic but Steph took my car keys."

"Get the wheelbarrow. That'll have to do."

CHAPTER 10

It took sheer grunt and determination to get Shane and the wheelbarrow across the path and down the driveway to the clinic.

I unlocked the door and switched on the light.

Shane was unconscious. Blood trickled from his nose, and his face had a blue tinge.

I needed to work quickly. It didn't take a genius to work out he was in a bad way. I had to remove the stick and insert a chest tube to drain off the blood from his injured lung.

Frank shuffled into the clinic.

I screamed and dropped a stainless steel dish to the floor making a loud crash. "Oh, Frank, you made me jump."

"You said you needed help. I may not be the best, but I'm better than no one."

"I need to get him up onto the table to remove the stick. It's in quite far, so that may be easier said than done."

"Undo him from the chair first," Frank said.

I found a pair of snips in the tool box Jon had left under the counter, and cut the ties.

Shane's arms flopped to the floor, and he almost fell off the wheelbarrow. The gurgling sound coming from his chest sounded like someone blowing bubbles down a straw.

My whole body was shaking. Frank took hold of my upper arms and shook me roughly.

"Calm down, lass. Think of Emily."

"Okay." I nodded. The mention of Emily had the desired effect, and I took several deep breaths.

"Frank, we need to get him up but he's heavy. Any ideas?" I held my breath, trying to prepare myself for what we were about to do. The adrenalin had kicked in and the professional in me was finally in control.

"If you help me lift his top half as far as we can, I can hold him in place while you grab his legs," Frank suggested.

"Okay, let's do it then. We're running out of time."

We managed to get Shane up onto the table. Frank's good arm was strong. I doubt I'd have got him up on my own.

"Right, I need to get a few things and then can you hold him while I try to pull the stick out?" I said.

He nodded.

I gathered all the equipment I needed, plus a stack of towels. "Okay, are you ready?" I glanced at him, taking a deep breath.

Another nod.

"When it comes out there'll be a lot of blood so be ready, and shove these towels onto the wound right away." I placed the towels on the table beside Shane.

The broken stick splintered as I tried to grip it.

Frank found some adjustable pliers in the tool box and handed them to me. "Try these."

The stick came away with a sickening squelch and Frank rammed a towel into the hole.

"Press down hard while I organize myself," I said.

Shane began to groan.

"Oh shit, Frank. If he wakes up, we're screwed."

"Can't you drug him?" Frank asked.

"We're already up to our eyeballs in trouble, Frank."

"Exactly, so what difference will a bit more make? Better to be hung for a sheep than a lamb," he said, in a matter-of-fact tone.

I stopped and glanced around at him. His eyes were more alive than they had been in ages, and if I didn't know better, I'd think he was actually enjoying this.

However, Frank was right. If Shane woke up, things could get a whole lot worse. A little bit of anaesthetic would have to do. "What would you say he weighs?"

"He's a big lad, but more wiry than heavy. I'd say around ten stone, maybe eleven."

I quickly worked out the quantities and prepared the medication.

"Okay, let's hope this is right. If not, it could kill him anyway."

"It'll work. This is the opportunity we've been waiting for. I think Jon sent him our way."

Immediate memories of Shane shoving his dirty penis into my mouth flashed through my mind, followed by the feelings of disgust I'd had when he violated my body. I shuddered. Wanted nothing more than to sink into a steaming hot bath and scrub away every last trace of Shane.

I didn't think Jon would send him to me, not like this.

But if it worked, if it helped get Emily well again, every disgusting second would have been worth it.

After I applied the chest drain, Shane's breathing steadied. My next step was to remove the Proteum. I'd already studied the location of the Proteus.

Shane lay face down on the operating table. I shaved a small area at the base of his skull and cut out a square of skin with a scalpel. Then with a tiny, high-powered hand drill I made a circle of holes and cut through the remaining bone with a fine wire saw, making a bone flap.

The proteus gland was easy to find. I inserted a needle and drew off the yellowish blood-tinged fluid, ten mil in total. I found it hard to believe this little bit of gunk could be the difference between life and death for my gorgeous girl. And for Shane, too.

I had to decide what to do with him next. We had two choices. To monitor him until he died naturally—which could take up to twenty-four hours—or administer a euthanasia solution.

My priority was to get this liquid gold into my baby, as I didn't know how long it would be viable. "Frank, I'm going over to the house. I might need you. Can you follow me?"

"What about him?" Frank nodded at Shane, who already looked dead to me.

"He shouldn't be a problem for a little while. We'll be back in no time."

I raced from the clinic, praying Shane hadn't got any other terrible disease such as HIV. But it was too late to concern myself with all that now. This whole thing was a huge gamble, but less of a gamble than doing nothing.

Emily didn't stir as I entered the bedroom.

I stroked her hair. "Mummy has to give you some medicine, my baby. You'll be okay," I whispered as I took out the syringe and attached a clean needle. Using a surgical wipe, I cleaned inside of Emily's arm before inserting the needle into her vein.

She made a tiny sound and my heart contracted, but she went straight back off to sleep. I said a quick prayer before injecting the fluid.

I was still sitting in the same position on the floor next to the bed when Frank entered. Tears streamed down my cheeks.

I shook my head, putting my fingers to my lips as I got up, my legs threatening to buckle under me.

"She didn't even wake up." I sobbed as I fell into Frank's arms.

His breath caught in his throat. "I thought you were about to tell me you'd changed your mind," he whispered.

I tipped my head towards the hallway and walked out of the

room, taking one last look at Emily before closing the door. "I hope we've done the right thing. What if it doesn't work? Makes her ill even? I may be a vet, but there's a world of difference between treating animals and treating humans." I had palpitations in my chest as the enormity of what we'd just done suddenly hit me. Bile rose into my mouth, and I raced to the bathroom, falling to the side of the toilet as my stomach contents splattered into the bowl.

Frank stepped into the room behind me and rubbed my back. "Are you okay?"

I nodded, wiping my mouth on my sleeve.

"It can't hurt her, lass, and besides, this is her only hope."

"But now we have to deal with Shane. In fact I'd better get back to the clinic," I said, pulling myself to my feet and linking my arm through Frank's, drawing strength from him.

"What do you think we should do?" he asked.

"Maybe a lethal injection is the kindest way," I said. "I know he's a nasty piece of work, but I hate the thought of causing any unnecessary suffering."

Even this would still haunt me. I had a rule to never euthanize pets in the clinic if they were fit and well. It amazed me how many people refused to rehome unwanted pets. They'd prefer to put them to sleep rather than suffer the distress of losing their owner and their home. I would try to convince them that lots of pets are rehomed successfully, but if I still couldn't sway their decision, I'd send them to the opposition to do the dastardly deed.

I found it hard enough to put a sick and distressed pet to sleep. It always tore my heart out to have to administer that fatal shot. However, in Shane's case, one fatal shot was better than leaving him to die naturally. There was no telling how painful or drawn-out that would be.

Frank nodded. "You go on ahead and I'll follow."

"No, get your wheelchair, and we'll go together. You must be worn out." I linked my arm through his.

Frank started laughing halfway down the stairs, and I thought maybe he'd gone mad. He braced himself against the wall to prevent him toppling down the stairs.

"What are you laughing at?" I asked, shaking my head, concerned I would have to cope alone if he'd lost his marbles.

"I didn't think to use the wheelchair earlier. Instead, I suggested the wheelbarrow and the next thing you had him strapped to the wheelbarrow and pegging it down the path," he howled.

I shook my head, "We weren't in our right minds, were we?" I smiled shakily, relieved he hadn't cracked up.

Once Frank recovered from his hysterical outburst, I helped him into his wheelchair and pushed him back to the clinic.

Shane was still out cold.

I prepared a dose of pentobarbitone, a short-acting barbiturate I often used for animal euthanasia. I knew it was still used for death by lethal injection in some American states.

My hands shook uncontrollably as my earlier nerves returned. It was one thing operating on him, but another thing entirely to inject him with this fatal dose. Tears streamed down my cheeks as I approached Shane.

I gripped his wrist, feeling for a pulse.

Nothing.

I checked the pulse at his throat.

Still nothing.

Grabbing the stethoscope from the hook on the wall, I listened to his chest.

Silence.

A sob escaped me, and I realised I'd been holding my breath.

"What's wrong, lass?" Frank said, getting to his feet.

"He's dead, Frank." I threw the syringe back into the tray, as though it were a hot rock.

I grabbed the table to steady myself, taking several deep breaths as I tried to clear my head.

"Already?" Frank's eyes were wide open as he shuffled past me to examined Shane himself. Satisfied Shane was indeed dead, he made his way back to his wheelchair and sat down heavily. His fingertips pressed to his mouth.

"So what now?" I asked, a strange numbness spreading through my limbs.

"Maybe the offal pit would be the easiest option.

"I thought about that, but they're still looking into Jon's accident. What if someone finds him?"

There had been lots of comings and goings the past week as they examined the scene and the digger. They had no reason to examine the offal pit, but I didn't want to risk it.

Frank wiped at his mouth with the back of his hand, his eyebrows furrowed. "Okay, we have no choice then. We'll have to dismember him and feed him to the pigs. They'll eat him, bones and all. We'll need to send Alex away for a few days, in case he notices something."

Frank had a home-kill business before he got sick. He would also slaughter and butcher his own animals in a slaughterhouse on the other side of the farm. We sent our cows away nowadays, so the slaughterhouse hadn't been used in a number of years.

"I can't do that!" I shook my head. "Can't we feed the body to them whole?"

"Maybe, but to be honest, I wouldn't want the pigs to make a connection between human beings and food. They might try to feast on anyone who dared to enter the sty if they did."

"I guess," I said. "But Frank, there's no way I can chop him up." I shook my head.

"The equipment is easy to use. Maybe I can manage with a little bit of help."

"How will we even get him there? Plus we can't leave Emily on her own." I felt my hysteria rising.

"If we get him over to the cold store tonight, we can finish the rest tomorrow. No one uses that area now, so he'll be okay. Can you drive the quad?"

"I suppose, but no one's been in there in years. How do you know the tools are still there? What if the power's been turned off?" My head spun.

"Because I didn't arrange for anything to change at the time. We just shut it up. I'll need the large bunch of keys in the garage. Do you want to get them when you fetch the quad? I'll wait here," he said.

I was grateful to be told what to do. Even though Frank wasn't physically strong any more, he'd taken control of this situation.

"Okay, but first I'll check on Emily," I said.

I raced towards the house, my thoughts in turmoil, dreading what I would find. Had I injected an animal with a powerful potion, I would monitor them closely in case of a bad reaction.

Instead, we'd left Emily all alone.

CHAPTER 11

The house had an eerie stillness. Steph wasn't home, thank God. I don't know what I'd have told her if she had been.

I could hear Emily's soft snores as I opened her bedroom door. Relief flooded my entire body as I slumped to the floor beside her bed, my breath coming out in pants.

"What have I done?" I whispered stroking her head. The sheer magnitude of my actions blew my mind. But if … if … I shook my head and inhaled deeply. I needed to pull myself together: this night wasn't over yet.

Confident Emily was comfortable and not having any terrible reactions to Shane's Proteum, I left.

I grabbed the keys and the quad, and was back with Frank and Shane's body within minutes.

Concerned about unbalancing the quad, we decided Frank would drive to the slaughterhouse with Shane on the back while I followed on foot.

When I arrived, Frank had already entered the building and a single light shone from the outer room.

Between us, we managed to heave Shane's body onto the butcher's block inside the cold store.

When I dropped Frank off at home afterwards he almost bounced up the path, as though he suddenly had a renewed zest for life.

I went back to the clinic to clean everything Then, I gave the house the once over, eliminating any signs of Shane ever being there, from the overturned rubbish bin and splintered walking stick, to pools of blood in the snug and up the hallway. I'd watched enough episodes of CSI to know the blood would still be visible with Luminol or a black light, but I hoped nobody would have the reason to look.

Surprisingly, the telephone wasn't damaged, except for a black scrape along the side. I put it back onto the hall table.

Almost finished, I took the rubbish bag out to the wheelie bin, and almost screamed when I came across a push-bike leaning against the back of the house.

I hadn't even thought about how Shane got here. I stashed the bike in the back of the shed.

Happy I'd done all I could for now, I locked myself in the bathroom. Standing under the high pressure shower jets, I scrubbed my skin until I thought it would bleed.

The gnarly puncture marks on my breast had already begun to weep, which didn't surprise me. Shane must have had untold amounts of bacteria in his mouth considering his putrid yellow teeth. I dabbed the wounds with an antiseptic solution and covered the area with a sterile dressing.

The sun created an orange glow in the room as I dragged myself into bed, aching from head to toe.

A ring-necked dove began cook-a-looing outside the bedroom window. I groaned—I was so shattered my bones ached. I heard a car pull up and a door slam. Steph's timing couldn't be more perfect.

I lay staring at the ceiling, sleep evading me. I began going over and over the night's events. Shane had raped me, and who knows what he'd have gone on to do. But had he deserved to die?

I'd thought so, as I impaled the walking stick into his back. I needed to stop him, come what may. Maybe if he'd died of his injuries after calling the police and ambulance, I wouldn't feel so bad.

What we ended up doing to him instead was terrible, but Emily would die without this chance. She might still die if the Proteum didn't work. Frank was right: Shane would have caused more trouble for us if we'd let him go. He was that sort. He never would have accepted defeat by a mere woman and an old man.

I was amazed I'd gone through with it. I'd managed to switch into professional mode, enabling me to perform the actual operation. It felt no different than if I'd been working on a dog, and if the said dog had died, I would feel immense sadness just like I did now.

I didn't think the police would come looking for Shane. He wouldn't have told anybody what he intended to do. There was nothing to connect him to us at all.

Almost asleep, I heard a tap on my bedroom door and Steph calling my name. I sat up as her head poked round the door. "Oh, hi, Steph, what's wrong?" My voice sounded gritty and hoarse.

"Emily's not well. She said her head hurts and she's crying for you."

I shot out of bed and down the hallway to her bedroom.

She was lying on her side and rocking, holding her head.

My heart was jumping out of my chest. I couldn't think straight. This was obviously connected to what we'd done.

"Hey, baby, are you okay?" I said as I slumped beside her on the mattress.

"My head hurts," she cried.

"I'll get you some medicine. Wait there." I ran into the bathroom and returned with a bottle of infant Paracetamol. I gave her a large dose and prayed it would have some effect.

Frank stood in the doorway. "What's happening?" His eyebrows furrowed together.

"She has a headache," I said. Our eyes met and held for a few seconds. "Try to get back to sleep, my baby. I'll get in with you, if you like?"

Emily nodded and wriggled over, giving me room to slip in beside her. Frank and Steph crept from the room.

I snuggled in next to her tiny body and rocked her gently. Her whimpering continued for a few minutes and then began to subside as the medicine kicked in.

My thoughts raced. I must have been out of my mind. To murder a man, even a disgusting and worthless excuse of a man, and remove his Proteum had seemed reasonable in the thick of the situation. I hadn't been thinking straight, obviously still in shock from being attacked and raped. But now I knew we'd made a huge mistake.

Although I'd researched all I could about the trials, the details were sketchy and I didn't know if something should have been added to the hormone before being injected into the patient or if it had been diluted and given over a period of time. All these factors were relevant, but I never even considered them last night.

Now she was in a lot of pain. I couldn't even call a doctor. What would I tell them? *Oh, by the way, I injected her with a rare hormone I stole from a guy I murdered, and now she's sick.*

Emily's breathing steadied and I noticed she'd fallen asleep. I held her tightly and closed my eyes.

I stretched and yawned. Light poured in the window and I squinted, surprised not to see my bedroom, and the whole situation landed with a thud on my shoulders.

I reached to the side of me and found an empty space where Emily had been.

I shot upright.

I ran downstairs, my feet barely touching the ground, my mind in a frantic spin.

The sound of Emily's giggles stopped me in my tracks.

She sat on the rug in front of the gas fire. Magazine cuttings and paper were strewn around her. A large piece of purple card had several pictures glued to it.

Making collages had been one of Emily's favourite hobbies before she got sick, but she hadn't been interested lately.

"Mummy!" Emily squealed as she got to her feet and launched herself at me, hugging my legs.

"What's going on here then?" I ruffled Emily's hair and raised my eyebrows looking at Frank and Stephanie. They both smiled and shook their heads.

"I'm making a surprise for you, Mummy," she said, taking my hand and leading me back to the rug.

"So I see, and a beautiful job you're doing too." I was amazed. I tried to stay calm, not to jump to conclusions. It was early days yet. But she seemed totally different from a few hours ago. She even looked different.

Emily plopped back down and continued with her collage.

I poured myself a strong coffee, still feeling bog-eyed. I would have loved nothing more than to crawl back into my bed for a couple of hours, but it was ten o'clock already. Frank and I had an appointment with a dead body and a dozen pigs. I shuddered. I didn't know how I was going to be able to do this.

I needed to speak to Alex, but by now he would have already done his rounds, and Saturday afternoon and Sunday were his days off. We'd have to work out an excuse to get him away for a few days next week. This would make the running of the farm quite difficult, but we'd have to make do.

My stomach was in knots and the blood surged through my veins. I took a deep breath trying to clear my thoughts and act, on the outside at least, as normal as possible.

"Where did you get to last night, Steph" I smiled and wiggled my eyebrows.

"Oh—umm—we had quite a lot to discuss." She blushed, glancing from me to Frank and back again, and flashed me a *stop-it-right-now* look.

I grinned. "Is that what they call it?"

"What did you guys do?" she asked.

"Nothing," I said, a little too quickly. "Tried to have an early night, but I couldn't sleep."

Frank nodded. "Me too."

"Are you busy today, Steph?" I asked.

"Hector said he may come over this afternoon, if you don't mind? He's staying at a bed and breakfast in town."

"Fine by me. Frank said he'd help me with a few things around the farm. Any chance you can look after Em for a couple of hours?"

"Course I will, but can't Alex help you? Frank can stay here with me."

"I'm actually looking forward to getting out on the farm again." Frank jumped in.

"Oh," Steph said. "Of course, if you're sure."

"We had a little chat last night, didn't we, Frank? And he wants to start doing the odd thing about the place now he's feeling a bit better," I said.

"That's a great idea. You don't want to overdo things though. I've noticed you're a bit unsteady on your pins today. Where's your walking stick?" Steph asked.

I'd forgotten all about his walking stick.

"I want to try without it for a while," Frank said. "I'll never get any stronger if I don't try."

"I guess," Steph replied. "Oh well, I'm glad you're feeling up to it. Great to see the little miss is feeling a bit better too." She nodded towards Emily, who was still busily cutting up different bits of paper.

"Yes, amazing really." I flashed another glance at Frank and he shrugged.

"How about after lunch then, Frank?" I asked, eyebrows raised.

"How about now? I might be too tired later," he said.

"You want to go now?" My stomach flipped.

Frank nodded. "May as well while I'm a box of birds."

"Okay. Let me get a quick shower and I'll be with you in ten."

I raced up the stairs.

Frank met me at the front door less than ten minutes later. We walked slowly to the shed and I took two sets of disposable overalls and a box of surgical gloves from the storage shelves. The clinic storeroom wasn't big enough to keep everything in there so we kept the bulk of the non-medicinal supplies out there.

"We'll need to get you a new stick." I looked around for something he could use for now. I found long metal pole that wasn't ideal, but better than nothing. "I forgot all about it in the excitement. But Steph doesn't miss a trick, does she?" I handed it to him.

"I know," he said, trying the pole out for size.

It was too long and the way he held it reminded me of a shepherd.

"We'll need to be a bit more careful around her, lass."

I moved my car out, then helped Frank to climb into Jonathan's truck. "Are you gonna be able to do this, Frank?"

"I'll have to be. I can't say I'm looking forward to it, but what we are about to do has been made so much easier seeing the way Emily's bounced back today."

"Could the Proteum be working already?"

"What other explanation is there?"

I shrugged, shaking my head.

I pulled up outside the converted stone barn, dreading going inside.

"Okay, Frank. The way I dealt with everything last night was by imagining Shane was an animal," I said, more to myself than anything.

"He was an animal," Frank growled. "I could have killed him with my bare hands for what he did to you. Would have done too, if this pathetic old body of mine hadn't failed me.

I rubbed his arm. "You did well, Frank. We stopped him together, that's the main thing. Anyway, let's focus. If we're gonna get through this, we can't think of him as a person," I said, trying to psych myself up, but I was already trembling and my breathing much heavier.

Frank had done this hundreds of times with a beast and didn't seem at all fazed by the situation.

I, on the other hand, had always been squeamish around raw meat. As a girl, I'd come over all faint whilst standing in the queue of a butcher's shop with my mother. I ended up staggering outside and flaking out on the pavement. I decided to be a vet that day, intending to save all the animals in the world. I also turned vegetarian, which lasted all of a week. I came home from school one day to the aroma of my mother's Carne Guisada, a Puerto Rican beef stew, and that had been the end of that.

Frank made his way to the butchery door and produced a large bunch of keys from his pocket.

I reluctantly stepped from the truck, took a deep breath, and followed him inside.

The outer area was dark and cool, and approximately four metres square.

Frank flicked a series of switches and the whole area lit up making me jump out of my skin. I was a complete nervous wreck. How *was* I going to do this?

The entire back wall had been fitted with wooden shelving from floor to ceiling.

A door stood open to the left and led to a storage shed. The cold store stood to the right, like a room within a room. A heavy white fridge-like door with a large metal handle made my heart hammer. I'd seen a film once where someone got locked in a similar room and died.

"Frank," I cried.

Frank stopped, his hand on the handle and glanced at me, eyes wide.

"What if the door closes behind us?"

He smiled and exhaled loudly. "There's a safety on the handle, lass. When we're inside we place the handle just so," he said, unlatching the handle and closing the door again. "As you can see, the handle prevents the door from locking until we come out and reset the lock from the outside."

"Are you sure?"

"Yes," he said, looking into my eyes and nodding. "Don't worry."

Frank opened the door and walked inside.

Although I'd been in the cold store last night, I couldn't remember anything about it. I'd been on automatic pilot, focused on dumping Shane's body and getting back to Emily as fast as I could.

It was a similar size to the outside room, except for the thickness of the walls, which were tiled in small white squares with grey grout. A black metal plate approximately one inch wide surrounded each wall, and had grotesque looking hooks fixed to it, sticking out every so often. A large wooden butcher's block took up the whole left hand wall, a variety of power tools hung beside it. And a blue wheelie bin stood in the corner.

I expected the smell to be quite bad, even though I knew Shane hadn't been there long enough for the rotting process to begin. I took my hand from my face and almost gagged at the sight of him.

Shane had been crudely hoisted onto the butchers block.

He lay face down, and his bare, blue legs and behind the first things I saw.

My legs buckled.

Frank reached out and steadied me. "You okay, lass?" he held my arm and once again, staring intently into my eyes.

I nodded and swallowed noisily. It felt as though my throat had closed up.

"Come on then. Let's get this over with," he said.

I helped Frank organise the tools he would need. I focused on Frank's face, tried not to look at Shane, and managed to keep myself together.

The loud saw in the empty room made my feet leave the floor.

The first cut was the worst part for me.

I screamed as Frank removed Shane's head.

Once his arms and legs were gone, the rest could have easily been a side of pork.

Frank needed me to help him hold Shane's carcass a couple of times. His left hand was still very weak, but on the whole, he managed alone.

As he removed each section, he threw it into the huge blue bin where it landed with a sickening wet thud that made my stomach lurch.

I kept imagining Emily's beautiful smiling face, and when that no longer helped, I forced myself to remember what Shane had done to me last night. What he probably would have done to Emily and Frank if he hadn't been interrupted.

Once all the bits had been chopped into smallish pieces and placed into the bin, I helped transfer several pieces into a separate plastic bucket that I put into the back of the truck. Then I wheeled the blue bin back into the fridge and hosed the area down.

Frank had designed the room for a quick clean up, and it came in handy now more than ever.

Once everything was back the way we found it, we drove to the pigsty.

I knew Alex would have already fed the pigs this morning, but they were always hungry.

As we emptied the bucket, they dove into it as though they hadn't been fed for weeks. The noise they made was horrific.

The portions mostly looked like large joints of meat, but I almost passed out as one of the pigs began chowing down on a foot.

I sat down at the side of the sty and placed my head between my knees, gasping for breath.

CHAPTER 12

It took almost half an hour before I could face driving the short distance back to the house, and I sat in the car for a further ten minutes, preparing to face anybody.

We sat in silence, both absorbed in our own thoughts.

The matter-of-fact way we'd dealt with the disposal of Shane's body had now hit me. I couldn't get the image of the pig and the foot out of my head.

We walked into the house to the sound of people talking. Frank headed straight up the stairs.

Stephanie and Hector sat at the dining table.

I forced a smile, struggling to behave as normally as possible.

Stephanie, chatting with her guest, flashed me a quick smile, her attention diverted or she would have noticed my strained grimace

"Hi there, Hector. I'm Victoria"

Hector jumped to his feet and took my hand, shaking it several times. "Please to met wiv you," he said.

I nodded, taking a good look at this stranger who had been a big part of my best friend's life for the past two years, and finally understanding the appeal. He had the kindest dark-brown eyes I'd ever seen.

I smiled, glancing at Steph. "Where's Em?"

"She went up to her room a few minutes ago."

My heart missed a beat. I prayed she wasn't sick again.

"Are you feeling okay, Vic? You're a funny grey colour."

"I don't know. I've come over all queasy. It's probably a stomach bug. I think I need to lie down for a little while. I'll check on Em when I go up."

"No problem. Can I make you some lunch? We were waiting for you to come back before I made something."

My stomach contracted. "Not for me, thanks."

As I pushed Emily's bedroom door open I expected to see her lying on the bed, sick again.

But instead the bedroom looked as though a toy bomb had exploded. Every single plaything Emily had accumulated in her five years lay strewn across the floor. My daughter sat in the corner, playing with her doll and a tea set, chattering in two dialogues, her expression intense and happy.

"Goodness gracious! What's happened in here?" I laughed.

"I couldn't find Filly," she said, looking up, her small face alive with delight.

"How are you feeling?" I touched her forehead. Warm, not hot. My back muscles relaxed. A normal temperature.

"I'm better now!" She ducked to avoid my hand.

My breathing hitched. "Are you?"

She nodded, concentrating on pouring a pretend cup of tea.

"I'm glad you're better, baby. Stephy is making you some lunch —are you hungry?"

She nodded again. "Can we bring it up here? We're having a picanic."

We'd been struggling for her to eat anything lately. Now she wanted food. My spirits lifted as hope crawled out of the dark space in my heart.

"Maybe you should take your picnic downstairs. Mummy's going for a little lie down." I stroked her curls. "Then I'll help you tidy up this mess if you like?"

I couldn't sleep.

Instead, I lay on the bed for a while. Emily's miraculous recovery played repeatedly in my mind. However, the guilt ate away at me. Even seeing how well Emily seemed to be recovering couldn't block out the awful events of this morning. I didn't think I'd ever forgive myself for being so selfish to take a life in order to save my daughter. It felt abhorrent to me, yet deep down I couldn't shake the tinge of relief.

From under my pillow, I pulled out the handwritten note Jonathan left less than a week ago. The empty ache I carried around with me since became almost unbearable at that moment.

All my breath left me, reminding me of a dog's toy being squeezed until it eventually twists in on itself, as happened every time I allowed myself to think about life without him. Sweet memories of him in my bed last night only added to my despair. I still couldn't believe it had been a dream—the way he cuddled me had seemed so real. I wished Jon could see how different Emily was today.

I folded the tatty piece of paper and made a mental note to put it into a snap-lock bag, otherwise there'd be nothing left to read.

An hour or so later I gave up the battle to sleep, showered quickly, dressed, put on some lipstick and went back downstairs to face life.

As I walked into the room, Stephanie had her hand down the

side of the sofa, Hector was on his hands and knees looking underneath the dining table and Frank was standing in the kitchen with a frown on his face.

"What's going on?" I asked.

"Hector's wallet is missing," Steph said.

"When did he last have it?"

"He showed Emily a photo of our place in Spain. Now it's vanished." She shrugged.

"That's strange. Did you ask Em?"

"Yes, she's playing outside in the garden." Steph nodded to the back door.

"Is she? Wow!" I walked to the window and watched Emily pedalling furiously on her trike. The colour had returned to her face and she looked like any other normal, healthy little girl. Tears pricked my eyes again.

I opened the back door. "Emily, come here a minute, baby."

She came zooming towards me, her hair blowing off her face in the breeze, and her cheeks rosy from the exercise. "Can we go to the park, Mummy? Steph said I had to ask you."

"Are you sure you feel up to it?" I asked, not believing any of this.

"Yes, I told you I'm better."

"Well okay then. But first, we need to help Hector find his wallet. Have you seen it anywhere?"

Her eyebrows furrowed. "No."

Something in her expression made me question her answer. "Are you sure, Emily?"

"I said no!"

"Okay then, can you come and help search before we go to the park?"

We searched the house from top to bottom. In fact, if they hadn't all seen his wallet earlier, I think I would have accused Hector of lying, for whatever reason.

"Oh well," I said. "It's bound to turn up sooner or later. I'm taking Em to the park. Does anybody want to come?"

Steph shook her head, taking her seat next to Hector again.

"I will," Frank said.

"Great. The fresh air will do us all the world of good."

"Can I take my trike?" Emily chirped, excited.

"Course you can." I smiled. It had been months since she'd had the strength to ride her bike

Emily and Frank were getting into the car as I placed Emily's trike into the boot. The trike seat lifted up, revealing Hector's missing wallet stashed inside.

My stomach lurched.

Why the hell would Emily do that? She'd never stolen anything before, never mind told me barefaced lies. Hiding the wallet behind my back, I opened Emily's door.

"Emily, do you remember what we were looking for inside?"

"Yes."

"What?"

"Hekkers wallip."

"Do you know what the wallet looked like?"

"Yes."

"Tell me."

"Like a purse," she said.

I nodded. "What colour?"

"Brown."

"Like this one?" I brought my hand from behind my back.

Emily's breath caught in her throat and her hand flew to her mouth.

"Any idea where I found it?"

She shook her head. Her huge eyes watched me, wary.

"In your trike seat.

She didn't say a word.

"What? Did you find it, lass?" Frank said, trying to turn in his seat to look at us.

I waved the wallet so Frank could see. "I'll be back in a tick."

I walked in and placed the wallet between Stephanie and Hector on the table.

"Where did…?" Steph shook her head, puzzled.

"Ahh!" Hector sighed.

"In Em's trike. She must have forgotten. I'm sorry."

"Oh, no harm done," Steph said. "All his cards and money are in there which is why he panicked." She laughed, before explaining to Hector in Spanish.

Judging from his huge arm movements and the sounds he made, he was overjoyed at the discovery.

"I'm sorry, Hector," I said.

"Hokay," he nodded and smiled, his brown eyes twinkling.

I touched his arm, then left.

CHAPTER 13

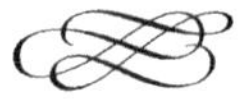

"Mummy, do you think Daddy's happy I'm better?" Emily asked.

"I'm sure he is, baby," I said as I parked the car outside the school gates.

Emily had got up early this morning and dressed herself for school. At first I refused, wanting to keep her home for at least another day or two. In the end, she begged and pleaded and although I didn't want to, I agreed.

"How does he know?" she said.

I switched off the engine and turned to face her. "Remember, I told you his spirit is in a special place. He can watch everything we do. He's with us all the time."

She wrinkled her nose. "Do you think he seed me take Hekkers wallip?"

"Maybe. Why did you do that, Em?"

"I was playing a game with my friend. Am I very bad?"

"Not bad, if you were just playing a game. But you shouldn't tell lies. Hector was very upset. And besides, you had no friends over, baby, so that's another fib you are telling me."

"I did, he's my new friend, we had a picnic and he said I should take Hekker's wallip."

Mrs Farnworth, Emily's teacher, smiled as we entered the classroom and hurried toward us.

"Emily! What a nice surprise. Look everyone, Emily's back with us. Say hello to Emily."

A chorus of, "Hello Emily," followed.

Emily beamed from ear to ear, thrilled to be the centre of attention.

The children gathered around Emily, and all seemed to be chattering at once.

Mrs Farnworth pulled me to one side. "How is she? I planned to call you today."

"She's well, but call me if she gets tired and I'll come for her."

"Of course I will. I'm sorry about Mr Lyons. What a shock."

"Thank you, I don't think it's sunk in yet," I smiled and shrugged.

"When I lost my husband it took weeks, maybe months before I stopped expecting to hear his key in the lock. You have family around you, though, and that should help. I found the quiet moments and empty house to be the worst."

"Yeah, I can imagine. I'm trying to keep myself busy, so I don't have time to think."

She gave me a sympathetic smile and glanced at the children who had begun to get a little unruly.

"I'll let you get on," I said, bobbing out the door.

I raced home. There were several farm chores I needed to do before feeding the pigs.

Alex had gone to a three-day cattle fair in London. He seemed confused when we gave him all the details last night, but didn't complain. Especially when we told him we'd booked him into a hotel, all expenses paid, plus he would still get his wages.

Stephanie had been engrossed in her renewed relationship with Hector. She'd not spent any nights at home since he'd arrived, which had made things easier for Frank and me.

I ran into the garage and replaced my shoes with farm boots. As I hurried back to the front of the house, Frank stood waiting for me.

"You don't need to come with me, Frank. It's pretty straightforward."

"I want to."

I winced as I pulled on a jumper.

"Still sore, lass?"

I nodded. "Should begin to ease soon. I've started a course of antibiotics."

The bite had turned as nasty as I'd predicted, but in a way I needed the scar. At least I'd have a physical reminder every time I got a fit of the guilts about what we'd done. I needed to keep it real. Shane had been a monster.

We took Jonathan's truck because it handled much better on the farm than my Saab.

So much of Jonathan remained in the truck. His sunglasses hung hooked over the visor, there was a pile of his favourite CDs in the centre console, and several post-it notes had been stuck to the dash. I fingered them as if they were treasures, reading a reminder to take the truck for a service, the phone number of someone called Tom, and some measurements. Several receipts stuck out of the ashtray.

The cab even smelled of how Jon smelled when he came home from a hard day on the farm. It comforted me, and if I closed my eyes, I could imagine him sitting beside me. My heart swelled. Overcome with emotion, I blinked several times to stop the tears from flowing. I needed to stay strong.

I started up the engine and gave myself a mental shake.

"Penny for them?"

"Emily has an imaginary friend," I said as I backed out of the driveway.

"A lot of children do, lass. I remember Jonathan having one when he was a lad."

"I know, but she said he told her to take Hector's wallet."

Frank shrugged. "She's been through a lot, poor thing. I'm sure there's nothing to worry about."

I nodded. "Yeah, you're right, as always." I smiled at him as I drove through the farm gate, but I couldn't shake off a niggling doubt.

We stopped at the chickens first. We had two dozen free-range hens in a large fenced field to the left of the house. The henhouse sat at the edge of the field, making the nesting boxes easy to access without having to enter the field itself.

I hooked a basket over Frank's left arm and he lifted the hatch and began to fill it with eggs.

"How much food do they have?" I asked. I'd never had anything to do with the feeding rituals of the animals. Jonathan always fed them in the mornings, leaving me free to organise Emily and Frank.

"Fill the large green feeder with layer pellets and the trough with water and that should do. Oh, and scatter a jug full of mixed grain about the place and they'll be happy as Larry," Frank said.

"Great. Let's hope the rest of the jobs are this easy." As I said it, I knew of one in particular that wouldn't be.

Once I'd fed the hens, I met Frank at the back of the henhouse and helped him collect the last of the eggs. We placed them into several trays before loading them into the back of the truck.

Next we checked on the two hundred cattle grazing in the fields. A few of them had newborn calves.

Our neighbours, Carole and Nick, owned a dairy farm and they removed their calves at birth to hand feed them for six weeks. I couldn't bear that. All our calves stayed with their mothers for at least six months.

After making sure there were no obvious problems, we checked the water troughs and the fences and walls.

The next stop—the pigs.

This is what I'd been dreading. Frank didn't have the strength to do this alone. We hadn't fed them since Saturday morning and I knew they'd be ravenous. We stopped off at the barn and collected what remained of Shane in a large plastic tub.

As we pulled up at the sty, the pigs went berserk. They even climbed on top of each other to get closer to us and the *food*.

Once again my stomach lurched as I heard the wet slopping sounds of the meat slapping onto the ground. The deafening grunts and screams of the pigs as they fought to get their share. I shook and my knees began to fold.

I shut my eyes tight and clamped my hands over my ears, but it didn't make the experience any less traumatic. My imagination filled in the gaps and in my mind's eye I saw a huge pig chomping down on a foot. My memory added the overgrown yellow toenails and clump of ginger hair at the base of the big toe.

I gave up my breakfast down the side of the sty wall.

CHAPTER 14

"I don't know about you, Frank, but I'm gagging for a cup of tea," I said, opening the front door.

"You're not kidding. You've worked me like a horse today, lass," Frank smiled.

"You love it," I bantered.

"I do, actually," he said. "Not felt this good in a while if I'm honest."

"There you go then, stop bloody moanin'." I winked at him and he chuckled.

The phone rang.

"Hello?"

"Hello, Mrs Lyons. Rosemary Jackson here, head mistress at Emily's school."

"Oh, hi. What's wrong? Is Emily sick?" I stopped breathing as I waited for her reply. Frank stood in the doorway, his eyebrows wrinkled together and one hand at his throat.

"No she's fine, but I do need to speak to you about Emily. I wonder if you could come in a little earlier today for a chat?"

"Yes of course. What time?" My heart raced.

"Say two-forty-five?"

"Okay. See you then." I hung up.

Frank stepped forward. "What was that all about?"

I shrugged. "I don't know, some problem at school. Emily's fine though. The head teacher wants to see me this afternoon."

Alex came in behind Frank.

Alex had been doing most of the work around the farm these past two weeks. Frank and I mainly organised the feeding of the animals. Except for this morning, when several cows had broken through a fence and we had to help round them up.

With me being probably the only vet in the world to be scared of cows and Frank hobbling about on his new walking stick, it had been a sight to behold.

"Right you two, how does ham sandwiches washed down with copious amounts of tea sound?"

"Sounds like heaven. I'm starving," Alex said.

"Yes please, lass." Frank looked tired out.

"Are you not eating, lass?"

"I'm feeling a bit queasy." I rubbed my stomach.

"Again? You need to eat something. You're wasting away."

"As if!" I laughed, clearing up the table.

I tidied the kitchen, and had just enough time to change before leaving for the school.

"Do you want me to come?"

"That's okay, Frank. You can have a well-deserved rest. Will you be okay on your own?" I felt silly saying this after what I'd seen he was capable of the past couple of weeks. But after six years of caring for him, it was a hard habit to break.

He cocked his head to one side, his mouth in a straight line.

"Okay, okay, but call me if there's a problem," I smiled.

I flicked through a magazine as I sat outside the Head Teacher's office.

It brought back memories of my own childhood and the only

time I'd been in trouble at school. All I'd done was pass a note to my friend, asking her if she wanted to hang out after school, but the teacher intercepted it and sent me out of class. I was mortified.

Mrs Jackson opened her door and beckoned me in. I'd never met her before, as she only joined the school after the Christmas break. From the sound of her voice I'd imagined a tall dark-haired woman, but in reality she was a dumpy redhead, dressed in a beige skirt suit that was at least a couple of sizes too small.

"Hello, Mrs Lyons. Sorry to keep you."

I entered her office and sat on the chair offered. A couple of seconds later Mrs Farnworth came in, looking flustered.

She bobbed her head at Mrs Jackson and placed her hand on my arm, giving it a gentle squeeze before taking the seat next to me.

"Okay," Mrs Jackson began. "I'm sorry to call you in, Mrs Lyons, but Emily has been behaving oddly since returning to school."

"What do you mean 'oddly'? Why didn't you tell me about this before now? I see you every day." I shook my head as I looked at Mrs Farnworth.

"We didn't work it out until today," Mrs Jackson replied.

"I don't understand."

"There have been a number of instances of theft over the past couple of weeks. Some of the items had been reported but shrugged off as they weren't very important things and the children could have been mistaken. For example, items from lunch boxes, a painting one of the girls had done—that sort of thing. But then Mrs Farnsworth's mobile phone vanished from her drawer, and her silver pen, a gift from her late husband, went missing from her desk."

Mrs Farnworth glanced at me apologetically, her hands in a twisted tangle in her lap.

"A hair clip went missing from one of the children's bags. Then this morning, the receptionist's purse vanished from her handbag behind her desk. Emily had just been in the office to return the class register."

"This is ridiculous!" I said, horrified. "She wouldn't steal them. Why on earth would she?" As I spoke, I remembered Hector's stashed wallet.

"I know this will come as a shock to you, Mrs Lyons, but we located all the missing items this morning. They were in Emily's cubby-hole in the cloakroom.

I shook my head, astounded. I couldn't work out why she would do something like this.

"She's been through an awful trauma—losing her father is bound to have some effect. Plus, I understand she's been sick."

I nodded, fingering my locket.

"We think she might benefit from a spot of counselling."

"Really? She's just a little girl. She's seemed all right to me. I thought she was coping."

"Nobody knows how a child will react to these things. It wouldn't hurt to use another resource the school provides. A counsellor comes here every two weeks. She works with children for a whole range of reasons, none of them more deserving than Emily. There's no reason to feel ashamed, I can assure you."

"I'm not ashamed."

"Great, I'll arrange for Janet Davies, our regular counsellor, to see Emily the next time she's here."

"Of course, if you think it will help." I shrugged, trying to make light of Emily's pilfering.

Mrs Farnworth smiled at me and once again placed her hand on my arm. "Don't worry. She'll be all right. Janet's amazing."

Emily was sitting alone on the mat as I entered her classroom.

My heart broke, seeing her looking so despondent after all

she'd been through. Her bright, smiling face had been all that had got me through the last couple of weeks.

"Hey, baby," I said quietly.

She looked up at me, her eyebrows furrowed and her huge eyes full of unshed tears.

I smiled, bending down, and held my arms out towards her.

She scrambled to her feet and launched herself at me. "I'm sorry, Mummy." She buried her face in my neck.

"Don't cry, my baby." I got to my knees and pulled her into my arms.

"Do you still love me?"

Jonathan's beautiful eyes gazed up at me from her face and my stomach clenched.

"Of course I do, silly. I'll always love you," I closed my eyes to stop the sudden rush of tears from falling.

"But Daddy will be mad at me if he see'd me take those things."

"I don't understand, Em. Why would you take them? You know you shouldn't steal."

She began to sob.

"Stop crying, come on. Go and get your bag. Grandad's waiting to see you at home."

She slowly left for her bag, dragging her feet as she did so.

Mrs Farnworth was standing across the room, deep in conversation with another parent and she waved at me.

I smiled and waved back, wondering what the gossipmongers would be saying.

Emily and I walked to the car.

"I need to ask you once more, baby. I need to try and understand? Please, you're not in trouble, but please tell me. Why did you steal those things?"

"I didn't mean to."

"But you *do* know it's wrong?"

She nodded.

"Come on, baby. I don't want you sad. I want to help you, that's all."

"I know."

"Let's make a deal, shall we? Next time you want to take something, you tell me and we'll talk about it. I won't be angry."

She nodded. "Okay."

Stephanie and Hector were at the house when we returned home. I chose not to tell them what had happened at the school. I didn't want Emily to overhear me. I discreetly shook my head at Frank as he opened his mouth to say something and he changed the subject. I winked at him and smiled.

I busied myself in the kitchen. I'd put a ham on the stove to boil earlier and I made some macaroni cheese for dinner.

Alex came in, and as I looked up I did a double take. I'd not seen him dressed in anything other than his farm overalls before, but tonight he wore a pale blue shirt and navy trousers. His messy brown hair, although clean, could have done with a good brushing, but I didn't think it was my place to say.

"Don't make me any dinner, Mrs Lyons. I said I'd meet a friend in Carlisle and I wondered, can I take the truck?"

"Course you can, Alex. About time you got out with someone your own age." I smiled. "Who are you meeting?"

His cheeky face flushed and he seemed tongue-tied.

I laughed. "Are you meeting a lady friend?"

"Kinda. Not like that though." His face went bright red.

"Ah, get outta here. You can't fool me."

He bobbed his head, mumbled something, and left.

I'd developed a soft spot for him. He was a lovely lad; incredibly shy but a hell of a good worker. I hoped he'd find a local girl and settle down. I couldn't bear the thought of him moving on.

With the lack of social events around here it would be inevitable unless he had a girlfriend.

Stephanie breezed into the kitchen and opened the pantry.

"I fancy a glass of wine; do you want one?"

"A bit early isn't it?"

"Not at all, five o'clock's not early." Her eyes twinkled.

"You go ahead. I'll have one with my dinner, otherwise we won't get fed." I laughed.

"Don't mind if I do." She poured a large glass of white wine.

"Are you staying here tonight?" I glanced up from the half loaded dishwasher.

Steph nodded, mid swig. "Hector's working tonight."

"I don't know why you're making him pay for bed and breakfast when we have more than enough room here. He spends enough time here as it is." I filled the detergent dispenser before setting the clock.

"He asked me to go back to Spain with him last night."

My head snapped up. "Are you going?"

"No. I told him I can't leave you yet."

"Is that the real reason? Because if it is, we'll be okay."

She shrugged. "I don't know what I want. Maybe I'll let him move in here for a bit. I'm not ready to go to Spain. I don't know if I'll ever be."

"When are you going to tell me what happened?"

"Later." She nodded towards Emily who was sitting at the dining table, drawing.

I nodded.

"Plus, I thought you wanted to get the clinic up and running again."

The clinic hadn't been in use since Jon died, apart from my own secret night-time procedure. There'd been a couple of call-outs that Steph had attended. We'd talked about re-opening, but nothing had been decided.

"I do, but you can't put your life on hold for me, Steph. We'll manage if you want to go."

"That's the point. I don't, not yet anyway."

"You can't expect Hector to be happy working at that pub for long. He's an architect, for God's sake."

"Not much call for a non-English speaking architect around these parts." Steph laughed.

"I know, but it's a bit of a come down. Washing glasses and mopping up slops wouldn't be my idea of fun."

Steph shrugged. "He'll live."

I placed a stack of plates and cutlery on the table beside Emily. "I'm going to have to ask you to tidy this up soon, baby. Dinner's almost ready."

"Okay, Mummy." She began clearing away her crayons and helped me to lay the table. Today's upset seemed forgotten, her mood back to normal.

Hector came through from the snug. I'd rarely set foot in there since that night.

"Okay, who wants wine? Frank?" Steph asked, the bottle raised.

"No thanks, lass."

I glanced up as Frank joined us.

"Hector?" Steph said.

Hector shook his head.

"Oh sorry, I forget you're working tonight." She affectionately stroked his face. "Victoria?"

I sighed. "Go on then, a small one if it will shut you up."

She ignored me and poured a full glass of wine. "Oops!" She giggled.

"Oops, indeed," I couldn't help laughing with her. She'd been wonderful these past few weeks.

"No Alex tonight?" Frank asked.

"He's meeting a friend in Carlisle. I let him take the truck."

I sliced the ham and transferred the macaroni from the oven

to the table. Everyone got stuck in, including Emily who had a hearty portion followed by a heaped bowl of ice-cream with sprinkles.

Afterwards, I ran her a bath and read to her for half an hour before tucking her up in bed.

I found Stephanie in the kitchen scrubbing the baked-on cheese off the pasta dish.

"I can finish off, Steph, if you want to go and spend some time with Hector."

"He's already left for work." She placed the dish into the dishwasher. "Did you finish your wine?"

"Almost, look." I held the glass up to show her.

She wiped her hands on a towel and despite my objections, refilled my glass.

"Okay, thanks. Where's Frank?" I asked.

"In the snug, watching a war film."

I screwed my face up. "What should we do then?" I sat down at the table.

"Drink!" She laughed.

My stomach lurched. "I don't fancy that either." I shuddered and placed my glass down, knowing I couldn't possibly take another sip.

"You always used to enjoy a drink, Vic. What's changed?"

"I don't feel like one. Plus, I'm only just managing to get through the days as it is, without getting all emotional on alcohol."

"You're doing fine, Vic. You amaze me, you really do. I was saying the same to Hector only this morning."

"Talking about Hector, what's going on with you two, Steph? You seem to get on well and you obviously want to be with him."

"It's complicated." She plonked down on the seat opposite.

"What? More complicated than my life?" I gave her a sidelong glance.

She took a deep breath before continuing. "We got on great for two years, and although he's young, I thought he was the love of my life. Until one night he shattered my illusions and made me see we couldn't be together."

"How? Something terrible must have happened for you to throw two whole years away. And if it was so bad, why are you even seeing him at all?"

"I don't want to tell you. I'd hate you to treat him differently." She downed her full glass of wine in one gulp.

"Stephanie!" I laughed. "I forgot what a classy bird you are."

She belched loudly. "I know."

Then we were both in hysterics. It felt so good to laugh. For a short time I forgot all about my troubles and the huge belly laughs replaced the continuous gnawing pain in my stomach.

Sitting down on the dining chair, tears streamed down my face. "Oh, that's better," I said, gasping for breath.

"I love seeing you laugh, Vic."

I nodded and smiled. "So tell me, missus. What happened with Hector in Spain?"

Her eyes narrowed, as she shook her head. "I can't."

"Yes you can. I won't treat him any different."

"Promise?"

I promise you."

"Okay, oh man." She took a deep breath. "He beat me up." She winced as she waited for my reaction.

"Oh my God!" I said, my mouth falling open. I'd promised not to treat him differently but I knew every time I looked at him now I would see a coward and a bully.

She nodded. "We'd gone out for dinner one night and had a wonderful time. We met up with one of his old mates in the bar afterwards and all got on really well. But when we got home Hector went mad. He accused me of flirting with his mate and he went crazy." She shook her head, close to tears.

"Oh, Steph." I moved to wrap my arms around her shoulders, now shuddering as she cried.

"I ended up in hospital. Had to have micro surgery for a cut on my arm—apparently the laceration was only a fraction of a centimetre away from a main artery." She lifted her sleeve and showed me a nasty three inch scar on her right arm, between her wrist and elbow.

"Fuck, Steph. How did he do that?" I said, horrified.

"He threw a vase at me. I held my arms up to cover my face and luckily this was my only real injury."

"I can't believe Hector could hurt you. He seems so lovely and gentle."

"He is, had been for two years beforehand. He'd never even raised his voice at me. But something caused him to lose his head, big time. I don't even know why, and neither does he. He swears he'll never harm me again and I believe he means it. But if he wasn't in control last time, how can I trust he won't do it again?"

I nodded. "I'm shocked. You must have been terrified."

"I was. Now drink up." She'd recovered her poise and waved the wine bottle at me.

"I'm okay, thanks. You have it." I truly couldn't face another drop.

She emptied the last of the bottle into her glass.

"Are you scared of him still?"

"No, not scared. He's lovely and he's given up his job and his life to come here to try and win me back, but I don't want to make things too easy for him." She took a mouthful and added. "Besides, deep down, I have this thread of mistrust, as if I've glimpsed deep inside him and seen the violence he's hiding. Can I ever really trust him again?"

Considering my activities two weeks ago, I couldn't bring myself to answer her question. I too had a thread of violence hidden under my shattered surface.

CHAPTER 15

"Hello again, Emily. How are you today?" Doctor Wilson asked.

"I'm all better," Emily said.

"You look as though you're feeling better." His well-groomed eyebrows rose as he scrutinised her over the top of his glasses.

"She's been a lot better for a while now. I'm not sure if you heard, but my husband passed away six weeks ago."

"No, I hadn't. I'm sorry, Mrs Lyons, that must be hard for you, with everything." He glanced at Emily and sighed.

"But that's just it. She's been better since around the same time —she's even gone back to school." It took an enormous effort to keep my voice as normal as possible, even though my delight and surprise was genuine. I'd gone over and over what I was going to say and decided to behave exactly as I would if the episode with Shane had never happened.

"I'm very pleased to hear it. I must admit though, I'm quite astounded."

"Could it be as Emily said, Doctor. Could she be better?"

"I'm sorry, Mrs Lyons, but that's quite impossible. We'll do some more tests to see what's happening. It'll be a full day again, I'm afraid."

"No problem." I smiled, my heart racing. I had no real choice but to let him go through all his tests again.

"Can I play with the dolly?"

"Not now, sweetheart. The doctor needs to do some more tests like last time. Do you remember?"

Emily nodded, tears welling. We'd talked about the possibility of more tests and the pain it could involve. "And can we go to McDonalds after?" This had been my bribe.

"We can, but only if you be a very good girl."

Emily sailed through the day. This time she knew what to expect. She didn't cry like the first time and I praised her bravery. I promised her I would buy her a toy if she lay still for the lumbar puncture, which seemed to work wonders.

Afterwards, Emily stayed with Diane, the receptionist, and I went back through to Doctor Wilson.

"Ah, Mrs Lyons. Come in and take a seat." He smiled.

My heart beat fast against my ribs and I dug my nails into my palms, desperate to appear calm.

"I had a quick look the scans and reflex test, results and Emily *is* showing signs of improvement. I must say I'm shocked by these initial results. I've never seen such a turnaround in a patient before."

"So she is better?"

"She is responding positively to something. We'll have to wait for the results from the lumbar puncture which will give us a more definite answer."

"When will that be?"

"I'll give you a call once the results are back."

He stood up. "I don't want to put a dampener on Emily's apparent remission. However, I need to reiterate there is no possible way she can get better.

"I know, doctor."

"She seems better right now, but this won't last. I want you to be prepared for that." He ushered me toward the door.

"I understand. Don't worry."

After filling up on a Happy Meal, Emily ran up the ladder and down the slide several times without stopping. Not like our last visit when she hadn't the energy to climb the ladder even once.

My heart twisted at the memory. Jonathan and I had been devastated at the news we'd just received. Not one of my happiest memories

Later, strolling up and down the aisles of the toyshop, a continual ringing followed us, getting louder. I glanced around to see who was allowing their phone to go unanswered. I realised the ringing was coming from Emily.

"Emily. What is that?"

"What?"

"The ringing!"

"Oh." She looked away, her eyes wide, and a worried expression crossed her face.

"Emily?" I held my hand out.

She pulled out an expensive-looking mobile phone from her jacket pocket and handed it to me.

"Where did you get this from?"

"I don't know."

"Are you lying to me?"

"No, Mummy."

"Remember what you promised only last week? After you stole Uncle David's watch?"

David and Lynn were our neighbours and close family friends. Emily took the watch when we'd called in for a visit, and I'd found it the next morning in the laundry basket.

"That I wouldn't tell lies." She sulked.

"So?"

"My friend took it from the lady with the dolly."

"Diane? At the hospital?"

She nodded.

"Come on, back to the car."

"I haven't got my toy yet."

"No toy today, missy. In fact, nothing for you until you stop this stealing."

She began to cry.

"I'm not going to change my mind, so you might as well stop that noise. You can apologise to Diane too. We're going back right back now."

"No, Mummy, please, I'm sorry."

"We have to. She's probably already noticed her phone's missing. I bet she's even called the police."

Emily took a sharp breath. "The police?"

I nodded. I didn't want to upset her, but this had to stop. She had taken lots of little things in the past few weeks, including my mum's St Christopher pendant from my jewellery box. I found the chain knotted around the neck of her favourite doll. Afterwards, she swore black was white she hadn't taken it.

We walked back into the Neurology department. Diane was still on reception.

"Hello, Emily, I didn't expect to see you again today," she said with a smile.

"Emily." I gave her a nudge.

Diane looked at me, her eyebrows drawn together in puzzlement.

"Emily wants to say something, don't you, Em."

She nodded.

"Okay." Diane clasped her hands.

"I'm sorry," Emily whispered.

Diane smiled. "What for, sweetie?" She glanced at me, her eyebrows furrowed.

"Your phone."

Diane's smile vanished as she turned back to Emily. "What about my phone? Have you seen it?"

Emily nodded again.

I reached into my bag and handed the phone to Diane. "Emily took it. I'm sorry."

Diane didn't say anything, but judging by her expression, she was obviously annoyed.

Emily began crying again.

"That was very naughty, Emily. I don't know why you took it, but I've been very nice to you haven't I?"

Em, still crying, nodded again.

My stomach was in knots. I longed to pull her into my arms and calm her tears, but I couldn't. No matter how harsh it seemed I'd come to the end of my rope. This had to stop

"Did you call the police?" I winked at Diane.

"Yes I did, and they are looking for a very naughty person who takes other people's things."

Emily began to wail. "I'm sorry. Please don't tell the police."

"If I agree, you must promise not to do anything like this again."

"I promise," Emily sobbed.

"Okay, I'll let you off, just this once. But if you do it again, I will tell them."

"Go and stand at the door a second, Em," I said.

She walked to the swinging door and stood waiting for me, looking sweet and innocent. I wanted to laugh out loud.

"Thanks Diane. I don't know what's got into her lately, but this isn't the first time she's done something like this. Hopefully, between us, we've frightened her enough to put an end to it."

"Hope so, love. Thanks for bringing my phone back, and good luck."

Stephanie arrived home from the clinic at the same time as we pulled into the drive. We'd started taking appointments again and had been getting a steady stream of animals through the door.

We stepped into the hallway as Frank came down the stairs. He looked pale.

"Are you okay, Frank? Have you been overdoing it?"

He shook his head. "I'm fine. You're late."

I realised he'd been worrying.

"It went well at the hospital. The tests show that Em's a bit better than she was. The doctor is puzzled by the change in her—he said he's never witnessed anything like this before. We're waiting for the results of the lumbar puncture to find out exactly what's going on."

"That's fantastic news, Vic." Steph ruffled Emily's hair.

Frank sighed and sat down heavily on the sofa. I bent and kissed the top of his head. "Don't worry. Everything's okay," I whispered.

"Can I play outside, Mummy?"

"I suppose so." I agreed in a stern tone, not wanting her to think all was forgiven.

In the garden, I pulled her trike out of the shed. Once I was back inside I told Steph and Frank about the mobile phone.

"I wonder what's going on in her head," Steph said.

"Got no idea. Today she said her friend made her steal the phone. I hope the counsellor can get somewhere with her. She has her second appointment tomorrow."

"She never stole anything before Jon died, did she?"

I shook my head. "No—never. I wish I could help her."

"She'll be okay, Vic. You'll see." Steph grasped my fingers.

"Hopefully, after today, she won't do it again. I tried a new tack with her and refused to buy her the toy I'd promised. Then I got her to apologise to the receptionist, who frightened her with talk of the police. I felt awful, but she can't be stealing every time she lays her eyes on something she fancies. I'm getting paranoid about taking her anywhere."

"She'll stop. It's obviously a cry for help," Frank said.

"I hope so," I said.

"Are you okay, Vic?" Steph asked.

"Yeah, I'm fine. Why?"

"I heard you being sick again this morning. You should see doctor," she said. "Here you are making sure everyone else is all right but you're not taking very good care of yourself."

"Just nerves, that's all. I was dreading going to the hospital."

"I can come with you next time, lass."

"Thanks, Frank. I'd like that. How were things here today?"

"Good, Alex is a belting little worker—he goes like a machine. Hector's a good help as well," Frank said.

Hector had moved in a couple of weeks ago and had been helping Alex around the farm in payment for room and board.

Frank enjoyed getting back out on the farm every day. Now he went with Hector in the mornings to feed the animals while I took Em to school and opened the clinic with Steph. This set-up suited me fine. However, if I never saw another pig as long as I lived, it would be too soon.

On the whole, we all worked well together, given the circumstances. We were a family, of sorts. All thrown together to make the most of a bad situation. A massive empty hole remained where Jonathan should be. I missed him so much. I tried to fill each waking moment, scared I would break down if I allowed myself to think about him for too long.

I glanced around as Steph left the room. "You looked terrible when I came in, Frank. Are you all right now?"

"I was worried. Wondering where you'd got to, and imagining all kinds of things. I'd hoped you wouldn't go."

"I thought about cancelling the appointment, but thought it would seem strange. I figured at least this way, even if they had questions, the condition is so rare I could act normally. Well, as normal as I would if … You know?"

"Yeah, lass, you're right. They'll probably question the initial test results before anything else."

I nodded. "What other conclusion could they come to?"

We hadn't spoken of what happened that awful night, not after the pigs had devoured all the evidence, and Shane's clothes and shoes were burned in the incinerator.

Then, one morning, as he and Hector were doing the rounds, Frank noticed teeth and clumps of gingery hair on the floor of the sty. He'd feigned illness and convinced Hector to take him back to the house.

I'd almost died of fright when Frank called me at the clinic. It never occurred to me that the pigs wouldn't be able to digest everything. We waited until Hector had gone into work and Steph was tied up at the clinic before we pegged it over there and did a full sweep of the sty. We put the hair and teeth into a snap-lock bag and buried it in the middle of the paddock.

I jumped out of my skin as Steph appeared in the doorway.

"I'm going to pick Hector up from the pub. Shall I get something for dinner while I'm out?" she said, shrugging into her jacket.

"Sounds good to me. I'm knackered—I don't fancy cooking." I glanced at Frank for his thoughts. He rarely ate takeaways.

"I don't mind. Whatever you girls decide is fine by me."

"Don't get anything for Em. She had a burger after the hospital."

"Didn't you get one?" Steph asked, a strange expression on her face.

"I wasn't hungry."

"You didn't eat any breakfast, and I'll bet good money you didn't have anything for lunch."

I shrugged.

"You need to eat, Vic. If you're not careful, you'll be ill." She scowled at me.

"I'm having some dinner, aren't I? I can't eat if I feel sick."

Steph sighed, and a glance passed between her and Frank.

I walked to the back door and called Emily in from the garden.

"Aw, but it's not dark yet." She skidded to a stop on her trike.

"It won't get dark until late, baby, because summer's almost here. You can watch a few minutes of TV with Grandad after your bath."

Steph had already left by the time Emily and I came back inside.

"She's only looking out for you, lass," Frank said.

"I know, but how can I tell her why I've got no appetite?"

"You can't. She's right about one thing, though. You will be ill if you keep this up. Your bones don't have a lot of cover on them lately."

I ignored him and led Emily up the stairs to run her bath.

Taps on full and bubble bath poured, I caught my reflection in the mirror. I did look gaunt, positively skeletal in fact. But I couldn't face eating, and not just for the reasons I told Frank; I felt nauseous all the time.

Emily appeared with a handful of bath toys and threw them into the water.

"Hang on. Let me check it's not too hot," I said, dipping my fingers into the water before turning the taps off.

"Mummy." Emily tried to bite me with the crocodile glove wash cloth.

I laughed. "Hey, cheeky."

Then she turned and did the same to the toilet seat.

"A crocodile wouldn't bite the toilet, silly,"

"He's not biting the toilet, he's getting my friend."

"Is this the same friend who told you to steal Diane's phone?"

Her arms dropped to her side, and she glanced at me warily.

"Well?"

Emily nodded and threw the crocodile back into the water. "Daddy said he's naughty and it's not my fault."

"Daddy said?"

"Uh-huh."

I ran my fingers through my hair, scratching my head. Prickles ran down my spine, and my heartbeat hammered in my ears.

Emily climbed into the bath and began giggling and throwing bubbles to what I now knew to be her invisible friend.

I silently observed her. Worried about saying the wrong thing, knowing the problems she had.

I cleared my throat and crouched at the side of the bath, splashing one hand in the water.

"Em, what else did Daddy say?"

She shrugged one shoulder and continued giggling at something I couldn't see.

"Emily!"

She turned to me. "He misses me and he's happy I'm better."

I nodded. "Okay. When did you see him?" The saliva in my mouth had dried up, making it a struggle to swallow the lump that had appeared in my throat.

"At night, when I'm sleeping." She shrugged again as if her words were nothing unusual.

I chewed the inside of my cheek, pushing the outside of my cheek with my index finger to enable my teeth to get a firm hold. The metallic taste of blood spread across my tongue.

I'd prayed for another visit from Jon. Even in a dream, like before, was preferable to this nothingness. An intense jealousy of my five-year-old daughter's visions or dreams consumed me. Whatever they were, I wanted them for myself.

I read Emily a story, tucked her up, and gave her a kiss. I left her whispering and giggling under the duvet.

Steph and Hector were buzzing around in the kitchen when I

got downstairs. Frank sat at the dining table, which had been set for four. A plate of bread and butter had been put in the centre, along with salt, vinegar, and tomato sauce.

"Sorry, are you waiting for me?"

"No, not at all, we've only just got back. Hector was delayed at the bar. Poor Frank thinks his throat's been cut, don't you, Frank?"

"I'm looking forward to it, that's for sure, lass," Frank said, his knife and fork already in his hands.

"I got fish and chips, Vic. Sit yourself down while we dish up."

My stomach growled with hunger pains, yet the sight of the food made me feel sick at the same time. I knew I would have to make a decent effort to put away my dinner with two members of the food police watching me.

"There you go, Frankie-boy. Get your old choppers around that little lot." Steph placed a huge plate of food in front of him.

"Don't give me that much. It'll outface me straight away." I panicked.

"I haven't, I've given you a lady portion, but just eat what you can." Steph handed me a smaller plate, and I sighed.

Hector produced a pot of tea and several cups before taking his seat next to Steph.

"Thank you, Hector." I nodded.

"K-you're welcome." Hector smiled and looked at Steph for confirmation he'd got it right.

Steph nodded and stroked his neck and shoulder.

"How's Emily after her hospital visit?" Steph asked, before filling her mouth with crispy battered fish.

I wiped my greasy lips on a paper serviette and nodded. "She seems fine, not at all bothered with the stealing episode. In fact, quite the opposite, and she just told me Jon has been visiting her in her dreams."

Frank coughed, his fork dropping to his plate with a clatter.

Steph jumped up, wide-eyed, reached for the teapot, poured him a cupful and added the milk before speaking.

"You're kidding me?"

I shrugged. "It's what she said."

"Probably a dream, do you think?" Steph asked. She had been scared of my mum.

"Yeah, I'm sure this is her way of coping."

Frank, composed again, resumed eating.

"I can't imagine losing someone close. I was just talking to a woman in the bar, while I waited for Hector, and her son has gone missing. She swears he's dead."

I gave a backwards nod and glanced at Frank. Our eyes locked. Icy fingers caressed the nape of my neck causing me to shudder.

"How awful," I managed to say as I grabbed for my locket.

"Yeah, that's what I said. Imagine not knowing where he is? That's got to be the worst part."

"Has she reported him missing?" Frank asked.

"Yeah, apparently the police are not interested. They know of him and reckon he's probably committed a crime and is lying low."

"He's a bad 'un?" Frank raised his eyebrows.

Steph nodded. "Seems he is, but even so, you'd want to know where he is."

"Probably as the police said, he'll turn up when he's good and ready." My voice sounded a little quivery and I cleared my throat and began eating again.

My mind spun at this random piece of information. One we normally wouldn't hear about.

I'd been watching the news and reading the local paper for any missing person's investigations, but nothing. Now, through coincidence this information was delivered.

At least it confirmed Shane hadn't mouthed off about his intentions. There was nothing to link him to us at all.

CHAPTER 16

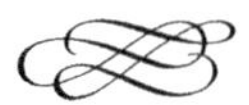

I came in from the clinic to find a message from Doctor Wilson. He'd left his direct dial number, and asked me to call him.

My heart thudded in my chest as I dialled his number.

"Hi, Doctor Wilson, Victoria Lyons here."

"Thank you for calling, Mrs Lyons. I've got Emily's test results in front of me."

"Yes?"

"Well, the most bizarre thing has happened."

"What?" I held my breath, my heartbeat pumping in my head.

"For some unknown reason Emily's results are normal."

"Oh my God! What does that mean?" I felt behind me for the hall chair and lowered myself down into it.

"I don't know. I would like to do some more tests in another couple of months, if that's okay. But as far as I can see, it's as Emily said. She's better."

"How can this ..."

"I'm just as baffled as you. This is the very last thing I expected the results to show. If I wasn't such a science geek, I'd say it was a miracle."

I felt terrible allowing him to be so excited but what choice did I have? I'd got myself into this and I needed to follow through.

"My advice to you would be to try and not raise your hopes too much at this stage. The problems were definitely there before and although her symptoms seem to have gone for now, they may return just as quickly. I'm looking forward to the next round of tests, and pray for the same outcome."

"Thank you, Doctor. I'm blown away. I'm sorry, I can't speak right now."

"I understand. I've had the morning to try to process the information myself, and I'm still astounded. I'll send you an appointment date in the post for six weeks or so. Let's hope, in the meantime, she continues to do well. If there is the slightest sign of deterioration, please ring for an earlier appointment."

I hung up. It was as I'd imagined—no explanations, but no accusations neither.

One more set of tests in two months. Hopefully, Emily would still be all right. It had been playing on my mind that in the trials, the patient's response only lasted up to six months. Up to six months! Which meant anything less than six months, but not longer than.

This piece of information didn't occur to me when deciding what we would do with Shane. I didn't even tell Frank about it.

So far all the lies—the murder, the disposal of Shane's body, the stress, the sleepless nights—and we would possibly only get six months' relief at best.

As I walked out of the bathroom, I almost jumped out of my skin.

Steph sat on the landing, her back against the wall.

"What the ..."

"Okay, Vic. This has gone on long enough. I think you need to go see the doctor."

"I'm okay."

"My arse, you're okay."

"I see. So that's your professional opinion, is it?" I giggled.

"Seriously, Vic. You're nothing but a bag of bones and I'm worried about you. You hardly ever eat, and when you do, you chuck it right back up again."

"It's nothing, just nerves."

"The doctor will be able to give you something for your nerves, if that's what it is."

"What do you mean, 'if' that's what it is?" I wobbled my head as my voice mimicked hers.

"Well, I'm not so sure," she said.

"About what?"

"I think you've got bulimia," she said, standing up tall—well, as tall as she could for a teeny five foot woman. Placing her hands on her hips, she glared at me.

"Oh no, not *the look*, Steph." I laughed. We'd always teased her about the way she could make a grown man quake in fear with *the look*.

"I'm serious."

"I don't have bulimia, Steph." I sighed.

"Humour me. Let's go to see the doc." She made a puppy dog face. "Please? For me ..."

"Fine!" I said, throwing my hands in the air.

I couldn't see the regular locum, who, ironically, was off sick. So an appointment was made for that afternoon with his replacement, another locum.

"I'm coming with you," Steph said, once I'd finished my rant.

"What for?"

"Because I don't trust you."

I shook my head. "Whatever."

Doctor Clifton turned out to be a slight dark-haired South African woman. I'd always preferred to have a female doctor, but since living at Frank's I hadn't had much of a choice.

"So what can I do for you, Mrs Lyons?"

"I need something for my nerves, doctor," I said. "Since my husband died a few months ago, I've not been able to eat or sleep very much."

"I see," she said, reading something on the screen in front of her.

"And she throws up all the time," Steph said.

Doctor Clifton nodded and continued reading. "It says here that you take a contraceptive pill," she said, glancing up at me.

"Not any more. I stopped it after Jon died."

"I see, and when was your last period?"

I shrugged. Panic setting in. "I can't remember."

"Do you mind hopping onto the table for me, Mrs Lyons?" she said, nodding to the examination table behind us.

The table was covered in a white cotton sheet which had been partially covered by a length of blue paper. I climbed up and lay flat, my mind in a whirl.

Doctor Clifton washed her hands, lifted my orange knitted top and began to palpate my stomach. Her eyes were fixed on the wall to the left of me, concentrating. She then pulled my top back down.

"Okay, Mrs Lyons, you can get down again, now," she said and re-washed her hands.

I sat, hardly breathing, waiting for her to return to her seat.

"How long ago did your husband die, Mrs Lyons?"

"Over three months," I said, my voice barely a whisper.

"And when was the last time you had sexual intercourse?"

"The night before he died." I quickly pushed the image of Shane, heaving on top of me, out of my mind.

"I will get you to take a pregnancy test just to be certain, but from what I can tell, I'd say your husband left you a parting gift, Mrs Lyons. You'll need to have a scan to confirm exact dates, but I'd say you are at least three months pregnant."

It was as though time had stopped along with my heartbeat and my breathing.

I vaguely became aware of Stephanie pulling me into her arms, tears running down her face.

The doctor continued talking, but I didn't have a clue what she said.

Moments later, I'd been shuffled into a toilet cubicle holding a plastic container.

I sat on the lid of the toilet, trying to gather my thoughts.

Just over three months ago, Jonathan and I had made love. And I would have given anything to know that we'd made a baby to mark that last precious night together.

However, there had been less than a week between that wonderful night and the night of his funeral, the night Shane raped me.

I knew that wasn't enough of a gap to make any difference on even the most detailed of scans.

I filled the container and met Steph in reception.

"Someone else has gone in, and she said to wait here," Steph said, smiling at me tentatively. "How are you feeling?"

"Shocked. Numb." I shook my head. "How did I not realise, Steph?"

"Let's face it; things haven't exactly been normal lately, have they?"

"I know, but it's just the same as when I was pregnant with Emily. As soon as she mentioned my period, I knew."

"I'm so pleased for you," Steph said, and gripped my hand again. "Are you excited?"

I shrugged. "Not really. Things are hard enough without a baby."

"You're joking. I thought you'd have been over the moon."

Doctor Clifton came into reception and beckoned me to follow her.

"I feel so silly, Doctor. It's so obvious now."

She smiled. "Sometimes it's difficult to see the very things that are right in front of your face."

She tested the urine, purely a formality at this stage, and nodded. "Okay then, I'll arrange for you to have a scan but judging by your dates and my examination, it seems we know exactly when it happened." She smiled.

That night, as I lay in a half-asleep slumber, Doctor Wilson's words suddenly struck me.

"If you have more children together, then yes, they will certainly have this condition."

I stifled a scream as I jumped out of bed. How could I have forgotten something as important as that? Blood rushed to my head and I staggered backwards, my legs bumping into the mattress and I slumped back down onto the end of the bed.

Since finding out about the baby, I'd been repeating a mantra over and over in my head, *the-baby-is-Jon's-the-baby-is-Jon's-the-baby-is-Jon's*. The thought of this new life growing inside me having anything at all to do with Shane made me feel physically sick. I'd always been against abortion, but in this instance what other choice did I have?

Family meant more to me than anything. After my mother died, I saw the world in an altered light. I felt different from the rest of my friends.

I now knew parents could *die*.

This knowledge made me vulnerable where my dad was concerned and when he too died, leaving me orphaned at an early age, I felt lost and rootless for a long time.

Then Jonathan came to my rescue.

He became my family and I embraced Frank as a substitute father. My second chance of being part of a normal family was complete when Emily arrived.

Now, my perfect life had crashed and burned. Jon was dead. Emily would soon follow unless a miracle occurred. And a tiny glimmer of hope in the shape of an innocent baby seemed doomed before it had a chance to be take its first breath.

The scan had been booked for next week. At least then we might find out for definite who the father is, depending on the due date they give me.

Steph had been acting strange, speaking to me in short, clipped sentences.

I knew why.

She thought I should be overjoyed about the baby. In her romance-addled brain Jonathan was reaching out to us from the grave.

CHAPTER 17

Doctor Wilson's appointment came around in a flash.

Frank came with us this time. Just last night I'd confessed about Emily's improving health having a time limit. He'd been distraught and I felt terrible for not telling him sooner, but I hadn't found the right time.

In the reception of the Neurology department, Emily and Diane were going through the special toy box. To my relief, Diane didn't ask about the stealing. I didn't want to admit Emily now stole anything that took her fancy.

Stephanie had lost make-up and costume jewellery from her bedroom. Emily had brought a bracelet home from school, plus a calculator and two more mobile phones.

The school counsellor said Emily showed classic signs of kleptomania, a compulsive disorder. She said a sufferer will have a sense of tension or anxiety before stealing, a relief or gratification during the actual event, followed by feelings of guilt afterwards. Then they would often discard the stolen items, which is what Emily did, stashing them in odd places before forgetting all about them. She acted shocked when they showed up, as though she couldn't remember taking them.

I found myself forever apologising to people and returning their belongings.

Doctor Wilson came into reception. "Mrs Lyons, would you like to come through?"

I jumped up, surprised out of my daydream. "What about Emily?" I asked.

"Leave her with Diane, if you like, for a couple of minutes."

Diane nodded.

"Won't be long, baby."

"Okay, Mummy."

I helped Frank up off the low chair, and followed the doctor into his office.

"This is my father-in-law, Frank Lyons."

They shook hands. "Pleased to meet you, Mr Lyons. Take a seat," he said as he settled into his leather chair. "Well, how is the little marvel? She's been the talk of the Neurology department since your last visit."

"She's the same as last time, although I've noticed her speech slurs when she's tired again. But still not as bad as before."

"That's good news. Have you noticed anything else?"

I shook my head.

"The stealing," Frank said.

"I don't think the stealing is connected to the illness." I placed my hand on Frank's, wishing he hadn't mentioned it.

"Stealing?" Doctor Wilson scribbled in a file in front of him.

"Emily began stealing a while ago. She's been seeing a counsellor who thinks she's a kleptomaniac," I said.

"Seems strange for such a young girl." He put down his pen and glanced at us over the top of his glasses.

"Probably due to her father's death—it began around the same time."

"Possibly. Who knows how such a thing will affect a youngster," the doctor said.

I nodded. "That's what I thought.

"Right, I want to do the tests once again, to see how the results compare. Is that okay?"

I nodded.

"Good. You know the drill. If you go up to the ward, they'll be expecting you. And I'll see you back here later."

"Thanks, Doctor."

We borrowed a wheelchair for Frank, the ward being a good fifteen-minute walk away on the other side of the hospital.

They were, as Doctor Wilson had said, expecting us, and we had the same nurse we'd had the previous times.

The day progressed smoothly with Emily in good spirits. She explained to Frank what she had to do in each test, and his presence was a welcome distraction for both of us.

"Hello again. Come in and take a seat," Doctor Wilson said.

Frank shuffled into the office. It had been a long day, especially for him, and it showed on his face. He usually had an hour on the bed after lunch most days.

"Once again, we only have some of the results. But we can see that Emily is still showing a massive improvement since the first set of tests. However, there's a significant change since last time but in the opposite direction I'm afraid."

My heart dropped to my feet. I reached for Frank's hand.

"Her reflexes are quite a bit slower, possibly because she's tired today, or distracted—it could be for any number of reasons. You said you noticed her slurring. This also makes me think she's on the decline again. But, as I said, the more detailed results are around a week away yet, so I'll call you like last time?"

"Okay." I wanted a more definite answer. "So in your opinion, right now, you think she's getting worse again?"

He shrugged and shook his head. "Who can say at this stage?

Emily has proven to be an exception in everything we know about this illness up to now. We'll continue monitoring her and see how she goes."

I had expected Emily would become sick again, but that didn't ease the steel band around my heart. We were on board an emotional roller-coaster.

"Don't be disheartened. Emily may surprise us again. As I said earlier, she's already the talk of the Neurological unit and several other hospitals are also following her remarkable turnaround."

I glanced at Frank, half-smiled and sighed. "Oh well, I guess we'll wait to hear from you." I stood up and held my arm out for Frank. "Oh, one last thing. I recently discovered I'm pregnant, and I remember you mentioning a sibling of Emily's could have the same condition. Is there a test I could do?" I'd not mentioned my fears to Frank, having thought it best to come from the doctor.

Doctor Wilson gasped. Looking from me to Frank and back again, he sat back down and indicated I do the same.

I sat, my eyes boring into Doctor Wilson's, dreading what I knew he'd say.

"Is the baby your husband's?" he asked.

I nodded.

"As you know, this illness is extremely rare, but in a lot of cases, it does tend to run in children born of the same parents."

"So there's a chance the baby could be sick too?"

"I'm sorry, Mrs Lyons, but the baby is most likely going to have the same condition as Emily."

I could tell by the look on Frank's face that he felt devastated, but he didn't say a word, clearly concerned about my feelings more than his own.

My heart broke for him.

Frank and I walked out of Doctor Wilson's office as though nothing had happened. Anybody watching us would never guess we'd received such devastating news.

We took Emily to McDonalds, as promised.

Frank didn't like fast food. He screwed his face up when he saw me watching him. "It's tasteless."

"Emily likes it, don't you, Em?"

She nodded, as she played with this week's toy. Her tongue stuck from the corner of her mouth comically as she concentrated on trying to make a plastic figure stand up on oversized feet.

"Can we go to the toyshop now?" Emily asked. I'd promised her a toy again if she lay still for her lumbar puncture.

"I'm sure we can. So long as you didn't take anything that doesn't belong to you this time." I smiled to soften my comment.

She shook her head but the expression on her face said different.

"Emily?"

She looked at Frank, her eyes filling up.

"Emily, what did you take?" I pressed.

She pulled a black pager out of her pocket.

"What the hell … Where did that come from?"

"I'm sorry, Mummy. Please can I have a toy? I didn't mean it. I didn't want to."

"Then why did you?" I felt like tearing my hair out.

"I don't know."

Frank placed his hand on top of mine and shook his head slightly. "Where did you take it from, lass?"

"From the spaceship."

The spaceship was what she called the scan.

"We'll have to take it back," I said.

"Oh no, please, Mummy. I promise I won't do it again." She sobbed, almost hysterical.

I didn't know what to do. I wasn't a psychologist, but I thought if I made her admit what she'd done and to apologise, she might learn from it. So far, it hadn't made the slightest bit of difference. I put my hand on my forehead and looked away, shaking my head and sighing deeply.

Frank wiped Emily's face on a serviette. "Maybe if we take the pager back and Emily apologises, maybe we could still go to the toyshop?"

I shrugged. I'd run out of ideas. My instincts told me to say no, to punish her again, knowing if we rewarded this bad behaviour she'd never stop. But a niggling voice in my head kept saying, *let her have what she wants. She's getting sick again and probably won't be around for much longer.*

"Whatever, but you've got to promise me with all your heart you won't do it again." I pulled Emily to me and bent looking intently into her eyes.

"I promise."

I knew she meant every word, but she obviously couldn't help herself. I had no choice but to start frisking her everywhere we went. "Come on then, we'd better get a move on."

Later that evening, with Emily in bed and Stephanie and Hector in the snug watching a movie, I tapped on Frank's bedroom door before poking my head inside.

Frank sat upright in bed reading a paperback.

Jonathan had redecorated this room just before Emily became sick. The walls were papered in slate grey and white. The three-quarter bed had a deep pillow-topped mattress and the headboard featured wooden panels, painted white gloss. A very manly room, clean and uncluttered.

"Hi, Frank. Sorry to bother you. I just wanted to check you're feeling all right. You were very quiet earlier."

"Come in, come in." Placing his book down, he removed his glasses before patting the bed to the side of him.

"Gosh, I need a stepladder to get up there," I laughed.

"I prefer a high bed. My legs are long, so it's easier for me to get up and down."

I nodded. "I remember."

He boinked the heel of his hand against his forehead. "Of course you do, you were there when I bought it." He shook his head and laughed.

"I've been thinking about what the doctor said. About the baby and how Em …" I rubbed at my eyes. "It's only a matter of time before she's sick again."

"I know, but it may take months before she's as sick as she was before."

"But all we went through. I'm sorry I forgot about the length of time it lasted. Why would I forget something as important as that?"

"Victoria, it doesn't matter. If it gave us the tiniest amount of extra time with Emily, then I'd have still done it—wouldn't you?"

I nodded. "I would."

"Then stop beating yourself up over it. And don't write Emily off just yet. She's still okay for now, and who knows what's around the corner."

I took a deep breath and exhaled loudly. "But what about the baby? I've been hanging out for this week's ultrasound, just in case they can be definite with the date the baby was conceived. I've prayed every night that it's Jon's. So now what? If it is then it'll probably have Emily's illness. If it isn't … well, if it isn't …" I shook my head, unable to go on.

"Let's wait for the ultrasound, then we can discuss the best way forward, lass."

"Yeah you're right, of course." Taking Frank's hand, I kissed his fingers.

An overwhelming love for this man made eyes fill with tears. I turned away, not wanting to upset him any more, and headed for the door.

"Goodnight, Frank.

"Goodnight, lass."

CHAPTER 18

"Do you want me to go to the hospital with you?" Steph asked.

"Thanks, but Frank's coming," I smiled.

"Frank?" she said, tipping her head to the side, her eyes narrowing.

"I know it seems strange, but he asked—he's excited about Jon's baby."

"I s'pose," she shrugged. "Just a bit odd, taking your father-in-law to the scan. But hey, if it works for you." She smirked.

I grabbed a cushion from beside me on the sofa and threw it at her. "Shut up, idiot." I laughed.

"Make sure you get a photo. Our Carole got one when she went for a scan and you could see his little face really clearly."

"Okay." I got to my feet as I heard Frank coming down the stairs. "Em's at Lyn's, I'm not sure what time I'll be back but if she …"

"I'll be here. Don't worry."

Heavily pregnant women filled the waiting room. I held Frank's hand as my pregnancy felt real for the first time.

I'd spent the morning on the Internet researching due dates. I'd worked out: Friday 17th January if it was Jon's, Friday 24th January if it was Shane's. I just needed confirmation from the scan.

However, I didn't know what the hell I would do either way. If I found out the baby was Jonathan's, it could mean going through this hell over again. And although I wouldn't miss one single moment with Emily, I knew I wasn't strong enough to do it a second time.

If the baby's development tied in with Shane's date I couldn't imagine continuing with the pregnancy, despite being totally against abortion.

"We're never away from hospital waiting rooms lately, are we, lass?" Frank said.

I smiled and shook my head.

"Don't worry. It'll be all right."

"I don't see how, Frank. If the baby's Jon's ..." I shrugged. "But if not, then ..."

"I know, I know, lass," he said, putting his arm around me and pulling me close.

I must have looked a right sight, in a maternity hospital with a man more than twice my age. Several of the women gave us strange looks.

"Victoria Lyons," a small Asian woman called.

I helped Frank to his feet before following her through to a room with pink walls that held nothing more than a bed, a monitor and a sink.

"Please climb up and undo your clothing. I'll be back shortly," the nurse said, pronouncing each word carefully. She shuffled around Frank and bobbed out of the door.

"They must think we're together," Frank laughed.

"Who cares what they think? It's none of their business."

I climbed onto the bed and lifted my loose green summer top up and pushed my elastic waisted skirt down slightly.

Frank looked away, but I wasn't a bit embarrassed. He'd seen me in worse states of undress than this one.

The nurse came back in and washed her hands. "My name is Flo, I am happy to meet you."

"Hi, Flo. I'm Vic and this is my father-in-law, Frank."

"Ah … your father-in-law." She nodded.

Frank chuckled.

Flo bent down and produced a large white tube from underneath the bed. "This will be cold," she said before squirting a large blob of gel onto my stomach.

When she switched the monitor on, a lot of static sounded from the speakers before settling into a rhythmic thumping sound as she placed a handheld device onto my stomach. My baby's heartbeat.

I looked at Frank and he reached for my hand, his eyebrows furrowed.

Flo moved the device around and suddenly the screen was filled with an image of our baby.

My breath hitched. "Oh, Frank," I said.

A tear ran down Frank's face. He smiled and rubbed my hand again.

"Your baby has a very strong heartbeat," Flo said. "And he's wriggling."

"He?" I asked.

"Oh, sorry. It's too early to tell, I always say he," Flo said.

She took a few measurements. "All seems perfect. Would you like a copy?"

"Yes, please," I said. "Do you know when it's due?" My heart almost stopped as I waited for her response.

"Yes, due date is twenty-first of January."

It took a few moments for me to process the information. I don't know why I was surprised. The dates she'd given me were slap bang in the middle of the ones I'd worked out for myself. I still had no clue who the father was.

CHAPTER 19

"Breakfast's ready," I called, and within seconds they all descended like a herd of starving animals.

Steph and Hector ran down the stairs, giggling like the young lovers they were. Frank came out of the snug, Alex from the bathroom, and Emily from the garden.

"Wow! That's a first," I said. "It normally takes at least three yells before you respond. I'm not quite ready yet."

"We're starving," Stephanie laughed.

"Stavin," Hector repeated. Steph had been trying to teach him English and we all joined in around the dinner table. This often confused the poor guy. Steph and I had Mancunian accents, Frank a broad Cumbrian one, and Alex an American one.

"St-aar-ving," Emily said, breaking the word down for him.

"Starvig," Hector said.

"That's close enough, Hector." I smiled and nodded. "We don't want to know what you've been doing to create such an appetite, do we guys?"

There was a resounding "No!" from everyone, including Emily, which made us all laugh more.

"Right, how about I pile it onto the table and you can help yourselves?"

"Kkhelp yourselp," Hector continued, obviously enjoying us all laughing at his expense.

"Help. Ha-ha-help," Emily said, mimicking what she'd heard Steph say in the past.

"Khe-khe-khelp."

"You're funny, Hekker," Emily laughed.

I placed a heaped plate of bacon and fried eggs into the middle of the table, and a stack of toast.

"Hegs."

"Eggs!" Emily squealed.

"Okay, you two, enough. Get eating before it's stone cold," I said.

"Hegs," Hector said again, looking at Emily for her response.

Stephanie said something to him in Spanish and nudged him in the ribs. Then Hector and Emily burst into fits of giggles again, in a joke of their own.

Frank filled Emily's plate for her as I produced a pot of tea and sat down.

"You not eating, Vic?" Steph asked, her eyes squinting at me in an unspoken reprimand.

"I had a slice of toast earlier. I'm not that hungry," I said, eyeballing her right back.

The morning sickness seemed to be settling down but I still couldn't face a full breakfast, especially bacon. I could barely face cooking it.

We hadn't told anybody else about the baby, especially after Doctor Wilson's shocking revelations. However, I was almost seventeen weeks gone already and although it was possible to have a termination up to twenty-four weeks, the procedure was much more difficult. After the twenty-week mark it would mean I would have to deliver the baby as normal. Prior to twenty weeks meant they could perform a D&E, still horrible, but a much easier option.

But in truth, although I hated the thought of having Shane's baby, how could I kill an innocent little child? The fluttering sensations I'd felt over the past few days made the situation even more real.

"So what do you have planned today, Alex?" I asked.

"I'm going on a trip with some friends to Gretna Green," he said.

"Ooh, anything you want to tell us?" Steph pitched in.

"Sorry?" He shook his head, puzzled.

"Are you eloping?" she said, "You know, getting married."

"Oh, no," he shook his head.

"Just kidding," Steph said. "You do know that's where people used to run away to get married, don't you?"

"I had heard about it. Not me though. I'd need a girlfriend first."

"I thought you had a girlfriend," I said. "You went to meet someone a few weeks ago."

He shook his head, finishing what he was eating before wiping his mouth on a napkin. "I told you; she was just a friend."

"You must have girls falling over themselves to be your girlfriend."

"No chance of that I'm afraid. Besides, I'm too busy for girls right now. They just complicate things."

"Very sensible, Alex. Girls *always* complicate things." Frank laughed.

"Watch it you … or you'll end up cooking your own dinner."

"Present company excluded, of course," Frank said, still laughing.

"Of course." I gave him my most stern look.

"Grandad's in trouble." Emily laughed.

"Did you recognise that expression, Em?" Stephanie said, amused.

Emily nodded, frantically chewing.

"What should we do today, Emily? Any suggestions," I asked.

"A picanic."

"A picnic? Do you honestly think you'll fit any more in after all that breakfast?"

She glanced down at her plate. "Oops." She laughed.

"We can have a picnic next week if you like. Any other suggestions for today?"

The weather had been amazing. It was the height of the summer holidays and I'd been feeling a bit guilty that I hadn't taken her away as we usually did. So I tried to make an effort on the weekends.

"How about fishing? We could go down to the river and have a paddle too," I suggested.

"Nah." Emily shook her head.

"Shopping?"

"Nah." She laughed.

"You're spoiled, miss."

"I know."

"Nah," Hector mimicked, creating a whole new bout of giggles from Emily.

"There's a summer fete at the pub. They're having a bouncy castle and a bucking bronco. Hector's working there but I'm going. I'll be propping up the bar," Steph said.

"I don't know. I don't like the thought of taking her to the pub."

"Please, Mummy?"

"It's a family day, and it's mainly in the garden," Steph continued. "There'll be loads of kids there. Early on there will be anyway—it might get a bit messy afterwards."

"I don't know. What do you think, Frank?"

"Oh, don't involve me, lass. I'm looking forward to a day in front of the box. Back-to-back football for me."

"Please, Mummy?"

"I'll think about it."

"Yes!" Emily punched the air.

"Right you. If you've finished eating I want your bedroom tidied, or we won't be going anywhere."

"Okay, then can we go?"

"We'll see. Now scoot." I began clearing the table.

Alex handed me his plate. "Thanks, Vic. That was lovely. I'd best be off, my buddies will be here soon. Have a nice weekend."

"Are you back tonight, Alex?"

"No, tomorrow night. We're going clubbing tonight and staying with a friend of a friend."

"Oh, to be young and carefree," Frank said, folding his newspaper.

Emily got to the door and stopped. "Hekker?"

Hector stopped his conversation with Steph and said, "Eh?"

"Hegs!" she said, and giggling, ran up the stairs.

"So, we may see you later?" Steph said.

"If we do come, it'll be early and then we'll go on somewhere else. I don't want Emily around a load of drunks."

"Fair enough. See you there, if you make it." She left with Hector in tow.

"Okay, Frank. Are you going to be okay alone?"

"Are you kidding? I'm looking forward to the peace and quiet."

"I'll have my phone if you need me for anything."

"I won't. But thanks."

I went upstairs to check on Emily and helped her finish the last of the tidying. "I'll make a deal with you." I said. "We'll go to the pub and have an hour there, and then we'll go on to somewhere else. Is there anything else you fancy doing?"

"Dunno." She shrugged.

I had to park ten minutes down the road and walk back. From the door the inside of the pub looked like wall-to-wall people.

I really didn't want to go in.

This had been the first crowded place I'd been to since Jonathan's funeral, and I seemed to be having some kind of panic attack. My legs were shaking and I wiped my sweaty hands on my jeans. I had to concentrate on my breathing, and it took several deep breaths to get my lungs working properly.

I gripped Emily's hand, and bent to talk to her over the loud hum pulsing through the door.

"It's busy, Em. Maybe we should come back later?"

"Aw. I just saw Kaylie. Can we go in, please?"

As we reached the door my head started swimming. I had to steady myself on the doorjamb before entering.

The small pub was filled with kids. The back doors and windows were opened up, showing the beer garden was also chock-a-block with families.

We passed the bar and noticed Hector busily loading the dishwasher.

"Hector, hi," I called. Emily waved frantically.

"Khello." Hector's face lit up and he waved as though he hadn't seen us in weeks. Then pointed to Steph, who was propping up the bar, as she told us she would be.

"Vic, come over here," she called.

I shook my head and pointed to the beer garden and then to Emily.

She nodded and hopped off her stool and joined us. "Mayhem, isn't it?" she shouted.

I nodded, needing to get outside to stop the panic rising in my chest. We shoved our way through the crowds.

Emily soon met up with several of her friends and they were having a wild old time on the bouncy castle.

Stephanie and I watched them for a while but then the bucking bronco soon distracted us, and we laughed hysterically at some of the sights we saw.

One guy confidently climbed on, dressed to kill in his skintight black jeans and fitted shirt. Gelled-back hair and cool dude shades told us he imagined himself God's gift to women.

He started out well, but the operator must have had a mean streak as one minute he was giving a good old show, and the next he'd been unceremoniously splattered onto the mat. His glasses were skew-whiff on his face. He jumped up too quickly to look cool and vanished into the toilet.

Next, a large girl sat astride the mechanical bull who had the crowd in hysterics before it got started. She wore a denim miniskirt and a short gypsy-style top, both at least two sizes too small. When she tipped forward, her bottom raised in the air, giving all and sundry a look at tomorrow's laundry. She landed moments later, flat on her back, legs akimbo, in a very unflattering position.

"Why would anybody do this?" I laughed.

Steph shook her head. "I have no idea."

It amazed me that the queue of people prepared to make fools of themselves hadn't diminished at all. In fact, it kept getting longer.

"Can I have a drink, Mummy?" Emily had come up behind us, her little face bright red from chasing her friends around the bouncy castle.

"Course you can, baby. Hold on."

"I'll come too," Steph said.

"You stay here with Kaylie's mum till I come back."

I followed Steph to the bar. We waited for at least ten minutes before we were served. I ordered two glasses of orange juice and a vodka and coke for Steph."

Two men sidled up to us. One was a short and dumpy, square-shaped bloke, the other lanky and thin. "Can we get you pretty ladies a drink?" the taller of the two asked, winking at me.

"No thanks," I smiled lifting my glass up.

"Vodka and Coke, please."

"Steph!" I said, eyeballing her.

"What? There's no harm in buying me a drink."

"Oh well, see you outside." I made my way back to the beer garden.

Emily was sitting next to Kaylie's mum and looked a little peaky. "Here you go, baby. Are you not feeling well?"

She shook her head, sipped at the juice and handed it back to me.

"Is she okay?" Kaylie's mum asked. "I'd heard she wasn't well, but she seemed fine running around earlier."

"She has been fine, but she must have overdone it." I smiled.

Emily leaned her head onto her arms.

"I'd better get her home." I placed the glasses down on the table and lifted Emily into my arms. As I fought my way through the bar, I noticed Stephanie still engrossed in conversation with the two guys.

I hiked back to the car, Emily a dead weight in my arms, and my legs threatened to collapse. My body shook with the sheer effort, and a strange twinge pulled in my lower stomach. Probably just a stitch, but I didn't want to push it.

"Shall we get you home, my baby?"

Emily nodded. "I think I'm not better anymore."

My stomach hit the floor. "You've just tired yourself out that's all. You'll see."

As I carried her in to the house, Frank met us in the hallway. "I didn't expect you back this soon," he said, his head cocked to one side.

"Emily's not feeling too well," I said. Our eyes held, and I shook my head, before carrying her up to her room.

I began reading her a story but she fell asleep before I finished the first page.

My feet dragged as I walked down the stairs. Just lifting them had become an effort. The last five months had been a reprieve, but it made me more aware of the future and the heartbreak that loomed.

Frank came out of the snug again.

"It's happening, Frank. Just like that—" I clicked my fingers, "—and she's sick again."

"Maybe she's just tired. It's hot out there—it saps your energy."

"Who are you trying to kid, Frank? Me? Yourself?" I didn't mean to snap at him. "We know how quickly she got better. Why would becoming sick again happen gradually? It won't."

He dropped his eyes to the floor and I saw I had hurt his feelings. Guilt hit me. He'd been so supportive and I'd be lost without him.

"I'm sorry. I don't mean to take it out on you. It just breaks my heart, that's all." I moved to hug him.

"I know, lass, mine too."

I found myself in his arms, sobbing into his chest. I was reminded of the night outside Emily's room and the way I had drawn strength from his embrace. He made me feel things would be all right, although I knew they couldn't be.

"Come on, lass. Let's sit you down." He made to go into the snug but I stopped abruptly and he changed direction to the kitchen instead.

A couple of hours later Emily joined us in the lounge.

"Hey, Em, are you feeling any better?" I asked, holding my arms out to her.

Emily climbed onto my knee looking decidedly sorry for herself.

"Can I get you something to eat?" I kissed her cheek.

She shook her head. "Not hungry."

"Okay, what do you want to do?"

"Watch *Mary Poppins*."

My heart sank. She'd not had any desire to sit in front of the TV for months—she'd been much too busy for that. I recognised it as another warning sign.

I glanced at Frank sitting at the dining table, studying the *TV Guide*. "Come on, lass. I'll put it on for you.

I smiled in gratitude. I didn't want to set foot in the snug unless absolutely necessary. I knew I was being silly—after everything else I'd gone through, how could a room affect me so much? But I couldn't help it.

That night, I loaded the last of the dishes into the dishwasher while Frank emptied the rubbish bin before bed.

I started as the phone rang and looked at the clock. Almost ten.

"Strange," I glanced at Frank and wiped my hands on a tea-towel "Who would be ringing at this hour?"

"Hello?"

"Hello, Victoria. It's Stan from The Bells."

'Oh, hello, if you're looking for Hector, I'm afra—."

"It's you I need to speak to, lass. There's been an incident here this evening involving Hector and Stephanie. Stephanie has just left in an ambulance. She's in a bad way, I'm afraid."

"What?" My head spun. "What sort of incident?" I swallowed noisily.

"Hector attacked her as they left the pub, and we didn't realise what was happening until it was too late. He beat her. Badly, I'm afraid."

"Oh my God! Where is he?"

"He left. We heard the commotion and by the time we got outside, Hector had jumped in the car and scarpered."

My mind went momentarily blank. She'd told me about the last time, but having known him for five months and shared a home with him, even grown to love his fun-loving childish ways, I couldn't absorb this new information. He normally appeared a gentle and loving man.

"Victoria, are you there?"

"Yes, Stan. Thanks for letting me know. I'd best get to the hospital."

"Would you let us know how she is?"

"I will do." I hung up.

"What was that all about?" Frank said.

"Hector has attacked Stephanie, and she's in hospital. I'd best get there. Will you be …"

"I'll be fine. Just go."

CHAPTER 20

The accident and emergency department buzzed with the usual drunken Saturday night crowd.

One guy sat on the floor of the entrance, vomiting into a rubbish bin. He had blood smeared down his face and stank to high heaven.

Two more men stood in front of me at the reception desk, trying to hold each other upright. The poor young girl behind the counter couldn't understand a word they said. She called for an older woman to help her, who happened to be fluent in drunkspeak and understood every word.

It soon emerged they'd been playing around with a shopping trolley and one of them was flung out. He landed on the road, receiving a deep gash to his head.

Once they took a seat the young receptionist shrugged at me apologetically, raising her eyes to the ceiling. "How can I help you?"

"I'm looking for my friend. Stephanie Cross—she's been brought in by ambulance."

"One minute, I'll check for you. Ah yes. She's being seen now. Come through and I'll show you where she is." The door buzzed open to the side of her and she led me down a corridor. Then she poked her head behind a curtain, before holding the curtain open for me to enter.

Stephanie began to cry when she saw me.

She was a mess, her face mottled shades of purple and red. Her left eye had completely closed, and the large black egg-shaped lump below it was obviously filled with blood. Her nose looked broken and the right side of her face was badly grazed.

"Vic," she said.

I noticed, as she spoke, that half of her front tooth was gone.

"Oh my God, Steph. What the hell has he done to you?" I perched on the edge of the bed and pulled her to me. Both of us broke into floods of tears.

After a few minutes, Steph wiped her eyes. "I was drunk. I'd been chatting to those guys, but I didn't mean anything by it. Hector didn't … he seemed bothered until we left the pub and then—Wham! The first smack came from nowhere."

Her words were slow and disjointed, and had a funny whistle to them. She had to suck air in between sentences as her lips were swollen and bleeding.

"He dragged me across the car park by my hair. Look." She turned slightly, and showed me a bald patch where a massive clump of hair had been ripped from her head.

"I'll kill him," I said. "We never should have trusted him again."

"It's all my fault. I wanted to believe him. He could be so … so lovely. You saw that, right?" Another bout of sobs followed.

I nodded. "But he'd attacked you before, and out of the blue that time too."

She tried to sit up, but gasped and gripped her side. "I think he's broken my ribs. He kicked me in my stomach, over and over. I didn't think he was going to stop."

"What did the doctor say?"

"He said I'm lucky. There's nothing major—apart from my

ribs. They're keeping me in tonight. I'm waiting for them to arrange a bed in the ward.

"I'll stay with you till then," I said.

When I pulled up outside the house, I was flabbergasted at the sight Stephanie's car parked on the driveway and Frank standing at the front door.

"I raced from the car. "What the hell! Is he inside?"

"Hang on, Victoria—HANG ON!" His raised voice and stern tone stopped me in my tracks.

"What? I don't give two shits what he told you. He's not welcome here. You should see the state of her, Frank. He almost killed her."

"I agree, but it's not that simple. He's unconscious."

I pushed past him into the hallway. "Where is he?"

"In the bedroom."

I charged upstairs and burst into the room.

Hector lay face down on the bed, completely out of it."

"Hector! Hector!" I shouted.

Nothing.

I grabbed hold of his hair and yanked it back. Reminding me about the clump of hair he'd torn from Steph's head.

No response at all.

"What happened, Frank?"

"He came back just after you'd left. Let himself in and began searching the house for Steph. He seemed distraught. I told him Steph had gone to the hospital but he couldn't understand me."

"Did he seem drunk?"

"No, I don't think so."

"This isn't a normal sleep," I said, shaking my head.

"I think he took something."

I pulled back Hector's eyelids; his pupils weren't reactive, and were the size of pinpricks. "I think he's overdosed on something."

"That's what I wanted to say to you, lass. He was sick in the sink and it was full of pills."

I raced to the bathroom with Frank close behind me. A pool of mustard-coloured vomit filled the basin, along with several blue, oval-shaped pills. The vile stench hit my nostrils, causing me to gag.

"Shit, Frank. Why didn't you call an ambulance?"

"Because I was waiting for you."

"What for? He could die."

"For Emily."

"Oh my God. You can't be serious!" I stared at him, hoping I'd misunderstood him, but knowing, deep down, exactly what he meant.

Frank didn't move. His face didn't alter as he stared at me.

"We're not going through that again, Frank." I shook my head, my pulse racing. "No way—you hear me? No fucking way!"

"But . . ."

"No buts!" I screamed. Placing my hands on my head. "Are you for real? I'm still having fucking nightmares about Shane and pigs. I'll never look at a piece of meat in the same way ever again. And what for, eh? Emily's already deteriorating, and you want to do it all over again!"

"Look at the state of him, lass. He's going to die anyway. We could take what we need first."

"You're off your fucking rocker, Frank." I stared at him, unable to comprehend.

"Hector chose to do this to himself, and besides, he'd want us to save Emily. For all his faults, Hector loves her."

"Course he would. Only not if it meant *he* had to die in the process."

"We need to do this, lass. We owe it to Emily."

"She's dying, Frank. The sooner we accept that, the better. All we've done up to now, is prolong the inevitable. What will we do in another few months when Hector's Proteum wears off? Kill someone else?"

"No, of course not," he snapped. "But don't you see? We're not killing anybody. Hector's done this to himself."

"You're mad! Absolutely stark staring bonkers." I shook my head, astounded. "I need to call an ambulance. This man is dying."

"Wait. Please, lass, think about it for a second. No one will expect him to come back here. He has no family or friends. Steph won't want him after what he's done. He's taken an overdose and will probably die anyway. What if we can help Emily long enough for a cure to be found?"

"But it's murder, Frank. Do you not see how wrong this is?" I hugged myself, shaking uncontrollably, my voice sounding garbled to my own ears.

"No. You're wrong. It's suicide. We're just helping Emily at the same time."

I began pacing the short distance between the bed and the doorway, confused. Frank's words sounded so logical. Besides, this man could have killed my best friend tonight if he hadn't been stopped. He knew he'd lost her for good now, which I presumed was why he took the overdose. He wouldn't want to live without her. So it wouldn't be murder. Would it? I couldn't think straight. I needed some air.

I raced from the room heading for the stairs. As I passed Emily's room, I noticed her door was slightly ajar. How she'd slept through all the commotion was beyond me. I reached for the handle, paused, then pushed the door a little wider.

Emily was lying on her back, the duvet bunched at the bottom of the bed. I quietly entered and rolled the duvet over Emily's tiny body.

I thought about how lethargic she had been today. Knew we wouldn't have long before she was as sick as she had been five months ago.

I was suddenly struck by an overwhelming sensation that I wasn't alone. All my senses heightened, and my scalp prickled.

"Jonathan? Is that you?"

A sound behind me made my feet leave the floor.

"It's only me, lass," Frank said, reaching for my hand.

"I must be as crazy as you for even considering this, Frank." I was suddenly calmer.

"Not crazy, lass. Resourceful. He has something we desperately need. Why waste it?"

I joined him out in the hallway, taking one last glimpse of Emily before closing the door. Then we walked back to Hector.

"We need to get him to the clinic." I grabbed Hector's upper arms and dragged him off the bed. He was bigger than Shane, and a couple of stone heavier. Frank helped with his good arm and between us, except for a precarious moment on the stairs where the three of us almost toppled to our deaths, we got him down into the hallway.

I fetched Frank's wheelchair and we managed to get Hector strapped into it. "I'll meet you there," I said to Frank and ran on ahead with Hector.

The clinic was only a short walk from the house. Once in there, I busied myself preparing all the things I needed and when Frank arrived I was ready to get Hector onto the table.

I gave Frank a couple of minutes to catch his breath. "Okay, same as last time, but he's much heavier. Are you ready?"

He nodded.

"Go."

We both lifted the top half of Hector onto the table and Frank held him in place while I got his legs. The shirt Hector wore had a shiny finish and Frank had trouble keeping hold of him. He slid down a couple of inches, but we caught him and finally had him on top, lying face down.

The procedure was even easier this time. Within forty-five minutes I was back with Emily and injecting Hector's Proteum into her. She woke up this time and cried a bit. I sat with her for twenty minutes afterwards until she was sound asleep again. She probably wouldn't remember any of it.

Frank had stayed with Hector. Between us we got him onto the quad and locked in the butchery fridge just as before. With one difference. Hector still had a faint pulse.

We went back to the clinic to tidy up, then I left to put the quad back in the shed.

When I returned, Frank sat in his wheelchair waiting for me. He looked like a gentle and frail old man. Nobody would ever believe what he'd been up to tonight.

At the house, I threw all of Hector's belongings into a couple of bags and hid them in the boot of my car. I'd deal with them in the morning. I cleaned the vomit from the sink and sat down, exhausted.

"We did the right thing, lass." Frank shuffled in.

"Oh, Frank. You made me jump. I thought you'd gone to bed."

"I checked on Emily. She's fast asleep."

"What are we going to do when this lot wears off, Frank? Trawl the streets for runaways and criminals?"

"Of course not. We didn't plan to murder anyone, lass. Shane, on the other hand, would have gone on to commit a much worse crime than rape or robbery that night, I guarantee it."

I knew he was right, but it still felt so wrong.

"As for Hector. From what you said, he left Steph for dead. Maybe would have finished the job if he hadn't been interrupted. Plus, he took an overdose, essentially killing himself."

I nodded. I needed to believe him, needed to believe our actions were vindicated.

"I know what we've done is against the law, lass. But we were handed the chance to cure your daughter, albeit temporarily. It's an impossible dilemma. Save the nasty rapist, or the innocent five-year-old girl? Any mother would make the same decision in your shoes."

He was right, or was he brainwashing me? He sounded perfectly correct, justified even. He had a calm, knowledgeable and trusted voice.

"Should we go to bed? We have a big day ahead of us tomorrow," I said. The thought of chopping up Hector's body and feeding him to the pigs made me weak at the knees. I still saw Shane's foot every time I closed my eyes.

CHAPTER 21

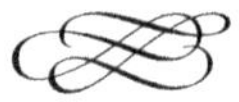

Emily woke in the early hours with a terrible headache like before.

I gave her some Paracetamol and climbed in bed beside her and rocked her until she was sound asleep. I prayed for what seemed like hours.

Lying awake in the dead of night always made my problems seem worse, but this one was already as bad as it could get. The most terrible part of the whole thing was that we'd left Hector in a fridge to die. I hadn't been in my right mind, obviously.

In the morning, Emily was her bouncing and bubbly self, once again.

Needless to say, I wasn't. I was jumpy and jittery, couldn't focus on any one thing and constantly on the verge of tears. I was petrified at what the next few months would bring. Transferring the Proteum was such an easy procedure, and with instant results.

How would I ever be able to allow Emily to get sick when I knew how easily I could cure her?

Was I cracking up?

Was this how serial killers were born?

After feeding the chickens, I dropped Hector's belongings at the incinerator. I planned to burn them all later once we had the clothing he still wore.

The phone rang as I arrived home.

"Hello?"

"Hi Vic, it's Steph. They're letting me out. Is there any chance you can come get me?"

"Course I can. You ready now?"

"If that's okay."

I found Emily in the kitchen. "I need to talk to you, baby."

She glanced up from her sticker book.

"Stephanie's had an accident," I said.

She gasped and her hand flew to her face, as though I'd just slapped her. "Like Daddy?"

"No. Oh I'm sorry, baby, nothing like Daddy at all. She's sore and bruised. I just don't want you to be upset when you see her."

"Okay, Mummy. Is Hekker bruised?"

"No, my baby. Hector is fine, but he's had to go home to Spain."

"Aw, but he's my friend."

"I know he is, but it couldn't be helped."

I found Frank soaking up the sun in the garden. He seemed miles away. "Penny for them."

"Oh hi, lass." He patted the cushion of the garden swing beside him.

"Steph's coming home. I'm going to get her now. Will you watch Em?"

He nodded.

"Then we'll go and see to the other matter once Steph's here. Leave them looking after one another."

"Okay." He attempted a smile.

"You seem deflated. Are you having regrets?"

"No, not at all, but I just wish we had a more permanent solution."

"I know, but we have a few more months, hopefully."

He nodded.

"Right, I'm off. Won't be too long."

Stephanie sat in an armchair at the side of the bed. The bruising looked even worse than last night.

"Are you sure you're fit to come home?"

She shrugged. "That's what the doctor said." She inched out of the chair, in obvious agony. "I'm fine once I get moving, honestly," she said, noticing the concern on my face.

"I think I'll get you a wheelchair, because the car's parked on the other side of the building," I said. "Wait there. I'll be back in two ticks."

Pushing Steph through the hospital brought back memories of last night, with Hector slumped in Frank's wheelchair. I steadied myself on the handles as I felt the corridor spin.

Back at home, Stephanie lay on the sofa in the snug with a blanket over her. Emily buzzed about, looking after her.

I had no choice but to go in there or risk questions.

Frank patted my arm and nodded as if to say, well done.

"Okay, if I set up the DVD are you sure you'll be all right while Frank and I see to the farm?" I said.

"We'll be perfectly fine, won't we, Em?" Steph said.

Emily nodded as the doorbell rang.

"If it's Hector, don't let him in," Stephanie said in a breathy voice, obviously petrified.

"Hekker's in Spain," Emily said.

"He is, baby. Stephanie's confused that's all. Wait there."

Two uniformed police officers stood on the doorstep. I stopped breathing and my blood ran cold.

"Yes, officers?" I was amazed at how normal my voice sounded.

"We're looking for Stephanie Cross," the older officer said, his kind blue eyes twinkling.

"She's only just got home from hospital. Do you really need to do this now?"

"Afraid so, miss." the other officer said.

"You'd best come in then." I stepped aside and led them through to the snug. "Please, wait here a second," I said, as I entered the room.

"Steph, the police are here. I'll just take Emily through to Frank and I'll be right back."

She nodded, wincing as she tried to sit up.

"Come on, Em. The policemen need to talk to Stephy for a few minutes. Emily took my hand and followed me into the hall. "She's in there, I'll be back in a tick." I held the door open for the officers.

I quickly explained what was happening to Frank and rushed back to the snug.

"—and he apparently came back for his belongings last night, left my car here. That's the last we've heard of him."

"Do you know where he might have gone? Does he have any friends or family in the area?" the older officer asked.

"No, he's probably gone back to Spain. Although I don't know how as I have all his money in my bank account. He hadn't got around to opening an account of his own yet.

My stomach hit the ground. My mind raced as I said, "I think he may have taken some money from my room."

Stephanie spun her head to look at me and winced again, grasping her ribs. "You didn't tell me that."

"Because I didn't want to upset you any more than you already are."

"Do you want to report the theft, Mrs...?"

"Lyons. No. If I'd have been here I'd have given him the money if it meant he'd be gone for good."

"And what about you, Miss Cross. Do you want to press charges?" he asked.

"No point, as he's gone. If he comes back then I will, but I've got a feeling we've seen the last of him."

"Okay, but if he turns up, call us right away."

"Will do."

They stood up and I walked them to the front door.

"Nasty piece of work's done a right number on her, hasn't he?" the younger officer said.

I nodded. "I can't believe it. He was such a lovely man."

"Do you have any idea how many times we hear that, Mrs Lyons? Salt of the earth, wouldn't hurt a fly."

"I can imagine," I said. "Makes it difficult to know who you can trust though, doesn't it."

"Anyone is capable of a serious crime if the circumstances are right."

"Yes, officer. I suppose they are."

I closed the door after them, my heartbeat pounding in my ears.

CHAPTER 22

"Are you sure about this?"

Frank nodded.

"Shall we do it then?" We'd been sitting in Jonathan's truck for half an hour already, and my mind was wavering with every second.

"Let's do it," he said.

We climbed out of the truck and Frank opened up the main door.

I followed him to the cold store.

Frank gasped.

I pushed past him to see what was wrong.

Hector had moved.

He sat on the floor next to the door, and his bloody fingers and the marks on the back of the door showed he'd been trying to get out.

"Oh no, Frank. This changes everything now. He wasn't dying. He didn't kill himself."

"Is he dead now?" Frank's face had drained of all colour.

I felt for Hector's pulse. Nothing. "He is now, but he wasn't,

Frank. Don't you see how wrong this is?" I almost screamed. I felt as though my head might explode as I ran from the shed, retching.

Frank joined me soon after. He clutched his bad arm to his chest and kept clearing his throat, clearly shaken by this turn of events. I had to stop myself from yelling at him again.

"Sorry, Frank. It's not your fault; it's mine. I didn't think he'd wake up—his pulse was so weak—but I should have given him a sedative to be sure. Imagine how awful it must have been for him waking up in here. Worse still, how awful would it have been if he was still alive now?"

"Well he's not, so let's do this." He was back in control. Thank God.

We cut Hector's clothing off and I put them in a bin bag. It was even more difficult to lift the body today than it had been last night. He seemed much heavier somehow. But where there's a will there's a way, as my dad used to say.

Frank didn't hesitate at all. I helped where needed but I kept my eyes firmly focused on Frank's face. I had to zone out the awful, wet, slapping sounds as he threw each piece into the blue bin.

When he'd finished, I washed everything down while Frank transferred half of the meat to a different container. We placed a lid on it and heaved it into the back of the truck.

At the pigsty I helped Frank tip the container in. But this time I didn't look at the contents and tried to block out the awful squeals. It worked. I wasn't sick this time.

Next stop, the incinerator. We burnt all of Hector's belongings, and our overalls. No one would know that he'd been back here at all—except for the half bucket full of body parts in the cold store of course, but even that would be gone by tomorrow.

We had discussed shaving Hector's head and removing his

teeth, but once it came to it we changed our minds. We'd have to remove them afterwards instead, like last time.

After heating a frozen pizza for Stephanie and Emily, I locked myself in the bathroom and ran a bath, immersing myself for two hours. I spent that time blocking out all thoughts of the last twenty-four hours with Hector and re-played my last contact with him in my mind.

Emily and I had gone into the pub, and he waved frantically at us and pointed at Steph sitting at the bar. I'd glimpsed him later on when he weaved through the crowd, collecting glasses in the beer garden. That was the last time I'd seen him. The rest I erased from my mind—or that's what I told myself, anyway.

As I stepped from the bath, my heart flipped as I spotted watery blood running down the insides of my thighs and pooling on the towel at my feet.

I couldn't believe it. After everything that had happened recently, now it looked as though the decision of whether or not to keep the baby had been made for me.

I sat on the toilet lid, put my head in my hands and finally allowed myself to cry.

Great racking sobs tore through me and hot salty tears washed down my face.

Initially the tears were for the baby and the injustice of the whole situation, but after a while I couldn't say which one thing in particular I cried for. In a way, losing the baby would be losing the final connection to Jonathan. Regardless of the fact the baby may not actually be his. Regardless of the fact I had been considering a termination. I knew at that moment I would never have gone through with it.

The gnawing pain that began in the bottom of my back confirmed my worst fears. I remembered that pain. Anybody who'd experienced labour would never forget it. I didn't know what to do. There was no way I would call an ambulance, not for a miscarriage. Ambulances were for emergencies. I didn't want to drive myself to the hospital just in case I took a turn for the worse. Steph and Frank were both incapable of driving me.

There was only one thing for it.

I got a facecloth from the drawer, raced to the bedroom and wadded the facecloth between my legs, holding it in place with a pair of panties.

Then I went downstairs and threw the bloody towels into the laundry.

Steph and Emily were still in the snug watching television.

"Righto, little lady, it's bed time," I said, trying to keep my voice as light and normal as possible.

"Aw, can't I just watch this?" Emily said, her eyes fixed to the television set.

"No, sorry, love. I need you to do as you're told. It's bedtime, no arguing. Now run upstairs, have a quick wash, brush your teeth and put your nightie on. I'll see you up there in a minute."

A sharp pain made my face contort as I spoke. Emily, still staring at the TV didn't notice, but Steph did.

I put a finger to my mouth and indicated to Emily.

Steph nodded and turned the TV off with the remote. "Come on, Em. Thanks for looking after me today, but I'm going to need you bright-eyed and bushy-tailed for tomorrow. That is, if you still want to be my nursemaid."

Emily laughed. "I don't got a tail," she said, hugging Steph as she stood up.

"So you don't. My mistake." Steph giggled. "But I need you to do as your mummy asks and get yourself to bed like a big girl. Do you think you can do that before I count to ten?"

"Uh-huh." Emily raced to the door as Stephanie began counting.

"One … two … three …"

Emily was upstairs before Steph reached four.

"Are you okay, Vic? You look terrible," Steph said.

I shook my head. "Where's Frank?" I asked.

"He went for a lie down. What's happening?"

"I'm losing the baby. I'm having pains and bleeding quite heavily. There's nothing anybody can do."

"Oh, I'm so sorry, Vic," she cried. "Can I do anything to help?"

"I'll go back into the bathroom until it's all over," I said, the words catching in my throat and fresh tears filled my eyes.

"Aw, Vic. Shall I call the doctor or a midwife or someone?"

"No point. I'll be okay."

"Call me if you need me," Steph said. "And Vic, don't dispose of anything. They'll need to examine everything to make sure nothing has been left behind."

I nodded, creased by an even stronger pain that had me doubled over.

I'd thought things would progress slowly like normal labour did, but now I wasn't so sure.

Emily was in bed by the time I got upstairs.

"Thanks for being such a good girl for me, Em, I'm sorry but I can't read to you tonight. I don't feel too well," I said, as I bent to kiss the top of her head.

"S'okay, Mummy. Maybe I'll be a nursemaid for you too."

"Goodnight, gorgeous girl."

"Goodnight, Mummy."

I'd barely made it back to the bathroom when I felt a gushing sensation between my legs. The facecloth and panties were no longer holding anything and as I stepped out of them I realised it was practically all over.

I sat on the bathroom floor, staring my tiny, perfectly formed baby boy. His entire body was no bigger than my hand.

My heart contracted.

The immense pain I felt was much worse than the actual pain of the miscarriage.

My rational mind knew it was a blessing, really.

Jon's baby would have been born with a death sentence hanging over it and Shane's baby would have been a constant reminder of that terrible night.

Nevertheless, as I held the fragile body of my son, I thought I might actually die with grief.

CHAPTER 23

The next couple of weeks were chaotic. Stephanie still wasn't able to work, and with Hector gone, we were two people down. Emily remained off school and the demand at the clinic had the appointments booked up solid. However, we somehow managed to muddle through.

I suspected I'd never totally get over losing baby Jonathan, a name I'd chosen to convince myself he was indeed Jon's son. And in the dead of night, I prayed Jon had been waiting for baby Jonathan, so he wouldn't be alone.

Emily didn't know about the baby; she'd had enough to deal with in recent months without having to understand the death of a baby brother as well. She would be back in school by next Thursday and I hoped Steph would be back on board by then too.

Seven of Emily's classmates were coming over the next day for Emily's sixth birthday party, and I had lots of girly finger food, pink cupcakes and jelly to prepare on top of everything else. I'd cheated and bought a birthday cake from the bakers in town, which I planned to pick up in the morning.

I'd left Stephanie on the floor of the snug, wrapping gifts for tomorrow's game of pass the parcel. In her utter boredom, she'd promoted herself to event organiser, using her ample time to plan all the entertainment for eight six-year-old girls and their optional parent or guardians.

We had a variety of fun party games set up. She'd also bought a piñata and filled it with lots of tooth-rotting goodies and had even bought Emily a new outfit off the Internet, a pretty white broderie-anglaise dress with blue ribbons and some white slip-on pumps to match.

As I finished mixing the batter for the cupcakes, I looked up and Alex was standing in front of me. I almost shot through the roof.

"Oh, Alex." I blew out dramatically and laughed, one hand steadying myself on the bench, the other on my chest.

"Sorry, I just wanted to show you this." He placed a small item on the bench and I bent towards it. When I realised what it was, I felt the room go topsy-turvy.

It was a tooth.

"What the ..." I couldn't continue. My mind raced and my heart partially stopped.

"A tooth," he said, mistaking my reaction for confusion.

"Have you just lost it?" I said. Amazed at how calm I sounded.

He laughed. "No, it's not mine."

"Oh. Where's it from, then?" How I kept my voice so steady was anybody's guess.

"I found it in the sty."

I cocked my head to one side and screwed my face up. "The sty?"

He nodded.

"How did it get in there?"

"No idea."

"How strange. Leave it there and I'll show it to Frank later," I said, doing my best to appear calm.

"Okay." He headed for the door.

"Maybe it's a pigs tooth?"

"No, don't think so. It has a filling," he said over his shoulder as he left.

I took several deep breaths, my mind racing. We'd cleaned the sty thoroughly and thought we'd removed everything, but obviously not. This one fucking tooth could have the whole mess crashing down around our ears. I had no idea what we could do about it.

I finished the cupcakes and placed them in the oven, before picking up the tooth and wrapping it in a tissue. Then I went upstairs to find Frank.

I knocked on his door.

"Come in."

"Only me," I said, as I entered his room.

Frank was sitting by the window on a white wicker chair, reading a book.

I perched on his high bed. "You'll never guess what."

"Tell me."

"Alex found this." I leaned towards him and passed him the tissue-covered tooth.

"Oh dear," he said, folding the tissue up again.

"He found it in the sty. I suggested it was one of the pigs' teeth but he pointed out it had a filling."

"It's okay. I'll tell him it's mine. That I lost it a while ago over there."

"Do you think he'll believe that?"

"Why not? He'd surely believe that before he'd believe we'd fed someone to the pigs."

"I guess."

"Don't worry, lass. I'll sort it."

"I hope so. This is all we need."

The party was a roaring success. Seven hyperactive guests and the birthday girl all had a wonderful time.

At the end of the day only Kaylie, Emily's best friend, remained and they both went up to Emily's bedroom to play while we waited for Kaylie's mum to arrive.

I heard a terrible scream above the sound of the vacuum cleaner and thought I was hearing things at first. I ran up the stairs as fast as I could, bursting into Emily's room.

Kaylie lay on her back, screaming, with Emily sitting astride her. Emily was hitting Kaylie repeatedly in the face.

"Emily!" I screamed and grabbed her arm, lifting her off Kaylie, whose face was bright red and a trickle of blood ran from her nose.

"What's got into you?" I shrieked, shaking my daughter by the arm, trying to shock her into calming down.

But Emily was furious. She kicked and squirmed, trying to get back to Kaylie.

Kaylie sobbed, "She-hic-told me-hic-to give her-hic-my hair-slide. When-hic-I said-hic-no, she-hic-hit me."

I shoved Emily towards her bed—she'd calmed down slightly. Then I picked Kaylie up from the floor and carried her from the room. "Stay there, Emily, and don't move until I come back," I snarled.

Emily's face was twisted into an ugly vision of pure evil—I'd never seen anything like it before.

I slammed the door.

Down in the kitchen I sat Kaylie on the draining board, wiped her face with a flannel and rested it on her bloody nose. "Hold that there a sec," I said, and bent to get a towel from the bottom drawer.

Her sobs had more or less stopped.

I wiped Kaylie's face on the towel, then brushed her hair, re-fastening her hairslide.

"Are you okay now?" I asked.

She nodded.

"How about a bowl of ice-cream or some sweeties?" I said. "Your mum should be here soon."

She shook her head. "No, thanks." A triple sob escaped her.

"I'm sorry Emily hurt you, sweetie. She must be very tired. She's not normally like that, is she?"

Kaylie shook her head. She'd calmed down slightly, her face returning to a near normal colour.

"Come on, let's get you down from there."

The doorbell rang as I placed her on her feet. "This must be your mummy."

Kaylie escorted me to the door and as soon as she saw her mummy, she began to sob again.

"She's had a fight with Emily," I explained. "I don't know—best friends one minute and fisticuffs the next." I grimaced.

"Kaylie. You mustn't fight with your friends," her mum scolded.

"It wasn't me; it was Emily."

"Never mind. You were here as a guest and it was Emily's birthday party. Where are your manners?" her mother said.

"Oh, don't blame her. Emily's extra tired. It'll be forgotten by next week." I smiled, knowing in my heart that my daughter had been the aggressor. "Okay, Kaylie, where's your bag?"

I felt terrible playing Kaylie's attack down, but Emily had already got enough bad press from the stealing. I couldn't bear for them to know she'd tried to rob her friend and beat her up when she wouldn't hand over the goods. However, I knew Kaylie would probably tell her mum everything as soon as they got to the car.

I walked back up to Emily's room and found her sitting on the floor, her back against the bed, arms folded in defiance.

"What was that all about, Emily?"

She shrugged.

"Oh no, I'm not having that. You know exactly what you did and if you don't tell me, there'll be no TV for a week.

"No, Mummy. It was an accident."

"Rubbish. I saw you punching Kaylie in her face. She's your best friend," I said, shaking my head.

"No, she's not!" she said stamping her foot.

"Where has this come from? I've never seen you so nasty."

"I'm not nasty," her top lip curled, showing her little teeth.

"Oh, really? I'll leave you to think about that. I don't want to set eyes on you until I have my nice little girl back."

"I am your nice little girl," she yelled.

I got up and walked to the door, closing it behind me.

"I'm your nice little girl!" she yelled again, and began banging on the back of the door.

I held it closed until I heard her move away, then I walked downstairs, unsure of what I'd witnessed, and where the hell it had come from.

Frank and Steph wouldn't believe me when I told them what she'd done.

Frank had been at the neighbours for the duration of the party. Although he adored Emily, the thought of another seven just like her was enough to send him into cold sweats. Steph had stayed for the entire party, and had done Emily proud with the effort she'd put into the party games. Afterwards, she went to drop a couple of Emily's friends off at home and planned to collect Frank on her way back.

An hour later, Emily walked into the lounge and sat next to me on the sofa. I put my magazine down on the coffee table and turned to look at her. Frank and Stephanie were now home and buzzing around in the kitchen.

"Well?" I said.

"Sorry, Mummy."

"What happened?"

"I got angry."

"You're not kidding. But why?"

She shrugged. "I don't know."

"What about what Kaylie said?"

She looked away.

"She said you told her to give you her hairslide and when she wouldn't, you began hitting her."

Still nothing from Emily.

"Is that true, Em?"

She nodded. "I wanted it. And it's *my* birthday."

"That doesn't give you the right to take her belongings and beat her up, does it?"

Nothing.

"Does it, Em?"

"No."

“No! I can't believe you did it. If I hadn't seen it with my own eyes I definitely wouldn't believe it."

"Sorry."

"I think you need to apologise to Kaylie, not me. She was very upset, and I don't blame her."

CHAPTER 24

I waved across the playground to Kaylie's mum and she turned her back, and flounced off in the direction of the classroom.

By the time we got there, several of the parents were standing in a group, obviously gossiping, and avoiding my gaze. I was worried how Emily would feel, but she didn't seem to notice anything untoward. I hoped it was just the parents acting like a bunch of bitchy schoolchildren. I could handle that.

I shook my head at them as I left the classroom.

The day flew by. It was great to have Stephanie back on board and we had a fun day in the clinic. We finished early and I dropped Stephanie off at the dentist, where she was having a crown fitted to her broken tooth, while I went to collect Em from school.

I knew as soon as I entered the classroom that there was a problem.

Mrs Farnworth abruptly ended her conversation with a middle-aged man, and headed towards me.

"Mrs Lyons, did you get my message?"

"What message?" I was frantically looking around the room for Emily, but she wasn't there.

"Emily had some kind of outburst this afternoon. We were playing games on the school field when she attacked several of the other children because she was losing."

"Where is she?"

"With Mrs Jackson. I had no choice but to remove her from the class. We couldn't calm her down. She even tried to attack me."

"I'm sorry," I said, shaking my head. "I need to sit down for a second."

"Yes, of course. Can I get you a glass of water?"

"No, thanks." I pulled a child's plastic chair down off the top of the table and sat heavily onto it, marginally concerned it wouldn't hold my weight, but it did.

I couldn't understand what was happening to my sweet little girl.

I didn't stay there for long. I couldn't bear the sly glances from some of the other parents. I wanted to yell at them, but that would just add fuel to the flames.

I knocked on Mrs Jackson's door and she opened it almost immediately.

"Ah, Mrs Lyons, come on in."

Emily sat at a desk off to the side of the room. She began to cry as she saw me. I held my arms out towards her.

Mrs Jackson, tight-lipped, indicated I sit. "I take it you've heard what happened here this afternoon?" she said, as Emily climbed onto my knee.

"Yes, I spoke to Mrs Farnworth."

"Well, I wasn't there when it all occurred. However, I did see Emily immediately afterwards and I must say I've never seen such rage from a young girl."

"I don't understand it," I said.

"Well, apparently this isn't the first time. We've had a number of parents insisting Emily is kept away from their children."

"What? That's nonsense. How can you do that? All kids fight and are best mates again two minutes later."

"We have a zero tolerance policy at this school, Mrs Lyons, and besides, this wasn't a couple of children having a squabble. Emily kicked, bit and scratched several of our children and even some teachers."

"Come off it. She's five years old."

"Six," Emily said.

"Six then, it's not as if she could do much damage."

"That's not the point. Besides, she could do a lot of damage to another six-year-old."

I shook my head and took a deep breath. "Okay, so what do you suggest?"

"I am suspending Emily for the rest of the week. She's welcome to come back in next Monday if she's willing to apologise to the children *and* Mrs Farnworth."

"You're kidding? Suspended! She's only six!"

"Not the point, Mrs Lyons."

"Come on, Em, we're going." I stood up, shaking my head. "See you next week then."

Stephanie was sitting on the wall of the dental surgery when we arrived. "Thought you'd forgot about me," she said, smiling.

"No, I'll tell you what happened when we get home." I hadn't said a word to Emily since getting in the car.

She was also very quiet.

"Hello, Em," Steph said.

"Hello," she said, and glanced out of the window.

I shook my head at Stephanie and she made an 'o' shape with her mouth, then winced.

I smiled. "How's your tooth?"

She opened her lips for me revealing teeth which were back to normal.

"Gosh, you'd never know it wasn't real," I said. The crown she'd had fitted made her smile complete.

"I know. I'm really pleased with it." She glanced into the mirror on the sun visor.

As we pulled up outside the house, Emily shot out of the car and ran inside, heading for the stairs.

"Not so fast, miss. You have some explaining to do," I said.

I walked through to the lounge and sat down on the sofa. Emily skulked in behind me and leaned on the arm of the chair opposite.

"Well?"

"They wouldn't throw the ball to me," she said.

"That's no reason to ..." I sighed, tired of repeating myself. She wasn't learning anything from the lectures and punishments. "You know what? Why bother? I can't deal with this right now. Just go to your room. Go on, get out of my sight."

"Fine then!" She stomped up the stairs and slammed her bedroom door. The kind of attitude you'd expect from a teenager, not a little girl.

"What's she done?" Steph whispered, as she sat down.

"She's had another temper tantrum and attacked a load of kids, *plus* her teacher this time. I don't know what to do with her. I'm out of ideas."

"When's she back at the hospital?"

"Next week, although it's nothing to do with that."

"How do you know?"

"Because ... I don't know, but why would it be?"

"Dur! She has an illness affecting her brain, and this is not normal behaviour for a six-year-old, Vic. The illness must be a huge factor in it."

"Maybe, but the doctor didn't say anything when I told him

about the stealing. He agreed it was probably because of Jonathan."

"Maybe they don't know it is connected. It's a rare condition, right?"

I nodded. "It does make more sense, I guess. If she really can't help herself, like she says." I shrugged.

"Can't you give them a call and ask?"

"There's no point. She's suspended from school anyway. I'll keep her home till after the hospital."

"I bet it's that—it's got to be. She's a good girl and this is so unlike her. She's taken on the demeanour of a thief and a bully."

As she said the words my stomach leapt into my chest.

A movement to the side of me caught my eye. Frank stood there, and from the look on his face I could tell he'd heard what Stephanie said and seemed to be having the exact same reaction as me.

"Frank! Are you okay?" Steph jumped to her feet and guided Frank to the chair, her arm around his shoulder. She looked at me, her eyebrows furrowed.

Frank sat down. "I—I'm okay," he said.

"You don't look okay," she said. "Can I make you a cup of tea?"

"That would be nice, lass. I just need to catch my breath."

"Do you want one, Vic?"

I nodded. "Please."

Frank met my gaze as Stephanie went through to the kitchen. "Do you think we caused it?" I whispered. Although it was an open-plan room, Steph was far enough away that she couldn't hear us.

"I don't know, lass."

"Think about it. She began stealing after we gave her Shane's Proteum. Everybody knows he was the biggest thief around. Then Hector—he definitely had anger issues. And now Emily is attacking people."

"It does seem strange."

"Steph thinks it may be connected to her illness, and that also makes sense. The other could be a coincidence."

"Maybe."

"But you don't think so?"

He shook his head. "No, I think she's got the worst traits of both of them."

We sat, absorbed in our own thoughts until Stephanie brought the mugs of tea through.

"What happened today, then?" Frank said.

"Emily has been suspended from school for attacking several of her classmates. She said it was because they wouldn't throw the ball to her. We're back at the hospital again next week. Maybe, as Steph said, it could be connected to her illness. I'll ask Doctor Wilson," I said, but in my heart of hearts, I knew different.

CHAPTER 25

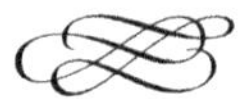

This time we went straight to the ward. We no longer needed the formality of meeting with the doctor first.

The tests went smoothly.

Emily, now used to it, only cried a little bit during the lumbar puncture.

The last results had shown a substantial drop since the previous ones. I knew these would be much better. Her health had once again been amazing since Hector. The only problems were the stealing and her temper, and although both of these things drove me to distraction, I considered the alternative much, much worse.

I left Emily with Diane when Doctor Wilson called us into his office.

"Okay then. Once again, Mrs Lyons, Emily's showing a huge improvement on last time. She's astounding the entire Neurology department. We can't keep up with her yoyo figures."

"That's great news. Isn't it, Frank?" I said.

He nodded, smiling. "It is, lass."

"We need the rest of the results of course before we get the total picture but these initial ones are quite remarkable. I have no doubt the others will confirm this."

"I was going to ask you, Doctor. Could Emily's illness be causing the kleptomania?"

"My initial reaction would be to say no, but with Emily, I don't want to say anything definite."

"She's also had terrible mood swings, and was suspended from school last week for attacking several of her friends *and* the teacher."

"Suspended? That is a worry. All I can say is that there have been no record of these symptoms before, but that could be because they weren't reported. People often come to their own conclusions about certain things and don't even think to tell us." He bounced his pen on the desk.

"I guess we're guilty of that ourselves. If you remember, it was Frank who mentioned the stealing last time, not me."

"Yes, and we all agreed it was probably connected to the death of your husband, which could still be the case. Nevertheless, I should have recorded the symptoms on the file."

I shrugged. "If it is the illness to blame, at least I'll be able to stop punishing her. I feel so awful. She says she can't help it and I *do* believe her, but the parent in me won't allow me to ignore the behaviour. All I seem to do lately is nag at her. She blames the worst of the behaviour on her imaginary friend."

"That's normal, I'd say. My own little girl had an imaginary friend when she was this age. Emily will grow out of it."

"I hope so."

"I wouldn't overdo the punishments. I'll arrange a psychiatric evaluation, if that's all right with you?"

I nodded again.

"See if they can shed any light on this behaviour. I'll also do some homework. Maybe we can find some more instances of this happening."

"What should I do then? If she attacks another child or steals, I shouldn't tell her off?"

"Try it, at least until she sees the psychiatrist. Praise her good behaviour. Ignore the bad, as much as you can.

"It's worth a try I suppose."

"In the meantime, I'll find out what I can and call you next week with the results."

"Thanks again, doctor."

I patted Emily down before we left the hospital. Frank laughed at me but I didn't intend to come back again if I could help it. She didn't have anything.

We stopped at McDonalds and Emily devoured her Happy Meal and went to play on the climbing frame while Frank and I finished our coffee. She found a new friend, and they ran up and down the slide, playing tag.

I drank the last of my coffee. "I'm going to the bathroom, then we can go—if you've finished?"

"Amen to that. Let's get out of this awful place." Frank grimaced.

I passed the play area. Emily seemed to be having a wonderful time. She missed playing with her friends from school. The young black girl she was playing with was probably a little older than Emily and she had the cutest face, chubby little cheeks and a wonderful pout.

I noticed a woman sitting opposite the play area who was obviously the girl's mother, as they were the spitting image of each other.

She smiled and nodded towards me as I walked by.

The sounds of screaming made my blood run cold. I raced back into the restaurant.

Frank was on his feet trying to control a hysterical Emily.

The cute little black girl was screaming the place down, blood all down the front of her white t-shirt. Her mother pressed serviettes to her face.

"What's going on?" I shrieked.

"Control your child before she kills someone. She's a monster!" the mother said.

"What did she do?" I asked. "Emily, what did you do?"

Frank was still battling with her and I snatched her by the arm and dragged her to me. "What did you do?"

"Kicked her," she said her lip curling once again.

"You kicked her? In her face?"

"She kicked and kicked my daughter until she fell backwards down the ladder. She's not right in the head," the woman continued.

"Actually, we've just come from the hospital and you're right. She's not well," I said, trying make excuses for my daughter.

"You don't need the hospital to tell you that. I'd have saved you a trip."

"I apologise for my daughter. She really can't help it."

"Then I suggest you keep her away from other children when she's not wearing her straitjacket."

I realised Frank had gone and I found him standing by the front door, his face a pasty grey colour. I walked over to him, dragging Emily behind me.

"Are you okay, Frank?"

He nodded but I didn't believe him.

"Come on, let's get home."

We drove in silence. Frank slumped in his seat, seemed to sink lower and lower as I drove.

I had to force myself to focus on the road. These past months I'd relied heavily on Frank for all kinds of things, forgetting about his illness. The thought of him having another stroke—or worse still, dying—made my heartbeat erratic.

Emily sulked in the back seat. I didn't say a word to her, attempting what the doctor suggested. However, I couldn't ignore what she'd done and be nice to her, so I opted to say nothing at all for now.

By the time we reached the house, Frank had deteriorated.

Stephanie had to help get Frank inside. It was difficult with Frank being such a large man, but between us we managed to get him into the lounge and lying on the sofa.

"I'm calling the doctor," I said.

"No, leave it for a few minutes, I'll be fine soon," Frank said, his voice weak and whispery.

"What's wrong? What are you feeling?" I demanded.

"I got a shock seeing Emily like that. I know you told me how she's been, but I didn't realise how bad she gets."

"But that can't be all. You look terrible. I'll give you five minutes while I make you a cup of tea, and if you're no better, I'm calling the doctor. Okay?"

"Okay."

Tea made, I got a pillow from the linen cupboard in the hall and placed it behind his back. "You're no better, are you?"

"Don't fuss, lass."

"I'll fuss all I want. I'm calling the doctor. No arguments."

I called the surgery and explained the situation.

"Can you bring him in?" the stupid girl on the end of the phone asked.

"No. I'm sorry, but I don't want to move him. He looks terrible."

"Right then, the duty doctor will come out after surgery, but if he gets any worse or complains of chest pain, call an ambulance right away."

"Thank you."

Less than an hour later, a burgundy Honda pulled up on the drive. Doctor Davies was taking his bag out of the boot as I opened the front door.

"Hello, Mrs Lyons. How are you?"

"I'm fine thanks. It's my father-in-law, Frank."

Doctor Davies shook my hand. His solemn gaze fixed on mine, his mouth turned down at the corners. "I was sorry to hear about your husband, Mrs Lyons. Shocking business."

I smiled. "Thanks, doctor. Come on through."

"Hello, Mr Lyons, I'm Doctor Davies. I don't think we've met." He held his hand out to Frank. "What seems to be the problem?"

"Probably nothing. I had a funny turn earlier and it knocked me for six."

"In what way?"

"Dizzy, short of breath, and my legs felt shaky—weak."

The doctor took his stethoscope from his bag and listened to Frank's chest. "Sounds fine," he said. Then he took Frank's blood pressure. "Hmm, that's a little high, but not too bad. Have you been overdoing things lately?"

Frank shook his head.

"He's had a busy day today, doctor. I'm shattered myself, so it must have affected you, Frank."

"What was today?"

"We've been at the hospital all day with Emily," I said.

"Oh yes. How is Emily doing at the moment?"

"They found she has an incurable illness." I glanced around, relieved Emily wasn't about. She'd gone into the snug with Stephanie.

"Yes, I received the notes from the hospital. How has she been?"

"Up and down, literally. The hospital staff are amazed with her."

"Oh, that's good then. Right?" he asked.

"We hope so, doctor."

Doctor Davies nodded and turned back to Frank. "Mr Lyons. I need you to take it easy for a couple of days. Doctor's orders. If you're not feeling better by Wednesday, come in to see me at the surgery or call and I'll come out again, but I think you'll be right as rain."

"Thanks, doctor."

"How did you get on with that Shane bloke?" Doctor Davies said, looking straight at me.

Had I heard him right? "Shane bloke?" I said.

"Yeah, outside the surgery that day. The receptionist said she heard your car alarm going off and saw you having trouble with Shane Logan. We were about to call the police when he took off and you and your husband left. I presumed you'd report him."

"Oh, I get you now. Sorry, I didn't know his name. We didn't report it—we were so worried about Emily. I'd actually forgotten all about that."

"I wish I'd called the police now," he said. "He's a local deadbeat and we'd had a few cars broken into around that time. No problems for a while now though, he's on the missing list."

"What do you mean?" My heartbeat felt jittery.

"His mother's trying to get the police to launch an investigation. Apparently he's been missing for months. Nobody's seen sight nor sound of him. I guess we should thank heaven for small mercies."

After Doctor Davies had gone I sat next to Frank on the sofa. "Oh, my God. I never knew anybody saw anything that day. When he asked about Shane I almost collapsed—I couldn't believe my ears."

Frank chuckled. "Me too."

"What if the police do launch an investigation? There's a connection to us now."

"Yeah, but how many other people would have come across Shane? He was a nasty piece of work."

"I'd have preferred absolutely no connection."

"The police won't be interested in that. You told the doctor you didn't even know who he was. He didn't go missing until weeks after. Don't worry. They won't suspect you of anything."

"I hope you're right, Frank."

CHAPTER 26

I rang Mrs Jackson first thing the next morning.

"Good morning, Mrs Lyons, how's Emily? We expected her back in school yesterday."

"She had a hospital appointment yesterday. You are aware she's a very sick little girl, aren't you?"

"Erm, I knew she'd had some kind of illness but I thought she was okay now."

I hadn't officially told the school about Emily's illness, but Mrs Farnworth knew.

I blew through my lips noisily. "She's far from okay. Her illness is terminal, and although she's not *as* sick in herself right now, I can assure you it's just a matter of time."

"I'm so sorry. I had no idea ... What is it?" Although her voice seemed cool and impassive I noticed a slight tremor.

"She's not producing an essential development hormone. It's very rare and there's a chance that the stealing and the temper outbursts are connected. The specialist is arranging for a psychiatric evaluation. I was wondering if you would prefer me to keep her at home in the meantime?"

"That's entirely up to you. I don't want to say you can't bring her in, but we must think of the safety of the other pupils."

"So you're saying I should keep her at home?" I couldn't believe my ears.

"No. I don't think that's fair either. In fact, if I'd known about the illness last week, I wouldn't have suspended her in the first place. We've got a staff meeting this evening. I'll put Emily at the top of the agenda and see what we can do. Can I call you in the morning?"

"Of course."

"Don't worry, Mrs Lyons. We'll sort something out."

Frank seemed more like himself this morning, but I insisted he put his feet up on the sofa again.

"I'm fine, lass. Don't fuss."

"You heard what the doctor said; just do as you're told. You've been amazing lately and I'd hate for you to take a backwards step now."

He tutted, shook his head and sat down on the sofa, smiling at me as if to say, *happy now?*

"Good boy." I laughed. "Just for today. If you're feeling okay by tomorrow, I'll leave you alone," I said. "Now, Emily?"

Emily lifted her head from the colouring book on the table.

"I need you to watch Grandad while I go and feed the animals. Do you think you can do that?"

"Yes, Mummy."

"Can I trust you both?"

"Yes, Mummy," they said together, giggling.

"Ha ha, very funny," I grinned at the two of them.

Stephanie was holding the fort at the clinic today. I intended to join her later to do the wages and the accounts—we were behind with several invoices.

Alex was on his hands and knees and up to his armpits in

muddy water at a water trough in the middle of the paddock. I tooted the truck horn and waved as I passed him.

He nodded his head.

True to her word, Emily's headmistress called back the next morning.

"I had a chat with the rest of the staff last night and we've decided to put an additional teacher's aide into Emily's classroom. It will be easier to keep on top of any situation and to intercept before any problems arise," she explained.

Intercept? What was this woman on? We were talking about a six-year-old girl for Christ's sake. "Will she be made to feel different?" I said.

"Of course not."

"Will other parents be told?"

"Well, no. It's nobody else's business."

"I guess we can give it a try then. When should I bring her in?"

"Tomorrow, if that's okay. That will give me today to organise things."

"Okay, thanks, Mrs Jackson."

Emily danced for joy when I told her she could go back to school. There hadn't been any more angry episodes since McDonalds, but she'd only been around us. I worried how she would cope in a classroom of kids.

The change in the other parents was amazing. The ones who had colluded with Kaylie's mum now waved and acknowledged both Emily *and* me. Mrs Jackson had said she wouldn't say anything, but someone had clearly blabbed about Emily's illness.

The teacher's aide was a slip of a thing with a gentle, girly voice. She would sit at the back of the classroom and keep an eye out for any potential conflicts with Emily.

Emily was thrilled to be back with her friends and they all seemed pleased to see her—all except Kaylie, who kept her distance.

I reluctantly left Emily in the classroom.

Everything ran smoothly over the next few days. There were a couple of occasions where the teacher's aide had to intervene but nothing major.

Doctor Wilson called the following Wednesday. He told me, as expected, that Emily's test results were amazing.

"I'd like to perform further tests next time, if possible."

"What kind of tests?" The hair stood up on the back of my neck.

"I want to try to establish why Emily is having fluctuations with her results. Maybe she's eating something or doing something herself that's having a positive result. I want to ask if you could keep a diary for me. A daily record of what she is feeling, her attitude, when she steals and her reasons, what makes her angry, and everything she eats and drinks. We will try to establish if there is any kind of pattern to help with the studies into this illness."

"Yes, that's fine," I said.

"Emily's results are making a lot of people very excited, Mrs Lyons. Next time I'd like a colleague to examine her and see what he suggests."

"Okay." I didn't like the idea of extra tests and heightened interest in Emily's results, but what could I say? There was no reason to suspect they'd be able to discover what we'd done. Plus the extra attention could turn up some kind of cure, and that would be wonderful.

"I've made a few enquiries about the behavioural issues and on the whole, there is nothing to report. Except, that is, in the early trials and the children that received the Proteum transplants."

My stomach lurched. "Really?"

"Yes, but that wasn't stealing or anger so I guess it's irrelevant."

"What was it then?"

One of the parents commented on a complete personality change. Her son went from an introverted boy to the class clown overnight. They weren't bothered—they actually liked the transformation."

"Were there any others?"

"One other, and she was the complete opposite. She withdrew into herself and sadly committed suicide two weeks later."

"Oh wow. That's terrible."

"Maybe it's just coincidence that these two children had been the ones who completed the trials, but they were the only ones to show any character changes at all. I am inclined to say at this stage, that the behaviour is probably connected to the condition."

He wasn't suspicious, thank goodness. But then again, why would he be? The idea that we'd performed our own transplants was too far-fetched to comprehend. It felt unreal even to me.

"I've arranged an appointment with the psychiatrist next week, on the twenty-fifth of September. I'll send confirmation in the mail. It's at ten o'clock, at the hospital."

"Thanks, Doctor."

"You're welcome. I look forward to seeing you in six weeks or so. Don't forget the diaries, will you?"

"I won't." I replaced the receiver and sighed heavily. So we *had* caused Emily's behaviour. She wasn't to blame. At least Emily could live with these symptoms, unlike the poor girl who'd got the suicidal tendencies.

Doctor Christine Forbes had a laid-back demeanor. Probably in her thirties, her flawless peaches and cream skin made her look much younger. She wore a brown gypsy-style skirt, a frilly white blouse and beige waistcoat, dressed up with lots of bangles and a brown bead necklace. Her loosely tied, sandy hair was held with a clip at the nape of her neck. A few stray curls framed her face.

I liked her immediately.

"Come in, you must be Emily," she said to me and winked.

"No *I'm* Emily. She's Mummy." Emily laughed.

"Oh hi, Emily. I'm sorry. I'm such a silly billy.

That was all she needed to do to hook my daughter. They were the best of friends before we entered her office and sat down.

"How old are you, Emily?"

"Six."

"Six. Wow! You're the same age as my daughter, Megan. I bet you like Raggedy-Ann."

"Yes." Emily's eyes lit up. "Does Megan like it?"

"Yes, it's her favourite."

"Does she like the Power Puff girls?"

"She certainly does, and My Little Pony. Excuse me for a second, Emily. I need to talk to your mummy. Is that okay?"

She nodded, smiling.

"I'd like to spend a couple of hours alone with Emily, if you don't mind? Do you have any shopping you need to do?"

"I'm sure I can find something."

"Great, see you back here at say ... Twelve-thirty? Then we'll have a chat."

I wandered around the local shopping centre, enjoying the time to myself. After a while, I stopped for a coffee, *a posh coffee* as Steph called them. I sat people-watching while I drank.

I never tired of this pastime, although I hadn't done nearly enough of it lately. Jonathan and I would try to guess what people did for a living. If they were married, divorced, had children. We used to end up in hysterics as Jonathan always went too far, inventing way-out scenarios and back stories with such detail. I often thought he was wasted as a farmer, as he'd have made a fantastic fiction writer.

Sitting at the table beside me, a middle-aged couple studied a tablet computer.

They both had dark brown hair—his was greying slightly at the temples which made him appear distinguished, and hers was straight and curled under at the chin. They wore the exact same shade of blue, her in a pinafore dress and he a shirt and trousers. I doubted they had children–too much time on their hands to colour coordinate their wardrobes to be parents.

I imagined their house would be organised and immaculate, lawns trimmed and edged to perfection, hanging baskets spilling over with an abundance of blooms. No pets. Pets would be too much of an inconvenience to a couple like them.

I couldn't see what was on the screen but I imagined they were booking an all-expenses paid Mediterranean cruise.

Two Asian females sat in an alcove across the room. I guessed they were mother and daughter as their hair was the same shade of black, and had been styled the same. Although the older woman's colour wasn't as vibrant, she was still a very attractive lady. She wore a thick, white cotton shirt and grey slacks.

The young girl wore a pale pink top in crinkly material with a hair bow to match and a white skirt. I couldn't see her face as she sat at too much of an angle.

Their conversation seemed intense, with the older of the two doing most of the talking while the younger nodded her head. Even though I couldn't hear what they were saying, I could tell they spoke in a foreign language.

She was probably in trouble for bunking off school, or mixing with the wrong crowd. I guessed the mother had brought the daughter out to discuss the problem, rather than let her father know what she'd been up to. Hence the reason for her mother chewing her ear off.

They finished their drinks and stood up. My stomach flipped and a pang of hurt gripped at my core as I noticed the huge pregnant belly of the girl as she turned to face me. I stood and hurried from the café and back into the mall, blinking back a sudden flood of tears.

Losing the baby had hit me harder than I thought it would. Somehow, through all the uncertainty, I'd developed a bond with my unborn son, and the grief of losing him hit me in waves when I least expected it. And because nobody, except Steph and Frank, knew about it, I had to behave as normal, even though I was experiencing all the stages of grief—the numbness, the anger and most of all, the guilt. I'd been considering terminating the pregnancy, and although some might say nature lent me a helping hand, made it easier on me, I didn't think so.

Feeling lost and jittery, I still had over an hour to kill. A hair salon caught my eye. I entered without much thought. It had been ages since I'd had a trim.

The young blonde girl gave my hair a thorough washing, followed by a mind-blowing head massage. Then she led me to a seat in front of the mirror.

"How much do you want off?"

A moment of madness overcame me. "All of it."

"I'm sorry?"

"Do something different, surprise me."

"But ..." She held my golden brown tresses in her hands and stared at my reflection.

"It's okay. I need a change." I nodded.

She beckoned to a middle-aged woman who stood at the back of the salon mixing some hair colour. The woman walked over to us, eyeing me suspiciously.

"What is it?" she said to the girl."

"Nothing's wrong," she said. "It's just that this lady wants me to cut all her hair off, and surprise her. I don't know what to do."

"Are you sure? You have beautiful hair," the older woman said to my reflection.

"Yes, I'm sure. I just want a change. It's been tied up for years."

She shrugged and nodded to the young girl and went back to the back of the salon.

"How about I cut it to your shoulders first and see what you think?"

"To my chin. I don't want to be able to tie it up."

When I returned to the hospital, I sported a fantastic new hair-do. I loved it. With the bulk removed, my curls had sprung to life and it altered my face completely. But not only that, I felt as though a weight had been lifted.

Emily did a double take when she saw me and began to cry. "Mummy, where's all your hair?"

"I've had it cut, baby. Don't you like it?"

She stopped crying, her eyebrows furrowed and looked at it again.

"I liked it before."

"I think it's beautiful," Christine said.

"Thank you. See what a couple of hours on my own can do? I'm not fit to be let out." I laughed. "Any longer and God knows what I'd have come back looking like."

"Well, we've had a wonderful time haven't we, Emily?"

Emily nodded, still staring at my hair.

"We've played lots of games and Emily's shown me how clever she is with her sums and her writing."

"And I played with a dolly," Emily added.

"If I gave you the dolly and a couple of books, do you think you could sit outside the door for a few minutes? I need to have a chat with your mum."

"Okay."

Emily seemed happily ensconced in her own world when we went back into the room. I took the seat Emily had vacated.

"Well, as I said, we had a wonderful time. You have a very bright little girl there," she said.

"Thanks."

"I've had the reports from Doctor Wilson, so I know what's been happening over the past few months. Losing her father like that in itself is enough to cause untold amounts of damage to a little girl. However, I believe your main concern is the stealing and violent outbursts?"

"Yes, that's right."

"She claims she can't help it, and from what she describes, I believe her. I think it's a lot more than being badly behaved, although it's hard to tell in this environment. I would prefer to visit Emily in the classroom and also at home if that's all right with you?"

"Okay." I nodded.

"But, from what I've seen up to now, I'm fairly certain Emily's problems stem from her illness. We can work with you and her teachers to try to establish ways of living with it, and how you should react when she does behave this way."

"That would be great. It's so difficult to know what to say or do. I don't know if I'm causing more bad behaviour by the way I deal with things. She blamed her imaginary friend for a while, although he doesn't seem to be around recently."

She smiled. "It's often easier to say you were made to do something rather than doing it off your own bat."

I smiled. "I thought that."

"I discussed her illness with her and she tells me she's better."

"Yes, she says she's better when she feels okay, like she does at the moment."

"I asked her why she thinks she's better and she said it was the medicine you gave her when she was in bed."

"Medicine?" My stomach dropped.

She nodded.

"I haven't given her any medicine … Oh yeah I did. Paracetamol, when she had a headache."

"Then that's what she thinks is making her better." She smiled.

My heart raced. I felt as though I had an army of jittering termites running through my veins. Did she believe me? There was no way of telling. Was I just being paranoid again?

"Okay, Mrs Lyons. I'll need you to sign one more form, giving me permission to approach the school."

"No problem."

"I'll be in touch over the next few days to let you know what we arrange."

"Great, thanks." I tried to keep my voice as steady as possible but I could hear the quiver in it. The doctor didn't seem to notice. Emily had never mentioned the medicine I gave her before. I didn't even know she remembered. My mind raced.

I couldn't get out of that place fast enough.

When I told Frank later, he shrugged it off again.

"Nobody knows anything—it's just your guilty conscience working overtime, lass."

"I hope you're right."

"Of course I'm right. How many mothers give their children medicine when they're sick in bed?"

"I suppose, when you put it like that."

"Think about it, lass. Nobody in their right mind would suspect anything like what you're thinking."

"But Christine's a psychiatrist. She's trained to notice the unspoken answers as well as the ones that leave your mouth."

"Only if they know there's something to look for. She's assessing a six-year-old girl for behavioural issues. All she would have been looking for, as far as her home life is concerned, is some form of abuse. And Emily is the most loved and well cared for little girl—anyone can see that.

"What would I do without you, Frank?"

"You'd manage just fine is what you'd do."

"I don't know. I'd probably walk into the police station and hand myself in." I smiled then sighed.

"It won't come to that, lass. I promise you."

CHAPTER 27

The next few weeks were uneventful, apart from the odd little scrape at school and several stolen items, but we didn't make a big deal about it. Once questioned, Emily confessed all, so there was no harm done.

Christine Forbes visited the classroom twice, and came to the house afterwards to meet the family. Emily gave her a guided tour of her bedroom and it all went well.

Just as I was beginning to settle down, the phone rang in the clinic. It was Rosemary Jackson.

"Mrs Lyons. You need to collect Emily. She's attacked another little girl so badly she's been taken to hospital in an ambulance."

"Oh my God! What did she do?"

"She kicked her repeatedly and then smashed a chair on top of her."

"You're joking!"

"Sadly, no." Her tone was flat.

I raced from the clinic, and hurried into the school a few minutes later.

Emily sat outside Mrs Jackson's office, still very angry. She snarled, "Go away," at me as I entered.

"What have you done?" I hissed.

"It wasn't my fault." She spat the words at me. The fury in her eyes shocked me.

"Don't tell me, you were forced. You couldn't help it?"

"No I couldn't. Kaylie started it."

"Kaylie? Oh no, not again." Kaylie's mother had been cool towards us since the party and refused to allow her daughter to play with Emily.

"She started it."

"How, Emily? How did she start it?" The anger was evident in my voice.

"She said I'm gonna die."

All the air seemed to be sucked out of the room. I couldn't breathe—couldn't speak. I shook my head from side to side, unable to respond to what she'd said. I knew how cruel some people could be, but why would anybody tell a child that another child was going to die?

"Nonsense!" I finally mumbled as I sat down next to her.

"She said that's why I'm allowed back in school, because I'm gonna die, just like Daddy." Her voice broke as she began to cry.

"Come on—we're going." I grabbed Emily's hand and headed for the door.

The receptionist stood up and leaned over the counter. "Mrs Lyons, Mrs Jackson wants you to wait here. She's on the phone with Kaylie's mother."

"Tell Mrs Jackson to whistle."

I walked from the school with my daughter and drove home.

At the house, Frank was talking on the phone. "She's here now, hold on." He covered the mouthpiece. "It's Emily's teacher."

"Would you take Emily please, Frank?"

"Course I will. Come on, lass, let's go into the garden. It's a lovely day."

I waited until I heard the back door close before speaking. "Hello," I snapped.

"Mrs Lyons, Why did you leave? I needed to speak to you."

"Because I was worried what I might do to you and your blabber-mouthed staff if I stayed."

"Really—what's that supposed to mean?"

"Did you find out why Emily did what she did?"

"I didn't have a chance. It was quite stressful and Kaylie's mother is distraught."

"I couldn't give a toss about Kaylie's stuck up, toffee-nosed mother to be quite honest with you."

"Mrs Lyons, I really don't ..."

"You really don't ... what? You don't know how Kaylie's mum found out about Emily's illness? Or you don't know why Kaylie told Emily the only reason she's allowed back at school is because she's dying? Or is it you don't know why someone would dream of telling a six-year-old girl all of these things? Which is it, Mrs Jackson?"

Silence on the other end of the phone.

I continued. "Because *I don't know* how a respectable head teacher could shoot her mouth off to all and sundry about my daughter's illness. So you can call Kaylie's *distraught* mother back and tell her that she caused today's attack, and the way I'm feeling right now, I'd say it was justified. Goodbye, Mrs Jackson."

I hung up.

CHAPTER 28

I refused to take Emily back to school. I applied to homeschool her and found a group of children living in the Cumbria area who met up in Penrith town once a week, to keep the children socialising.

I received a written apology from Mrs Jackson. I think she was worried I would report her, but I couldn't be bothered. It's not as if I even knew which teacher had blabbed.

However, this grand gesture on my part caused a problem at home with the running of the farm and the clinic. Frank offered to supervise Emily if I set up the work I wanted her to do, and I decided that would have to do for now.

The paperwork had been piling up in the clinic, as well as the ordering and invoices. I always made sure Alex and Steph's wages were paid on time though—I couldn't afford for them to get fed up with me and take off.

I intended to start looking for a young person to help on the farm in the mornings and the clinic in the afternoon. This would free me up to sort Emily out at home and also get on top of the admin.

However, dreams are free. Living in the country, miles from

the nearest village made finding help difficult. I could ask around and maybe even place an ad in the local paper but that would all take time. We'd have to cope whichever way we could for now.

It was best I kept myself busy anyway. Emily's hospital appointment loomed and it had been playing constantly on my mind.

"You don't look too well, lass. Is something wrong?" Frank asked.

"Didn't sleep a wink. I'm okay though. Are you ready?"

Frank stood up from the table and folded his newspaper.

"Em, come on. We're going," I yelled.

Emily bounced down the stairs.

We piled into the car and headed to the hospital. We had to meet Doctor Wilson at his office again. My stomach gurgled and my head felt thick. I hoped I wasn't coming down with something.

Doctor Wilson called us in. I gestured to Diane to watch Emily and she nodded.

"Oh, Mrs Lyons, could you bring Emily in with you this time?" Doctor Wilson said.

"Of course, come on, Em."

An Indian man sat behind the desk.

We sat opposite him and I returned his smile.

"This is Doctor Prajesh. He's come from Birmingham especially to meet Emily today," Doctor Wilson said as he sidled in behind the desk and pulled up a chair next to the Indian doctor.

"Hello, pleased to meet you. I've been looking forward to it," Doctor Prajesh said. His Brummy accent shocked me as I was expecting a sultry Indian lilt to his voice.

"You are very famous in our hospital, Emily," he continued.

Emily laughed nervously and looked at me, reaching for my arm.

I smiled, and nodded encouragement.

"We're all amazed at how well you've been, because you were very sick before, weren't you?"

Emily nodded.

Doctor Wilson cleared his throat. "We want to do a few more in depth tests this time," he said. "Doctor Prajesh, has state-of-the-art equipment and will carry out these extra tests for us."

"What are the tests?" I asked. The familiar jittery feeling had returned.

"As far as Emily is concerned today, there will be little or no difference. The difference is in how we perform the tests and the information gathered. We will be taking a closer look into the cells, trying to work out what is going on at a deeper level," Doctor Wilson explained.

"Okay." I nodded, still none the wiser. I would have to allow them to go ahead with their tests. How would I explain otherwise? Plus, after a sleepless night, I'd come to the conclusion that even if they could go deep into the Proteum that's floating about in Emily's body, how would they know it wasn't hers? If Proteum was different from person to person, then not everybody's Proteum would work. They would have to match it, like bone marrow or blood. It was all pie in the sky anyway. They seemed clueless too, as if they were just hoping and praying for a breakthrough for this terrible illness.

"Did you complete the diary for me?"

"Oh yes." I dug out the notebook I'd completed from my bag and passed it to him.

"That's great. Okay, shall we get cracking?"

Back in Doctor Wilson's office later that day, both doctors were perusing a graph. We'd left Emily with Diane this time.

"I'm showing Doctor Prajesh all the test results from the very beginning. Showing him all the fluctuations, including today's."

"So there are more fluctuations?" I asked.

"I'm afraid so. Have you noticed any signs with Emily at home?"

I shook my head. "No, not really."

"Her results aren't as bad as they have been but they are significantly decreased from two months ago. It's an absolute mystery. We've gone over the diary you did for us and at first glance we can't see any patterns with her food and behaviour. Which, to be honest, we didn't expect to find, yet we needed to rule that out. But we will have them properly analysed."

My stomach leapt to my mouth. I glanced at Frank and smiled. My hands knotted tightly in my lap, trying to control the tremors I felt.

"We've also had a report from Doctor Forbes. She agrees that the behaviour is likely due to the illness. She was quite taken with your daughter, by the way. She said Emily has higher than average intelligence."

I smiled and nodded.

"All these results will be compiled and added to the results from the tests Doctor Prajesh will do over the next couple of weeks. We don't know what will come of it, if anything. But Emily's got us all sitting up and paying attention, which can only be a good thing."

After patting Emily down for unauthorised items, we left the hospital. Instead of going inside McDonalds we went via the drive-thru. Emily wasn't happy about this but she didn't continue with her sulking once she had her Happy Meal.

Things had calmed down into a steady routine. Frank was amazing with Emily, and the old-school way he taught seemed to have her mesmerized. She even looked forward to her lesson times.

"Might have to make this a permanent solution." I laughed.

"I enjoy it, and in fact, I'm good at it. It's nice to be able to do something well for the first time in ages."

"You've definitely got the magic touch."

He smiled. "I don't know about going that far, but at least I have a reason to get up in the morning."

"Suits everyone, then." I hugged his neck.

The phone rang. It was Doctor Wilson.

"I have the lumbar puncture results and it's as I thought, Emily's figures have dropped again, quite considerably."

"Oh no ..."

"I wouldn't worry too much. The way these results have been yo-yoing it's just as likely they'll have skyrocketed by your next appointment."

My stomach dropped. It was easy for him to be excited and hopeful. I knew the truth. The only way she'd get better results would be for some other poor person to die, and that wasn't going to happen again. We only had the decline of Emily's health to look forward to, and then ...

Doctor Wilson interrupted my thoughts. "Doctor Prajesh is in the middle of his tests and we will hopefully hear from him by the beginning of next week."

"Okay, thank you."

As I replaced the receiver, the clinic mobile phone rang. "What the ..." Stephanie hadn't made an appearance yet this morning. I had a feeling it would be one of those days, even though it was barely eight o'clock.

I answered the phone.

"Victoria, Angela here. Sam asked me to call. We've got a heifer that's been caught in a barbed wire fence, and she's a mess. Can one of you come out soon?"

"Yeah, no problem. We won't be long."

"Steph," I called from the bottom of the stairs.

Stephanie appeared on the landing with a large white towel wrapped around her body and a pink one on her head.

"We've got a call-out. Anderson's farm. A heifer has had a fight with some barbed wire."

"Give me ten minutes and I'll be right with you."

"Are there any bookings this morning?"

"Not till eleven—do you wanna come along for the ride?"

"Why not?"

The Anderson farm was only a couple of miles down the road. A dairy farm with two hundred head of cattle. They always used us because our call-out charges were cheaper than using the vet in town, plus they were good friends with Frank.

Samuel Anderson was a white-haired, white-bearded Cumbrian whose farm had been passed down through the generations. Farming was all he'd ever known.

"Nice to see you, lass. I didn't expect to see two of you."

"Don't worry, Sam, we won't charge you twice." I winked.

He laughed. "That's not what I meant. How's Frank? Been a while since I've seen 'im."

"He's doing great, actually. Thanks for asking."

"Do you want a cuppa while Stephanie looks at the heifer? I know Angie would love to see you, and I know you ain't too fond o' cattle." Not many people knew of my fear of cows but Sam did, and he found it hysterical.

I pushed the door of the farmhouse open. "Have you got the kettle on?" I said.

"Well, aren't you a sight for sore eyes. Come in, come in, lass. I love your new hair-do." Angela Anderson jumped up from her armchair by the fire and hugged me tight.

"Thanks. It's probably due to be cut again by now." I patted at my hair, as if I could tell what it looked like by the touch.

"Oh, it is nice to see you, lass."

"You too."

She poured the tea from a huge teapot that sat on the range and placed the two cups between us on the table, as well as a plate of biscuits.

"Thanks, Angie."

She nodded and sat down opposite me, wiping her hands on her blue apron. "How are things since—you know—Jonathan?"

I nodded. "Surprisingly okay. Frank's been amazing, to be honest. A real rock. And Stephanie, well I'm lucky, that's all I can say. Without them, I'd be up shit creek."

"We all need 'elp. I don't know what I'd do if something happened to Sam. But I guess it's inevitable—none of us are getting any younger."

"Do you employ anyone?"

"Sam gets the odd guy in every now and then, but on the whole he does the lot 'imself. Works 'imself into the ground, he does, and fer what? I'd prefer to sell up now while we're still capable of enjoying what time we 'ave left. Do a bit of travelling and stuff. I've always wanted to go to Canada."

"I definitely would if I were you. Life's so short. Look at Frank. Never a day's sickness in his life and then, wham! A stroke. It's taken nearly seven years to get where he is now. He's doing great and able to fend for himself again, within reason, but was all the hard work worth it? He almost killed himself and what for? To leave all his hard-earned money to his only son, who beat him to the grave."

"No, but you will. And God knows you deserve it. Are you thinking of selling up?"

"To be honest, it never crossed my mind. Not a bad idea, though."

The farm still belonged to Frank, and although we'd discussed it when he first had his stroke, Jonathan refused to take ownership. Since Jon died we'd just got on with it, but for what? It didn't make sense.

Stephanie and Sam came into the kitchen like a couple of whirlwinds. "Get this lass a nice hot cuppa. She has the most nimble fingers," Sam said.

"Oh, aye. Do I have to worry about you two?" Angela laughed, raising her eyebrows.

"Don't be silly, woman. Everybody knows you're the love of me life." He turned his back to her, grinned and shrugged at us.

"Nice save, Sam," she said, and we all laughed.

Later on at home, I sat next to Frank on the sofa. "Have you ever considered selling up, Frank?"

"I've been thinking of nothing else since Jonathan died, but you've been managing okay and I didn't want to upset you."

"It wouldn't upset me. I must admit, it never crossed my mind until today. Something Angela Anderson said when I was over there this morning."

"Do you think we should?"

"I don't know. It's up to you."

"Don't be daft, lass. It's up to us."

"It's your farm," I said.

"One that I haven't done a stroke of work on for over six years. It's our farm. Our farm. Our clinic. Our home."

"What would you want to do if we did?" I sat on the sofa beside him.

"I couldn't move into town into one of them shoeboxes. I've

loved living in this house. It would be hard to leave but I guess we have to be realistic, lass."

"I'd have to find work and juggle Emily—for now at least." The weight of that sentence hung between us.

"Would you move back to Manchester?" Frank asked.

"Would you want to?"

"No, but you don't have to worry about me."

"Frank, behave. If the farm sold, all it would mean is we would find somewhere else to live. It would make absolutely no difference to us."

"I have no hold on you, lass. It's not fair. You shouldn't have to tie yourself to me now Jonathan's gone. You have your own life to live."

"Would you listen to yourself. Aren't we family?"

"Of course we are."

"Well, nothing is set in concrete. We just need to think things through. The farm is hard without Jonathan. Alex is amazing, but what about when he wants to move on? We'll be in a mess."

"Should be worth quite a bit. We own it outright, so wouldn't have to worry about an income."

"That's your money though, Frank. I'd still need an income."

"Now who's being daft? What will I do with it? Leave it in the bank until I die, and then you'll get the lot anyway."

"Don't talk like that."

"We have to be honest. You need to know your future will be set financially, whatever happens."

"What if, and it's a big if, because I don't know the legalities. But couldn't we just sell off the land? Keep the house and clinic and sell the farm buildings, stock and land?"

"I don't see why not. It's been done before. It wouldn't hurt to look into it and I'd love to stay here. This house has a lot of memories for me."

"Me too. I'll find out what I can tomorrow."

The next few days were hectic. I made an appointment with the council and had a couple of estate agents around to give us an idea of price if we were able to split off the land. There were some restrictions, but it looked as though it would be possible.

The other alternative would be to rent the land out, which might be a good idea in the interim; at least we'd get rid of the work and get an income for it as well.

On Sunday evening, while Emily bathed I changed the sheets on her bed. As I removed the fitted bottom sheet, I heard a clunk as something fell down the back of the bed. I shoved my arm down the gap and pulled out a red-jewelled pillbox. I unclasped the tiny latch on the lid and found two rings inside, a diamond engagement ring and a wedding ring.

"Emily!" I marched through to the bathroom.

Emily lay on her back, her head under the water, blowing bubbles. When she saw me standing over her she sat up quickly, coughing and spluttering, and sending water cascading all over the floor.

Once she'd calmed down, I held out the box. "Where did this come from?"

"Dunno?"

"Don't start that again, Emily. Where did it come from? If you don't tell me, we're not meeting your friends tomorrow."

"Aw, Mummy." She began crying.

"Enough!"

She stopped, her beautiful eyes wide open. "From Auntie Lyn's."

Auntie Lyn was the next-door neighbour, Lynette Woods. She and her husband had been Frank and Barbara's best friends for years. Emily had gone over there with Frank a few days ago, and she must have taken it then.

"This looks expensive, Emily. Lyn must be very upset to have lost it."

"I'm sorry."

"Come on. Out." I unplugged the bath and wrapped my thieving little daughter in a fluffy white towel. I dried her and she dressed herself in her pyjamas while I finished off making the bed.

"Tell Auntie Lyn I'm shorry."

"Pardon?"

"Tell Auntie Lyn I'm shorry."

It was starting again. The slurring was the first thing I noticed every time.

"I will, my baby. You get to sleep now."

It had been four months. The same length of time as before. I'd noticed her slurring when she was tired for a few weeks before the pub party.

I walked down the stairs and sat on the bottom step, my head in my hands. I missed Jonathan with an intensity I'd never known, but I felt angry at the same time. Angry with him for leaving me like this, and for being so careless on that fucking digger.

Tears poured from my eyes and my chest constricted, as invisible fingers squeezed every last bit of air from my lungs. I had to fight to inhale. A few minutes later, I wiped my eyes and walked through to the snug.

Frank was watching *Antiques Roadshow*.

"Are you okay, lass?"

"Yeah, but I just found this in Emily's bed." I showed him the pretty, red box. "It's Lyn's. I'm going to take it back there now. Will you listen out for Em? Steph's reading in her room."

"Of course I will, lass."

I knocked at the door and the hall light came on almost immediately.

Dave opened the door and seemed pleased to see me. "Come in, lass."

"Thanks, Dave. Sorry it's so late."

"It's not too late, we're just having a cheeky gin. Do you fancy a snifter?"

"It's been ages since I drank gin—it's all I used to drink when I first met Jonathan."

"Go through to the lounge and I'll get you one. Tonic and a slice of lemon?"

"Lovely."

Lynette sat on the sofa with her feet tucked underneath her. She beckoned me into the room and patted the cushion next to her. "What a nice surprise. Is this a social call?" Her eyebrows furrowed. "Is something wrong?"

"Not wrong. Well ..." I took a deep breath before pulling the pillbox from my pocket. "I found this."

"Oh, Emily?"

I nodded. "I'm sorry."

"She's quick, I'll give her that. I hadn't even noticed it was missing. Are the rings still inside?"

"Yeah, they are. I found it in her bed."

"They were my grandmother's rings. I've had them for years." She opened the lid and smiled.

"She doesn't mean it. The specialist say's it's definitely her illness. She can't help it."

"It's hard on you."

"What is?" David said, handing me a glass.

"Emily, she's been stealing again." Lyn passed him the pillbox. "The doctor says it's her illness."

"Aye, lass. It's a terrible shame, so it is."

"We're coping. Frank's been amazing. He's found his calling, helping Emily with her schoolwork."

"Aye, every cloud they say. We've noticed he's bucked up a weebit."

"Did I see Jason Reid at your place this afternoon?" Lyn said.

I nodded.

"Thinking of selling then?" She raised her eyebrows.

"Just weighing up our options. It's difficult."

"I bet it is. You only have to ask if you need some help though. You know that, don't you?"

"I do, thanks, Lyn, and we appreciate it, but you have your own things to keep on top of."

"Did I tell you our Michael's coming home from Ireland next week?"

I shook my head. "No, how come?"

"He and Maria have finally broken up, for good this time. And although it's not a very nice thing to admit, I'm glad. They've not been happy for years."

"That will make things easier for you," I said.

"Yeah, it will, and you'll have a fit young man on hand if you need it. We're not much cop in that department nowadays are we, Dave?"

Dave shook his head.

"Oh he's gonna love that isn't he? You donating his services to the neighbours." I smiled.

"He's a good boy, had his own farm in Ireland. They've sold it now and split the profits. She's gone on her merry way with her fancy man. I said it all along, didn't I, Dave?"

Dave nodded.

"She's a trollop. I'm just glad they didn't have any kiddies," Lyn continued, off on a tangent now.

"When did you last see him?" I asked.

"Three years ago, when we went over there for a long weekend. He rings every week, though. I spoke to him just this morning."

"It'll be exciting to see him, then. When's he arriving?"

"Next Saturday. Yeah, it'll be strange to have him here. He left home when he was eighteen years old, almost twenty years ago now."

"Wow."

"I know." She laughed. "We have plenty of room here—we don't have to get under each other's feet. Our Ronnie has always lived no more than five minutes away, but she's been pregnant more often than not over the past five years. And as you already know, Vic, she doesn't have an easy time of it."

"Yeah, I know. I don't know if I'd ever have another if I suffered as much she does." I grimaced.

CHAPTER 29

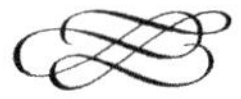

"Can I put the angel on top?" Emily asked staring up at the Christmas tree.

"Do you have a pair of stilts?" I asked.

"What are they?"

"Two long sticks that you stand on so you can reach the top."

She looked at me, her eyes screwed half-closed and her head cocked to one side.

"Never mind." I laughed. "How do you intend getting up there?"

"You can lift me up."

"You must be joking. It's too high, and you're too big."

"I can lift you up," Alex said as he walked into the room.

"Oh hello, Alex. How's things with you?" I smiled affectionately.

"Good, thanks. I'm just checking what time we're leaving tonight."

"The taxi will be here at seven-ish. Is that all right?"

"Fine. Right, where's that angel?"

Emily jumped up from her spot underneath the tree and

placed the red baubles on the coffee table before digging the tatty old angel out of the box.

"She's a little past her best, isn't she, Em?" I asked. "Maybe we need a new one."

"Aw no, Mummy. I like her."

"Okay then, we'll keep her this one last time but she won't make next Christmas." As I said the words, my stomach did a twirl, realising she might not be the only one not around by next Christmas.

Emily's slurring was worse and she'd been lethargic in the afternoons this past week. I was determined to make this Christmas the best I could. Who knew what the New Year would bring.

Alex lifted Emily up so she could put the angel in pride of place. Then he left to get ready for tonight.

Frank and I were taking him and Steph to The Bells for our Christmas bash, and we'd also invited a few of our more important clients.

Lynette was coming over to look after Emily for a couple of hours and I was quite looking forward to letting my hair down for a little while. Well, figuratively. It was still too short to put up.

We finished decorating the tree and I had a shower while Emily had a bath. I agreed to let Lyn put her to bed.

The taxi arrived bang on time. Stephanie looked amazing in a sparkly green off-the-shoulder dress.

I wore my old faithful black trousers and jazzed them up with a turquoise sequinned blouse I'd bought a couple of years before. I found a pair of flashing Christmas earrings in with the decorations and wore them instead of my gold hoops, surprised they still worked.

We were doing a secret Santa and I had an awkwardly shaped, terribly wrapped gift under my arm.

"Ready?" I called as I walked into the lounge in search of Frank. I found him chatting with Lyn. "Come on, mister, the taxi's waiting. Time for bed, Em."

"Auntie Lyn said she'd read me a story."

I glanced at Lyn, who nodded.

"Okay, but then it's straight to sleep."

"Okay, Mummy. You look pretty."

"Thanks, baby. Goodnight." I kissed the top of her head. "We won't be late, Lyn."

"Take as long as you like. I'm looking forward to watching exactly what I want on TV. I've got two of the buggers flicking channels at home now."

"Oh, of course. I forgot Michael's home."

We all shuffled into the hallway where we met Steph coming down the stairs.

The restaurant was full of party revellers, and the atmosphere was pumping.

We'd pre-ordered a set menu of with the choice of pâté and melba toast or prawn cocktail to start, followed by a traditional turkey with all the trimmings, and a choice of Christmas pudding with brandy sauce or trifle.

Sam and Angela Anderson were already sitting at our table.

"Hello, you two. Sorry we're late," I said, kissing them both before sitting down.

"You're not late. We're early, as per usual." Angela laughed, gazing pointedly at her husband and raising her eyebrows.

"I'd rather be too early than late." Sam attempted to defend himself. "Who else is coming?" He nodded at the empty chairs.

"Cathy and Martin Coombes from Sedgewick Farm, and Steve Allen and his current squeeze."

Steve Allen was the local Lothario. He'd gone through all the single women in the area—and some not so single—and broken many hearts. He owned a deer farm which had a venison butchery and shop on the premises.

Cathy and Martin Coombes were popular with all the young girls in the area. Cathy was a riding instructor and they owned a pony trekking business.

As we spoke, a suave-looking Steve Allen walked in with a blonde beauty on his arm. She must have been half his age, if that. I smiled as he approached us.

"Steve, glad you could make it."

"I'd never stand up a pretty woman," he said, bending to kiss me.

I groaned. "Cheese alert!" Everyone laughed.

"Don't be like that, Victoria. You could hurt my feelings." He feigned injury.

"Shut up and introduce your guest." I smiled, extending my hand to the young girl at his side.

"This is Sally-Ann. Sally-Ann, this is Victoria Lyons, our very own wonder vet."

Sally-Ann gripped my hand with surprising strength for such a little thing. I introduced the rest of the guests to her as we sat down.

A couple of minutes, later Cathy and Martin arrived with their arms full of gifts.

"What's all this?" I asked. "You're supposed to bring one each, that's all."

"We've got a few goodies for Emily. You're still planning on her taking riding lessons in January, aren't you?" Cathy asked.

"If she's well enough, yes."

"Then she'll need these. I'll leave them here under the table—don't forget them."

"That's so nice of you. Thanks."

Martin shuffled around the back of the table and sat next to Frank.

We began pulling crackers, putting on the silly paper hats and reading out the corny jokes.

The waiters were told to keep the wine flowing, and by the time the dessert was being served, the table was in a raucous state.

Alex seemed to be the worst. Wine obviously wasn't his drink of choice, and it had gone straight to his head. His alter ego emerged as a confident and extremely funny young man.

Sally-Ann was clearly smitten with him and laughed as Alex and Steve bounced off each other all night, like a double act. My jaw ached from laughing.

Stephanie sat opposite Steve and they flirted blatantly, although Sally-Ann didn't seem to notice because she only had eyes for Alex.

I stopped drinking after a couple of wines. After eating too much food, I couldn't face it, but I didn't want to be a party pooper. I loved seeing Frank enjoy himself, catching up with his old mates, David and Martin. They'd all had a good go at the wine and were now hitting the whisky. Angela and Cathy were also putting the world to rights.

After the dessert, we went through to the bar. "One more, and then I'll ring a taxi," I said to Frank.

He nodded. "Aye, lass, it's well past my bedtime."

"Oh well, you can have a lie-in tomorrow."

"Chance would be a fine thing," he said. "All those years as a farmer messed me up for lie-ins."

Once in the bar, the group rearranged. Alex and Sally-Ann sat together and so did Steph and Steve.

I noticed a woman in her fifties trying to catch Sally-Ann's eye. Sally-Ann cringed and gave her a small wave.

The woman approached the table.

"Get ush a drink Shal."

"Leave me alone, Mam," Sally hissed.

My ears pricked up. Sally-Ann was a pretty, slim, well-dressed young woman. But her mother was as rough as they come, with rank, yellowing grey hair stuck to her head. Her clothes were smelly and stained.

"Aw, don't be like that wiv ya own mam."

By now, Steve had noticed the exchange and put two and two together. "Is this your mum, Sally-Ann?"

She hesitated, then nodded. All eyes on her.

"Get her a glass then, and pull up a chair."

"No, she's okay, aren't you, Mum?" Sally-Ann eyeballed her mother. "Haven't you got things to do? Come on, I'll get you a drink." Sally-Ann got up from her seat and ushered her mum to the bar.

I raised my eyebrows at Angela, and she swiped her brow with the back of her hand and laughed.

I nodded and smiled.

Alex began chatting to a group of girls on the next table.

Angela and Sam stood up to leave.

"I've had a wonderful time. Thanks, Vic." Angela said.

"Aye, lass. Thank you." Sam kissed me.

Sally-Ann came back to the table, having bought her mum a pint of something then left her at the bar.

Stephanie and Steve were engrossed deep in conversation, so Sally-Ann sat next to me.

"Are you okay?" I asked her once Sam and Angie had left.

"Yeah, sorry about that. She does my head in."

"Oh dear. Do you not get on?"

"Are you joking? Just look at her. She's a right pain in the neck."

I didn't know what to say. I felt awkward, so I focused on the hysterical laughter coming from the next table. I smiled at Sally-Ann and rolled my eyes.

She looked at Alex longingly, then at Steve and Steph. "I think I'll get going. Thanks for the meal. Would you tell Steve I had a headache?"

"If you're sure," I said.

"Yeah, she won't leave me alone now. Once she's necked her cider she'll be back over. I don't think Steve will even notice I've gone."

"I'm sure he will."

"No, and anyway, I wouldn't foist my mum on my worst enemy. She'll be mithering you soon, and you're too nice."

"Don't let her ruin your night."

"It's too late. I bet you think I'm a terrible daughter, don't you?"

"No, I don't. You obviously have your reasons."

"She's always been a pain, but since my brother went missing, she's even worse. She drives me mad."

"Your brother?"

"Yeah, our Shane. He was another scumbag, to be honest with you. My family's full of them. What? Don't look so shocked. I know what they're like."

"I'm not … I mean …" my heart clattered against my ribcage.

She laughed. "Yeah, I know what you mean. Don't worry, I'm used to it."

"How did you turn out to be so lovely?"

She shrugged. "My mum gave me away when I was two. My Auntie Kath brought me up."

"So how come you're back here?"

"Auntie Kath died last year and I had nowhere else to go. I don't intend to stay around. I'd have already gone if it wasn't for Shane vanishing. Mum's been distraught and I felt rotten leaving."

"What do you think happened to him?"

She shrugged. "Honestly, I think he's probably dead. But he could be anywhere. If there was a few quid to be had, Shane would be there. So long as it's illegal, that is. God forbid he'd get himself a real job. Anyway, he was partial to every drug going, and was also a dealer. He'd do anything for the price of a pint."

"Oh, right."

"Do you know him?"

"No. I don't think so."

She pulled a leaflet out of her bag and handed it to me.

My breath hitched in my throat as I stared into the cold eyes of Shane Logan.

"You know him?" she asked again.

"Seen him around. But no, I don't know him." I passed the leaflet back to her.

"Keep it—I've got hundreds. My mum makes me hand them out."

I folded the paper and shoved it into the side pocket of my handbag.

Sally-Ann hugged me and got up to leave. "Thank you for dinner. It was lovely and very nice to meet you."

"You're welcome," I said, standing up. I gripped both of her elbows. "Sally-Ann, I'm sorry if I'm speaking out of turn, but if I were you I'd get away from here, from your family, and try to make a decent life for yourself. They'll just drag you down."

She smiled, there was a pained expression in her eyes and she sighed deeply. "I have nowhere to go," she said.

"Call me next week—the number's in the book. I might be able to help you."

I don't know why, but I felt compelled to help this lovely young woman. She had the most awful family and I could clearly see that she wouldn't amount to much if she stayed around them. She would end up just another disgusting drunk if left to her mother's devices.

"Thank you, Victoria, I will." She smiled and walked quietly away.

"Pretty young girl isn't she?" Cathy said.

I nodded. "Such a shame to have ..." I cocked my head to the side, indicating Sally-Ann's mum.

"I know. All of them are trouble. She doesn't seem anything like the rest."

"She just told me her aunt brought her up, until she died. She's done a marvellous job with her too. Shame all that hard work will be undone by that lot."

"You're so right," Cathy said. "Poor girl."

I glanced around at the dwindling party. Frank was still chatting with Martin. Steph and Steve looked as though they'd completely zoned everybody else out, which surprised me. Steph had heard all the stories about Steve being a male slut. I hoped she realised what she was doing.

Alex came staggering over and sat down next to me. The table of girls seemed relieved he'd left.

"Are you okay, Alex?"

"I'm wonderful, and I want to tell you that you and your family are the best ever."

"Thanks." I smiled.

Cathy's eyes twinkled.

I shook my head at her and laughed. "Are you ready to go home, Alex?"

"Nah, I want to go dancing with some friends."

"Where are they?"

He looked around the room. "Where's Sally-Ann?"

"She left."

"Wha—"

"Come on, let's get you home."

I stood up and asked the girl behind the bar to order a taxi.

"Are you almost ready, Frank?"

"Aye, lass. Ready when you are."

"We'd best get Alex home before he throws up." I laughed, glancing at Alex who had turned a greenish colour and leaned against the bar.

I placed my hand on Steph's shoulder and she started. "We're gonna head off, Steph. What do you want to do?"

"Oh, I'll come too."

Steve glanced around. "Where's Sally-Ann?"

"She left—she had a headache."

"Oops." He shrugged, and they both laughed. "In that case, do you fancy going on somewhere?" he asked Steph.

"Okay." She smiled, her eyes sparkling at Steve.

We all made our way to the front door. Steve helped us get Alex in the back of the taxi and we said our goodbyes to Cathy and Martin.

"Emily's presents!" Cathy and I said at the same time, and then laughed.

I ran back into the restaurant and retrieved the pile of gifts from under the table.

Back outside, I saw Steve's black Aston Martin drive away with a wide-eyed Stephanie in the passenger seat. I waved but they didn't seem to notice.

I slid into the taxi beside Alex, who promptly began snoring.

Once home, I paid the driver who helped get the parcels into the hallway while I helped Alex.

"You check on Emily and let Lyn go, Frank. I'll get this one to his room."

"Can you manage?"

"I should be able to."

Alex was upright but leaning on me. By the time we got to the garage, he'd found his second wind, wanting to dance and sing. He tried to make me put my bag down but I swung it away from him, laughing and the leaflet I'd got off Sally-Ann fell to the floor.

"Whoops, you dropped something," Alex said, bending to pick the piece of paper up. He glanced at it then sat heavily on the bottom step of the spiral staircase.

"I got it off Sally-Ann. It's her brother. He went missing ages ago."

"I know him." He was a lot more sober than he had been a few seconds ago.

"Yeah, you probably do—he's lived round here all his life."

"No, I mean, I saw him *here*."

CHAPTER 30

I stood stock–still, staring at him, suddenly struck dumb.

He attempted to get up. "I need to tell the police."

"Wait, what are you talking about? He's never been here."

"Yes, he has—twice that I know of. The first time I told Jonathan about it and we chased him from the property."

"Jon didn't tell me."

"No, he said not to. Said you'd freak out."

I sat beside him on the step with a huff.

"Then I saw him the night of Jon's funeral."

"You must be mistaken. What would he want round here?"

"That first time we saw him Jonathan told me he was bad news and probably casing the joint."

"I need a drink," I said.

"Now you're talking," he said, standing up and heading for the door.

"Where are you going?"

"With you, for a drink."

I sighed. "Come on then. One, mind you, then bed."

We walked back towards the house as Lyn's car disappeared down the driveway.

Frank leaned into the fridge, picking at a chicken carcass we'd had for lunch. He glanced around, a quizzical expression crossing his face. "What's wrong?"

"We need a drink," I said, opening my eyes wide and raising my eyebrows at him.

He jerked his head backwards, as if asking what the problem was.

"Show him the leaflet, Alex."

Frank read it. He didn't flinch at all. His self-control surprised me. "What about it?"

"This guy is Sally-Ann's brother, and he's been missing for months."

"And?"

"Apparently Alex saw him around this house a couple of times. Once he told Jon, who warned him not to mention it to me. The next time was the night of Jonathan's funeral." I poured two stiff brandies and downed mine in one, handing the other to Alex.

"Why would he be here?" Frank asked.

"I have no idea."

"Tell us what happened last time, Alex."

He downed his drink and placed the glass back onto the bench top. I refilled it.

"I was standing outside having a smoke after the funeral. It was late, around ten o'clock. I heard a sound but I didn't see him right away. Then I heard his bike spokes clicking. That's when I saw him standing on the path, looking at the house. All the lights were out except the hall light."

"Go on," I said.

"I didn't know what to do. Didn't want to confront him but I couldn't ignore him, so I cleared my throat and switched the garage light on. I pretended I hadn't seen him because Jonathan said he was a nasty piece of work. Anyway, he didn't move at all for a few minutes, then he turned away and pushed his bike from the driveway."

"I wish you'd told us."

"I did think about it, but you'd just buried Jon and I thought you had enough to worry about. If something had happened I would have told you what I saw, but nothing did, and I never saw him again."

He knocked back his drink again.

"Slow down, Alex. You'll pass out." I laughed.

"Sorry, I've never been able to drink in moderation. That's why I don't normally bother. I'm an old soak once I get the taste."

"Oh well, you're not working tomorrow, so you'll be able to spend the day in bed." I poured him another, and a small one for myself. "Can I get you one, Frank?"

He shook his head. "No, but I wouldn't mind a cuppa."

"Go and sit yourself down and take Alex with you. Are you hungry?"

"I'm peckish. I know I shouldn't be after all that lovely food, but I am."

"Fancy a ham sandwich?"

"Oh, I'd love one, lass."

"How about you, Alex?"

"Nah thanksh." His legs were like bendy rubber as he followed Frank to the lounge where he flopped down on the sofa.

I picked up his drink and walked behind him, placing it on the coffee table. "There you go."

"Thanksh," he said again.

Frank sat in the armchair.

Back in the kitchen I set about making a plate of sandwiches and a cup of tea for Frank. Frank and Alex were chatting but I couldn't hear what they were saying above the sound of the kettle boiling.

Frank glanced my way a couple of times. He seemed a little agitated.

I joined them a few minutes later, handing Frank the plate of sandwiches and placing his tea on the table.

"Thanks, lass."

"Okay, so what have I missed?"

"Alex was just saying he thought he'd found that bloke's bike in the garage."

"What bloke?" My heart froze in my chest. I felt the contents of my stomach turn to liquid.

"The missing bloke," Alex said.

"Impossible. Why would it be in our garage? You already said you saw him leave on it."

"I know, but it's quite distinct. Part of it is silver and part of it pink, as though its two different bikes welded together. It also has two different coloured tyres. A white one on the front and a black one on the back.

"And you saw it in our garage?" I kicked myself for not getting rid of the bike, how stupid I'd been to forget all about it. My eyes flashed at Frank.

I walked back to the kitchen and brought back the brandy bottle, topped up my glass and then held the bottle out to Alex. He finished the dregs of his glass before holding it out for me to refill it.

"That's strange," I said.

"I know, then I found that tooth in the pigshty. I almost convinced myself something had gone on, until Frank told me it wash hish tooth."

I laughed with him, but the tone sounded flat and empty. Alex didn't seem to notice.

"I'll tell the policshe tomorrow. Look at the date he went mishing. I'm shure thatsh the date of Jon's funeral. Poor Shally-Ann," he said.

I also felt sorry for Sally-Ann. She'd never better herself while she was hanging around her deadbeat family. I felt somewhat responsible for that. If Shane hadn't gone missing, she'd have moved on by now. Instead she stayed out of some sense of loyalty to her alcoholic waster of a mother. The same mother who'd given her away in the first place.

"Do you have any brothers or sisters, Alex?"

His eyes were almost closed as I spoke and he sat up quickly.

"No," he said.

"What about your mum and dad?"

"Dead. I have no one left."

"Wow! That's hard on a young guy like you. I was the same at your age. Luckily I met Jonathan, and he and Frank became my family."

"I don't mind. I'm okay alone. Beshides, I have you guys." He necked the rest of his brandy and settled back onto the sofa.

We sat staring at him for a few minutes until he began to snore.

I got up and nodded my head towards the kitchen, eyeballing Frank.

He stood up slowly, his eyes not leaving Alex as he followed me to the kitchen.

"Oh fuck, Frank. What are we gonna do? We've had it now. They'll investigate, and once he tells them about the bike and the tooth that'll be it."

"Calm down, Victoria." His voice was harsh, so unlike him.

My mouth snapped shut, as I looked at him, shocked.

"There's no point getting hysterical. We need to stay calm."

I nodded, my mind racing. I began pacing backwards and forwards.

"We need to get rid of him," Frank said, calm.

"How?" I spun round to face him.

"How do you think?"

I shook my head. Opened and closed my mouth, but no words would form. "No."

"What choice do we have? He's the only one who saw Shane here. He saw the bike. He found the tooth. Without him, we're back to square one."

"But this time it's different—this would be murder."

"What were the others if not murder? Don't be so bloody naïve."

"One was self-defence, the other suicide. You said it yourself."

Frank laughed. "The court won't see it that way."

"But not Alex, Frank. He's lovely. We're all he's got."

"Exactly. All the more reason to do it. No one will be looking for him."

"No, Frank. No!"

"Okay, it's up to you. I don't mind. My needs will be met in prison. I'll be fed, have a TV and a toilet. That's as important as things get for me. You, on the other hand, won't find it that easy. And where does that leave Emily?"

I closed my eyes and took a deep breath. "We have no choice, Frank. We've done wrong and we need to suffer the consequences. We should have known we'd get caught—no one gets away with murder—not really, not forever."

"But what could go wrong, this one last time?"

"Everything. Everything, don't you see? What if Stephanie comes home? Do we knock her on the head too? What if another tooth is found by the new farmhand? Because we can't manage the farm on our own. Do we just keep bumping people off as they get in our way? Where will it end?"

"Make a choice then. I'll go whichever way you decide. But it needs to be tonight if we're doing it. As soon as Alex wakes up in the morning, he'll go straight to the police, and that will be end of the story."

"Don't put it all on me. That's not fair," I said.

"How's it not fair? I told you what I want to do."

Loud snores came from the sofa.

My senses were wired, and my eyes felt as though they were sticking out on stalks.

"We could use his Proteum," Frank said, his voice soft. "He's not a thief or a bully. He's a lovely lad, so there'd be no problems with him giving Emily any badness."

It was too much. I ran to the sink and brought up the contents of my stomach. I could smell the brandy, which made me retch even more. I splashed my face with water and used a spoon in the plughole to mash up the vomit lumps, which made me woozy once again.

I needed to think. Frank was right—it would need to be tonight if we were to do it at all. Tomorrow would be too late.

I couldn't believe I was actually considering it. This wasn't me. I was a kind, honest woman. A vet, a wife, a mother, a daughter-in-law, a neighbour, a friend—I had enough labels. I didn't want to add serial killer to the list.

I looked at Frank, who was still leaning against the bench, scrutinising me.

"No, Frank—it's over. I can't do it. We're so much better than this.

"Fair enough, come on—let's get to bed. You may as well throw a blanket over him—he's out for the count." He placed his arm around my shoulders and we walked to the hallway. Frank headed for the stairs while I got a blanket from the airing cupboard.

"Goodnight, lass."

"Goodnight, Frank." I walked back into the lounge and pulled Alex's shoes off and swung his legs onto the sofa, before covering him up. He was out of it, and didn't feel a thing. I could do anything and he wouldn't even know about it, but how could we do what Frank suggested? This young man had been a part of our household for months now, for the best part of a year. He was lovely, no harm in him at all. I stroked his mousy brown hair, and then quietly left the room.

CHAPTER 31

Climbing the stairs I realised that this would possibly be the last time my life had some kind of normality. In Emily's room, I bent to kiss her curly head. My nose filled with her scent and I inhaled deeply.

"I love you, my baby," I whispered, then walked to the door.

"I love you too, Mummy," she whispered, and it almost broke my heart.

I staggered down the hall into my room, sat on the edge of the bed, and cried. And cried. I leaned forward and picked up the photograph of Jon, Em and me together, taken at the beginning of the year. We looked so happy.

So much had happened since then; I found it hard to comprehend. My darling Jonathan was gone, taken so suddenly and cruelly. I placed my fingers over his face. Then, for the first time, I noticed how tight he held on to Emily. He would have done anything for her. But would he have committed murder? I didn't think so.

How would he feel if not doing it meant I would get locked up for years, leaving Emily to face the ravages of this awful illness alone, to die without any of us by her side?

I placed the photo face down on the dresser and jumped up, ripping off my clothes and replacing them with jogging bottoms and a sweatshirt.

I raced down the hall and tapped on Frank's door.

He opened it right away, still fully dressed. I pushed in and shut the door behind me, leaning against it.

"This has got to be the last time," I said. "The *very* last time."

He nodded, "Okay, lass."

"Promise me, that no matter what comes our way, we can't go through this again. I don't even think we should take his Proteum. We should just get rid of him and make Emily comfortable and let her die in peace."

"Why do it at all, if that's how you feel?"

"Because once Alex opens his big trap, we'll be hauled off, leaving Emily alone. I can't allow that, Frank. If Emily was already dead, I'd have no qualms paying for the crimes we've committed, but not yet. And for all that I do love Alex, he's threatening my family, albeit unknowingly. Emily may have to go through this, but she deserves to have us around."

"I can't allow you to waste his Proteum. If we're doing this we need to go the whole hog. What if they find a cure in the next few months?"

I knew he was right, but it felt much worse this time. "Whatever, but we need to get it sorted out tonight—the whole lot. I won't have the energy to get up tomorrow and go about getting rid of him."

Frank nodded. "Let's do it then. Have you thought of how?"

"Yeah, I'll go to the clinic and get some anaesthetic. I'll inject him where he lies and move him after that."

"Okay."

"I'll do that now—meet you downstairs in ten."

I raced off to the clinic. I didn't know how much he weighed, but I guessed he was approximately the same size as Shane. I made up the same amount and ran back to the house.

Steve's Aston Martin was parked up on the drive outside the house.

"Oh, fuck," I said under my breath, and slid the syringe up my sleeve. I smiled and waved at them both, trying to act normally before pushing the front door open and closing it behind me.

Frank was standing in the hallway with his coat on.

"Get that off," I said. "Steph's here. I'll put the kettle on."

He shrugged out of his coat and hung it over the banister.

"I have a bad feeling about this, Frank. Both other times, things went like clockwork but they were god-awful people and deserved everything they got. This time, it's me and you that are in the wrong."

"Calm down, We've done nothing yet."

I took a deep breath. "You're right." I filled the kettle then walked back into the hall and peeped through the window at Stephanie and Steve. They were still sitting in the car.

I walked back into the lounge. "If they come in, stall them—I'm gonna inject this now."

Frank stood in the lounge doorway, ready to head anybody off, if needed.

I carefully slid the syringe from my sleeve and removed the lid. I squirted a small amount out of the needle. I then bent over Alex and took his hand in mine, stroking it for a couple of seconds before turning it over, popping the buttons on the cuff of his yellow shirt. He didn't even flinch as the needle pierced his skin.

I pulled down his sleeve and covered him back up with the blanket, nodding at Frank.

I made us a drink. Strong black coffee for me—I could still feel the effects of the brandy, although I'd thrown most of it up. Frank had tea. We sat at the dining table waiting for Steph.

"I wish she'd bloody hurry up, or else I'm going to have a heart attack," I said. My hands were a twisted mass of fingers in front of me. "What could they possibly have left to say?"

Frank chuckled. "I'm not an expert, but as far as I know, the first few hours of a relationship is the only time a man enjoys talking. Don't begrudge her this time."

I laughed at him. "I've so underestimated you over the years."

"In what way?"

"I thought you were a simple man, no disrespect meant by that, but not complex—what you see is what you get. But I couldn't have been more wrong."

"No—you were right, but needs must, lass. If your family needs you, then you dig deep and find the strength and the way forward, regardless of what hurdles life throws in your path. You just have to jump as high as you can to miss them."

"What if we can't miss them? What if we fall flat on our face?"

"Then we stand up, walk around and take a running jump at the next, and the next."

"I wish I was as calm as you."

"You're doing just fine, lass. Jon would be so proud of you."

"Would he? I'm not sure—he'd probably report us to the police himself."

"No way—he'd have done the same as you. Don't kid yourself about that. He loved that little girl with every ounce of him. If the choice was her life or that nasty Shane's, I know he wouldn't have hesitated."

"I hope so."

"Every parent would, lass. It's human nature to nurture and protect your own."

"But Shane was somebody's son—that poor woman in the pub tonight."

"She left it a bit late for her maternal instinct to kick in. She had her chance to protect him and steer him on the right path years ago, but she failed him."

"What about Hector then?"

"He took an overdose, lass. His mother will be spared the knowledge of that. There's nothing more cruel on a family than suicide."

"Apart from not knowing—both of those parents will go to the grave not knowing what happened to their sons. Thank God Alex's parents aren't alive."

He shrugged. "I can't help that, lass. All I know is we did what we did for our Em."

The front door opened and Steph crept in, her shoes in her hands and her handbag hung from the crook of her elbow.

"Hello, you dirty stop-out," I said.

"Hi—sorry. You're not waiting up for me, are you? I had my key."

"No. We sat up talking with Alex, and as you can see, he left the party early."

She glanced around and laughed when she saw Alex under the blanket.

"Did you have a nice night?" I asked.

"I did—it was great."

"And?"

"And what?"

"Are you seeing him again?"

"Tomorrow. He's taking me to see the classic car he's just bought."

"He's filthy rich, Steph. But a player—be careful."

"I'm under no illusions. Does he own a decent amount of property then?"

"An indecent amount, more like. Just watch out, that's all."

"Don't worry, I'll play it by ear. Was Sally-Ann upset? I felt a bit awful."

"She didn't seem bothered. She's only a kid anyway, much too young for him."

"That's what he said. I still feel bad for her though."

"She'll get over it," I said.

"Right, I'm off to bed. Are you going up soon?"

"Yeah, I'll just finish off the dishes and then I'll follow you up. Goodnight, Steph."

"Night-night. Oh, by the way, what were you doing outside?"

"I thought I heard a noise and I went to check if I'd locked up the clinic. I had."

"Well, goodnight."

We waited for another half an hour before doing anything. Then we got the wheelchair from under the stairs and manoeuvred Alex into it quite easily. He was completely unconscious.

I ran to the clinic ahead of Frank once again. Frank arrived and helped lift Alex onto the operating table. He was much lighter than Hector but still quite heavy.

Within half an hour, I had his Proteum and I took it over to Emily right away.

As I injected her she turned over, her eyes flickered open and then closed again.

"Thank you, Mummy," she said.

I stroked her hair for a few minutes until her breathing settled.

I decided to take the car to the clinic instead of the quad—I didn't want to disturb Steph. Frank and I got Alex into the back seat and over to the butchery building.

As we removed Alex from the car, I noticed he wasn't breathing. I put my hand on Frank's arm. He stopped and looked at me.

"He's already gone," I said.

I felt relieved. I didn't want any danger of him waking up like Hector had.

We got him onto the butcher's block and I felt for his pulse. Nothing. I'd brought another syringe to give him an overdose but it wasn't needed.

"Goodbye, Alex," I whispered, and stroked his face. "Right then, are we doing this now?"

"If you're up to it," Frank said.

"We've got no choice." I helped him cut off Alex's clothes and threw them into a black bin bag.

Frank started the bone saw and I looked away. This was his area of expertise and I hated this part.

I stood still at the side of Frank but facing the opposite direction. I tried to mentally transport myself to another place far, far away from this awful room of death.

The screams, when they came, scared the shit out of me. I was so confused. I turned around just in time to see Frank lose his balance and crash to the floor. The screams continued, and not from Frank. I looked around and I couldn't believe my eyes.

Alex was sitting up. One arm was gone, chopped off at the shoulder and his other arm flailed wildly.

I screamed. An earth-shattering deafening scream that seemed to drown out any sound Alex made.

He seemed to see me for the first time and grabbed the neck of my overalls, pulling me towards him. His eyes were wide open. His screams had lost strength and were now a high pitched squeal. It horrified me.

How could this be possible? I'd checked him myself—he was dead! However, this one-armed naked man was far from dead. I gripped his hand and tried to pry open his fingers but they were stuck in some kind of spasm. I couldn't get him off me.

"Frank!" I screamed. "Frank, help me!" But Frank didn't budge. I couldn't take my eyes off the real-life horror movie playing out before my eyes.

I leapt backwards, but Alex came too. I pushed him but he held on tight. His squeals made it hard for me to think straight, hard to think at all.

I shoved back at Alex, needing to get him off me, to put as much space between us as possible, but I couldn't move him. I shoved him with every ounce of strength I could muster. He began to move backwards, and his pleading eyes tore my heart to shreds. I wanted to stop. To beg for his forgiveness, but it was too late.

I shoved and a roar escaped me. Alex staggered backwards, still holding my top, still screaming and I thrust myself forward. I slammed him into the far wall and suddenly the screaming stopped.

His eyes stared at me, unmoving. What had just happened? Why had he suddenly let go and stopped screaming?

I staggered backwards and fell to my knees. Alex stayed at the side of the wall, unmoving.

His eyes still stared, yet they were glazing over. I spun around to Frank who lay on the floor against the door, also unmoving. I scrambled over to him.

"Frank!" It didn't sound like my voice. "Frank. Wake up, Frank. Speak to me."

CHAPTER 32

I flicked at Frank's face—no response.

A gash on his forehead pumped blood out at a steady pace. He'd obviously hit his head on the way down. Thankfully he'd dropped the bone saw and the safety switch had cut off.

I tore a strip of fabric from Frank's shirt and tied it around Frank's head.

Alex was still rigid at the back of the room. I sat, leaning my body against Frank. Trying to weigh up what had just happened. What was still happening, and what I could—would—do about it.

Frank's pulse was strong but his pupils were unresponsive. Whatever I needed to do, I'd have to do it alone.

The room looked like a blood bath. The blood from Alex's amputated arm was all over the place, and all over me. The room could be washed down easily, but I'd have to hose myself down before I could step foot out of the place.

I put my arms under Frank's armpits and tried to drag him to the door, but I couldn't budge him. I needed to call an ambulance, but how could I?

I'd known from the start this was a bad idea. Known it would go horribly wrong.

I got to my feet, legs shaking. I could hardly move, but I managed to get over to Alex. His unmoving, unblinking eyes told me he was really dead this time, but I needed to make certain.

I placed my fingers on his throat. Nothing. I had no idea how and why he was still upright. I looked around the back of his head and solved the mystery.

A hook in the wall now stuck straight into the back of his skull, and had assisted in killing him off once and for all. I put my arms around his waist and yanked.

He came away easily, although with a nasty wet squelch.

A cry escaped me. I tried to place him on the floor with the grace and dignity he deserved, but he was too heavy for me. Instead, he fell in an ungainly heap, his head hitting the concrete and bursting like a ripe watermelon. I fell to his side and sobbed hysterically.

I don't know how long I sat there, but the blood that covered me and my overalls dried. I needed to pull myself together.

I located the large blue bin that Frank used for the body parts, and wheeled it over to Alex. Finding the strength from somewhere, I managed to lift him up and topple him over the side. Then I picked up his dismembered arm, holding it by the finger like a squeamish child picking up a worm. I shuddered, flinging it into the bin.

I pushed the bin out of the room, leaving a trail of blood behind me.

I hosed down the room as much as I could with Frank lying to the side. I stripped off my overalls, and the ones that Frank wore and threw them into the black bag which I also put in the bin.

Then I ran around the building, searching for anything that could assist me to get Frank to the car. I found an old plywood trolley. One of the wheels was missing, but it would have to do.

It took an age but I finally got Frank onto it, enabling me to get him into the main part of the building so I could finish hosing the blood down. Then, with a mop and bucket, I cleaned the trails the two sets of wheels had made.

I found another pair of overalls hung on a nail at the back of the toilet door. They were huge orange things but I climbed into them, rolling the arms and legs up to fit.

Once the room was clean, I pushed the bin containing Alex back into it and locked the door. Then I pushed the flat-decked trolley out to the car.

Frank's pulse beat strong. I tapped his cheek again. "Frank? Frank, I need you to wake up." The nasty gash above his right eye needed stitching. I could have stitched it myself if that was all, but it wasn't—he needed a doctor.

I tried my best to rouse him, and eventually he began to stir. "We need to get you into the car, Frank. Will you help me?"

He mumbled something that I couldn't decipher, but slowly got to his feet and staggered to the car. I pushed the trolley back inside, making a mental note to come back and clean it as soon as I got a chance. It was still covered in blood. I drove to the house.

Frank stayed in the car while I ran inside and quickly showered and changed my clothes. I thought I'd removed most of the blood from me at the butchery but the water still ran red for the first few seconds.

Afterwards, I wrote a quick note for Steph and grabbed my handbag and mobile phone, before racing back to the car.

By the time we reached the accident and emergency entrance, it was almost 4am. I ran inside and called for help. A porter and a doctor helped to get Frank onto a stretcher, then wheeled him inside.

I had to stay at reception to give his details and located him a short time after in a cubicle. Several doctors and nurses buzzed around him.

"Can you tell us what happened?" a tall effeminate doctor asked.

"I'm not sure. I found him like this, but he's obviously banged his head."

He nodded.

"He gets unsteady on his feet. He's recovering from a stroke."

"I see," he said as he examined the deep gash. "He'll need a few stitches, and we'd best do a scan to be on the safe side."

"Of course. Do you think he'll be okay other than that?"

"I think so. He's taken a nasty knock but his vital signs seem okay."

Nothing sinister showed up on Frank's scan. He would be all right, but he was still out of it at eight-thirty when Steph called.

"What happened?"

My stomach flipped. Oh shit, what would I tell her? "He fell and banged his head last night. It's a long story. I'll explain later. Is Emily all right?"

"Yes, she is now, but she had a terrible headache earlier. I gave her some Paracetamol and she brightened up soon after."

"Are you okay to stay with her until I get back?"

"Yeah, course. I'll take her to Steve's with me if she feels all right, otherwise I'll postpone it for another time."

"Thanks, Steph. I'll give you a call as soon as I know more."

I curled up on the armchair beside Frank and waited. A while later I sensed a movement. My eyes flew open. Frank's hand wafted the air in front of him and his eyelids fluttered.

"Frank! Thank God. Are you okay?" I jumped to my feet and leaned over him.

He seemed disorientated. I poured him a glass of water from the jug on the bedside cabinet and placed it to his mouth. He drank gratefully. I wiped his mouth on a tissue. "Are you feeling okay?" I repeated.

He nodded, eyebrows furrowed and his eyes darted around the room.

"You're in hospital. Do you remember what happened, Frank?"

He began to shake his head then stopped. His eyes grew wider as clearly his memory returned.

I glanced around, making sure we were still alone. "It's okay. I've sorted it. For now, anyway. You banged your head and had to have stitches, but you're okay, except you'll have a doozy of a headache for a while."

"Alex?" his voice sounded hoarse and scratchy.

"He's gone," I said, glancing around me once again. "I put him in the blue bin but he's still in one piece—well, two counting the arm. I'll have to sort out what to do with him later."

"Get me up."

"No way, Frank. You're staying put. No one goes there. It'll be okay for now."

He struggled, trying to get up, but he didn't have the energy and lay back down heavily.

"See, you're not well. Just do as you're told."

"But …"

"No buts—I'll sort it."

"Then wait for me. I'll be okay in a day or two."

"We'll see. Now, have you any idea what we're gonna tell everyone?"

He lay back, looking at the ceiling, deep in thought for a few seconds. "Say Alex attacked me when he was drunk. At least that'll explain why he's not around."

I nodded. "Okay."

I arrived home to an empty house. Steph had left a scribbled note on the kitchen bench, telling me that she'd taken Emily to Steve's.

Although I wanted to do nothing more than drag my weary

body upstairs and crawl into bed, shutting out the world, I needed to make use of the time alone.

Alex's room was surprisingly tidy for a young man. In fact the orderly way he'd folded his clothes, in colour order, would put most women to shame.

I found a bag under the bed and began throwing his belongings into it. I was amazed at how calm I felt. How far removed I had become from my feelings. I didn't take much stuff. I figured a young man in a hurry would only take the essentials. A full sweep of the place only took a few minutes.

In the bedside drawer I found his passport. The name inside puzzled me: Alexander Finnegan. I knew him as Alexander Snow. I shoved it into the back pocket of my jeans.

After one last look around, I threw the bag down the spiral staircase and loaded it into the truck.

I stopped at the shed, got out of the truck and ran inside. I returned with Shane's bike, the one made from cannibalised parts. I threw it into the truck, climbed back in, and drove towards the butchery.

As I opened the door to the butchery, the stench made me gag. I'd not thought to put Alex back in the cold store.

I held my breath and ran over to the blue bin and pulled out the rubbish bag.

It took several minutes back in the truck before I was able to breathe properly. Then I drove to the incinerator, stashed Alex's things inside, and lit it.

I took the passport from my pocket and studied it again. Alexander Finnegan. The photograph was Alex, and the date of birth his as well. I remembered him telling us he'd arrived in the country on a work visa from America. The passport he showed Jon when he first came to work for us, had been in the name we paid him under–Alexander Snow. I knew I'd probably never know the truth now. I tossed the passport into the incinerator and watched the blue outer cover melt and burn.

Next stop, the offal pit. I launched Shane's bike into the deep dark hole. I thought how easy it would be to dispose of Alex's remains down there, but I would always worry about them being found.

I didn't have the physical or mental energy to deal with the body today. I knew there was no way on this earth I could chop him up myself. However, I knew he'd be okay in the cold store for a while longer—no one ever went in there.

I needed some sleep.

"What the hell!" I yelled, as I swerved to miss the huge, black four wheel drive coming at full pelt towards me. I skidded to a stop before jumping out.

"Are you stupid? You almost smashed into me," I yelled to the driver.

"I'm sorry, I'm sorry." The man held his hands up to his head as he leapt from the vehicle. "It was all my fault."

"Damn right it was. What the hell are you doing here anyway? This is private property."

"I know. I'm looking for Frank." He held his hand towards me. "Michael Woods, David and Lynette's son." He smiled, his pale blue eyes twinkling.

"Oh, hi," I said, taken aback. I offered my hand limply.

"I called at the house first, then guessed you must be busy on the farm."

"What can I do for you?"

"Have you finished your work? Because I'd kill for a cup of coffee," he said, displaying that cheeky smile once again.

I shrugged. "I'm on my way back to the house. I'll put the kettle on if you want to follow."

"Great."

Michael parked his beast of a car beside mine as I opened the front door.

"Do you take sugar?" I asked as he entered the kitchen.

"No thanks, just a drop of milk."

He looked nothing like his parents. David was stocky with fairish skin, grey hair and light blue eyes. Lyn was blonde with brownish eyes. This guy was tall and lean, with a shock of dark hair and startling blue eyes.

I placed a steaming cup of coffee in front of him. "There you go, Michael. Now, what can I do for you?" I smiled as I sat opposite him at the table.

"Is this a bad time?" He screwed up his black eyebrows and a concerned look crossed his face.

"Your timing could have been a little better." I laughed. "I've been at the hospital all night with my father-in-law."

"Uncle Frank? Why? what happened?"

"He fell—banged his head. He's all right though. Should be home tomorrow."

"Bloody hell! The last time I was home he had a stroke."

"Yeah, the poor guy is only just coming right from that. Our farmhand left last night too, so we're in a bit of a mess."

"That's what I wanted to talk to you about. Dad tells me you're thinking of selling the farm."

"Nothing concrete yet. We're weighing up our options. Why? Are you interested?"

"I could be, at the right price."

"That's nothing to do with me. Frank's the owner. But we have been thinking about leasing the land out initially, then subdividing so we can keep the house and clinic."

"I see."

"Would that be a problem?"

"Guess not—I don't need a massive house like this one and it wouldn't affect what I have in mind."

"Which is?"

"Extending Dad's farm. I'd be able to stay there while I convert one of the disused barns. You still have the butchery and the outhouses, don't you?"

"I guess so. That's Frank's domain, I'm afraid. I don't have a lot to do with the farm."

"Would you mind if I have a quick squizz round?"

"No! I mean, I'd rather you wait until Frank's back. Why don't I call you tomorrow, once he's home? He has the keys and everything."

"Yeah, no problem," he said. "I was shocked to hear about Johnny. He was a great bloke. We were best friends growing up."

I sighed, nodding. "Thanks. I'd forgotten you knew him. How's it feel to be home after all this time? Were you in Ireland long?"

"Sixteen years in total. We stayed with Maria's parents for the first few years, then Maria and I bought a run-down farm just over ten years ago. We were able to turn it around and we sold it off for a decent profit, even with the recession.

"That was lucky."

He nodded. "I'm sure my mum's told you all about my marriage."

"She did mention it."

He slapped his thigh and laughed. "I bet she did more than that. She can be very vocal when she's a mind to, and makes no secret of the fact she hates Maria."

I shrugged. "She just cares about you, that's all. You're lucky. My mum died when I was a kid so I've never really had that kind of maternal concern, but I do envy it."

"She's not a bad old girl. And to be honest with you, it wasn't all her doing. Maria's a very hard woman to deal with, very self-centred. Mum read her like a book as soon as she laid her eyes on her."

I yawned behind my hand. "I'm sorry—but I'm gonna have to get some sleep."

He jumped up. "Of course. So I'll hear from you tomorrow?" He picked up both cups and walked into the kitchen and placed them in the sink.

"You will."

"Great. I've enjoyed our chat, Victoria." He held his hand out towards me and I took it. Our eyes locked, and the electricity that passed between us shocked me. I snatched my hand away a little faster than I meant to.

CHAPTER 33

I ran a bath and had a long relaxing soak, but it didn't even begin to relax my mind. I couldn't shake the image of Alex's body in that bin. I had no idea what I was going to do about it.

No way could I butcher him and feed him to the pigs on my own. I'd have to speak to Frank, but whatever we decided, we'd have to be quick if Michael wanted to have a look around.

The sounds of Steph and Emily arriving home, giggling and squealing, made me groan. I really wasn't in the mood for high spirits right now. There was already enough noise going on inside my head.

I slid further down in the bath, filling my ears with water in an attempt to shut out the world for a while longer.

When I finally went downstairs, I found them in the snug making Christmas cards. They had hundreds of pieces of card, bits of ribbon, stars, glitter and glue strewn all over the carpet.

"Oh, hello. I thought you were being quiet," I said.

"Mummy!" Emily jumped up off the floor and ran to me.

"We thought you were in bed," Steph said.

"I had a bath."

"You must be shattered. How's Frank?"

"He's awake now, and he should be home tomorrow."

"Yay!" Emily said.

"Are you girls all right if I go and have a lie down?"

"Course we are. We were going to get some fish and chips for tea. Do you want some?"

I hesitated. "No, I don't think so. I'm not hungry."

"Have you eaten today?"

I shook my head.

"One large portion of fish and chips for you then, and no arguments. I'll bring it up later."

I rolled my eyes to the ceiling. "Whatever."

The next morning I got up early to do the rounds with the animals and collect a pile of eggs.

It was Sunday morning, so nobody asked about Alex as I normally did the Sunday rounds. I made some breakfast before calling the hospital. They said Frank could come home.

"Okay Em, do you want to come to get Grandad with me?"

"At hospital?"

"Yes, if you hurry up and get ready. We've got to go," I said.

"Okay." Emily reached for her shoes and sat on the rug to put them on.

"You got any plans today, Steph?"

She smiled.

"Go on," I said

"I'm seeing Steve again. We had a good time yesterday didn't we, Em?"

"Yes, and we went for a drive in his new car. He said it was a new car but it was really an old one," she whispered the last part.

"Didn't you like it, Em?" I laughed.

"I liked it, but it wasn't new. I think he was tricking."

"You still haven't told me properly what happened with Frank," Stephanie said.

"Can I tell you later?" I nodded at Emily.

"Oh," she mouthed, and nodded.

Although Frank looked much better than yesterday, he still wasn't right.

"Are you sure he's okay to come home?" I asked the nurse as she brought us a wheelchair to transport Frank to the car.

"He's been discharged, so the doctor must think so," she said.

"I'm fine. I just need to get out of here."

"Can I push you, Grandad?"

"He's too heavy for you, Em," I snapped.

"No, he's not. I'm better again."

She obviously felt different every time we topped up her Proteum, even though her symptoms hadn't been as bad this time.

"Do you? That's good."

"So can I push him?"

We were halfway up the corridor. I stopped and lifted my hands off the handle. "Fine, you push." I was aware I was snapping but my nerves were all of a jangle and I really couldn't help it.

She hardly got him a foot further before she gave up.

"What? Too heavy?"

"Yes," she said, defeated.

"Come on, we'll do it together," I smiled.

I let her stand in between me and the wheelchair and helped her push Frank, making it twice as hard for me, but it made her feel as though she was helping.

Once in the car I mentioned to Frank about the visit from Michael.

"That would work, especially now," he said.

"Yeah. That's what I thought, but we have a slight problem."

"What's that?"

I glanced at Emily in the rear view mirror. She didn't seem to be paying any attention but I couldn't trust that. "He wants to check out the butchery and the outhouses."

"Oh."

"I lit the incinerator yesterday, but there's still the problem of the pig food to sort out."

"I getcha."

"I said I'd call him once you're home but I guess we can put him off for a couple of days."

"We'll sort something out, lass."

"It's so good to have you back, Frank. You frightened the life out of me."

"I can imagine."

"Imagine what, Grandad?"

"I was just telling him how worried we were when he hurt his head."

Back home. Frank lay on the sofa, exhausted. Steph had gone out and Emily went to make some more Christmas cards in the snug.

"So what happened?"

"It was awful, Frank. You fell, and Alex was screaming. He got hold of me and we fought. At least I think we did, although he didn't do much—he just wouldn't let go. I slammed him into the wall and impaled his head into one of those nasty hooks. I managed to get him into the bin but I couldn't chop him up. There's no way, Frank."

"We need to get him to the pigs."

"Whole?"

"I guess. When were they last fed?" he asked.

"Friday."

"They'll be starving. We'll have to do it soon."

"You're going nowhere. I'll do it."

"If you tie the bin to the tow bar of the truck and drive very slowly, it should work."

"I nodded. "Okay—I'll do it now. Are you all right to watch Emily?"

"Of course, but I'd rather help you. Are you sure you can do this alone?"

"There's no one else to look after Emily, and I'd rather do it while Steph's not here."

"Okay."

I got a set of disposable overalls, my farm boots, and a length of rope from the garage. I didn't relish what needed to be done, but I had to think of it as a piece of meat—just an animal carcass. Lord knows, I'd had to dispose of enough of them in my time as a vet.

When I got over to the butchery, I climbed into the overalls and tied an old rag around my face. I took a deep breath before entering.

The smell hit me like a freight train. I couldn't bear it. I spun away and back through the door, slamming it behind me. It was much worse than I'd imagined, but I had no choice. I had to do this.

Bracing myself once again, I entered, glad I hadn't eaten since breakfast. I grabbed the bin and wheeled it easily to the door and out into the open, but I couldn't leave it like that. I needed something to place in the top of the bin.

Rummaging around in the disused shed, I found an old tarpaulin in the far corner. It was full of cobwebs and spiders, which would have freaked me out a few months ago. Now I took it all in my stride—it would take a lot more than a few hairy spiders to scare me now.

I stashed the faded yellow tarp into the top of the bin and wheeled it around to the back of the truck, tying the handle of the bin to the tow bar with the rope.

I took my time towing the bin. It wasn't far, around eight

hundred metres. But the large chunks of gravel that made up most of the road surface would have made it a nightmare to pull the bin by hand.

The pigs must have smelled the decaying corpse, because they were squealing before I got anywhere near them. I wished I could turn my ears off. The sound brought visions to my mind, visions of a hairy foot and yellow toenails. I felt woozy.

There was no way I could lift Alex's body over the top of the sty, and no way I'd want to. That meant I had to unlock the side gate and push the bin inside, which was easier said than done. The gate hadn't been opened in a while, and the bolt was shut tight.

I found a large screwdriver in the truck and bashed the bolt a few times, which seemed to loosen the rust enough for me to release it.

The pigs were going bonkers by now. I pushed the bin through the gate and twisted the handle as hard as I could until it eventually tipped onto its side. The awful sounds that followed as the pigs tucked into their feast will stay with me forever.

I left it like that. The bin could be removed later. Tomorrow, even. I just needed to escape the gruesome sounds and the revolting stench.

I stripped off the overalls and stopped once more at the incinerator before returning to the butchery block, where I gave everything one last hose down.

Once satisfied, I returned home.

I met Emily in the hallway. "Ew, Mummy, what's that stink?" she said, holding her nose.

"I fell in the pigsty." I ran up the stairs to the sound of Emily's laughter.

Then I stood under the jets of the shower until the water ran cold.

After drying myself, I put on my fluffy white robe and slippers and went for a lie down on my bed, relieved it was all done, and positive it was the very last time I'd do anything like that again.

I must have fallen asleep as I woke to the sound of deep voices. My heart leapt out of my chest. Who the hell was here?"

I crept from the bedroom. The voices had faded slightly and were now coming from the snug. I found Emily sitting at the dining table, colouring.

"Who's here, Em?" I whispered.

"Uncle David and another man."

"Shit!" I said. "Sorry for swearing, Em." I ran back upstairs, annoyed with myself for not calling them to put them off.

I threw on a pair of tatty jeans and a bright pink breast cancer t-shirt, then rushed back downstairs. I took a few deep breaths to calm myself before walking into the snug.

"Oh, hi, you two. Sorry, I meant to call you."

Dave got up and embraced me but I quickly pulled away, paranoid I still stank.

"Frank's not up to a tour of the farm today—doctor's orders. He has to rest for a few days."

"Yeah, no problem," Michael said. "We were passing and just called in to see how the invalid is doing." He smiled, and my stomach did a little twirl. "Anyway, I only want to have a look at the butchery. I could go myself."

"No!" Frank and I said together.

Michael and Dave seemed taken aback.

"We can't find the keys," Frank said. "Jonathan had them last and we'll have to look for them."

"Okay, no hurry," Dave said. "We're only throwing a few ideas around anyway, Frank. Mike wants to buy into a farm and I told him you may be selling. Makes sense for him to look at this because it would only mean a boundary change rather than a full subdivision."

"Sounds perfect to me," Frank said. "If you can just give us a couple of days for me to get back on my feet, then we can look into the ins and outs of it."

"Course we can. Okay, we'll leave you to it. Lyn will have the dinner on the table by now and is probably cursing us anyway."

They both stood up and I walked them to the front door.

"Thanks, lass," Dave said. "He does look a bit peaky, doesn't he?"

"Yeah, he's been overdoing it and needs to take a bit more care—he's had to help out a lot more since Jonathan died. It would be fantastic to lose the farm responsibilities and to be able to look after him again."

"He's lucky to have you, lass."

"I'm the lucky one. God knows where I'd be without him."

I waved them off and went back through to Frank.

"How did it go, lass?"

"I did it. The pigs seemed to jump on him—they were starving. I hope they finish the job off."

"They should. If not, we'll sort it tomorrow. No one will be going near there before then."

"I hope not. Can I get you something to eat?"

"If you're making something."

"I need to feed Emily, so…"

"Shall we call for a pizza? You look done in," he said.

"I am, to be honest. Yeah, let's do that, and then I'm having an early night."

Stephanie arrived home as we were tucking in to a meatlovers, Franks favourite, and a Hawaiian, Emily's favourite. I had no appetite and spent most of my time picking the ham off, my stomach lurching at the idea.

"Frank—you're home!" Steph rushed in and hugged Frank from behind, kissing the top of his head.

"Grab a plate, Steph. Takeaways again, I'm afraid," I said.

"Yum, just the ticket for a Sunday dinner."

"I didn't expect you home this early."

"I thought you might need some help, but you look like you have everything under control."

"Ordering pizza is a doddle," I laughed.

"You don't seem yourself, Vic." She looked at me through squinted eyes.

"I'm fine, just tired. It's been a bitch of a weekend."

"I know." She glanced at Frank and smiled.

"Aw—Mummy said the b-word."

"Sorry, Em." I rolled my eyes to the ceiling.

Steph laughed.

The doorbell rang and Steph began to stand up.

"I'll get it. I've finished anyway," I said.

My stomach threatened to chuck up the little bit of food I'd eaten as I imagined a group of police officers standing at the door. Bracing myself, I held my breath as I opened it.

A short butch-looking blonde girl stood directly in front of me, beside a lanky guy wearing a black leather jacket and red cap.

"Hello?" I said, glancing from one to the other.

"Sorry to bother you, Mrs Lyons, but do you know where Alex is?"

My stomach flipped. It was as though time had stopped and I became aware of the most minute details—the large diamante earring in her left ear, the scuffed red plimsolls, the way she shifted from foot to foot. I didn't think these two were a couple—she looked more like a dyke, and him a nerdy geek.

The wind had picked up and blasted through the door, causing me to step backwards into the hallway. A loud sound in my ears puzzled me until I realised it was the pumping of my heart.

"Mrs Lyons?" she asked again, glancing nervously at her mate.

"I—erm—no. He's not here. He—he left."

"Left! Where to?"

"I don't know—he got drunk on Friday night and attacked my father-in-law. Put him in hospital in fact. He'd gone by the time I returned home on Saturday."

"Oh my God!" she almost screamed. Her reaction made me shudder.

"Man," the guy said.

"Do you know where he could be? He's not answering his phone," the girl said.

"I have no idea, I'm sorry." I made to close the door.

"If he gets in touch, could you ask him to call Alecia?"

"Alecia, no problem." I smiled and nodded then closed the door.

"Who was that?" Steph asked, back in the snug.

"Someone looking for Alex."

"Oh yeah, a guy called for him earlier. Said he's been trying to get hold of him since yesterday."

I cocked my head sideways at her, towards the kitchen. "Anyone for a cuppa?"

Steph took the hint and followed me to the kitchen. "What is it?"

"It's Alex. He had a funny turn on Friday night after you'd gone to bed. He was the reason Frank ended up in hospital."

"You're joking!"

"It's true, I'm afraid. After you went to bed he woke up, drunk, and attacked Frank."

"Where is he now? Did you tell the police?"

"No. I don't think he meant to do it. When I got back yesterday, he'd already packed up and gone."

"Oh my God! I'm shocked—he's normally such a gentle guy."

"I know, but that's booze for you. Now we're in a pickle with the farm. I don't know what we'll do."

She shook her head. "I'm sorry—I'm still trying to process it. He attacked Frank?"

I nodded. "I really don't think he meant to—we shouldn't tell everyone. It's not fair."

"I won't say a word. Maybe he'll be back tomorrow."

"Maybe, at least I hope so." I felt terrible lying to her like this. I was getting worryingly good at it—I didn't even flinch anymore.

Frank got up from the table and joined us in the kitchen.

"I just heard what Alex did to you," Steph said.

Frank nodded.

"I think it was an accident though." Frank nodded again. "So do I."

"Then why would he leave, if it was an accident?"

"He probably just panicked. I'd rather give him the benefit of the doubt," I said.

"Me too," Frank said.

"Well let's hope he does the right thing and comes back to face the music tomorrow," Steph muttered.

"Yeah—let's hope," I said, glancing at Frank.

CHAPTER 34

By the next afternoon, there was nothing left of Alex's body. The pigs squealed at me again as though they hadn't been fed for a week. I decided at that point that I hated pigs and knew I would never touch anything porky ever again.

I knew there had been experiments into using pigs as potential organ donors for human transplant. For decades, people have been fitted with heart valves from pigs, and diabetics injected themselves with pig insulin before they learned how to synthesise the human version of the hormone. I wondered if anybody had ever tested pig Proteum to see if it was a potential solution. But there again, knowing what I did about Proteum transplants, it would probably turn Emily into a trough feeder.

I had another look around. Everything seemed in order. It would be a day or two before the first of the teeth and hair would reappear.

We'd arranged to show Michael around the farm tomorrow. I hoped and prayed that he would decide to take it off our hands, and the sooner, the better.

Sally-Ann planned to come into the clinic first thing in the morning for a chat.

On the surface, life seemed normal. The farm and the extra workload wouldn't begin to affect us until next week, but as long as the animals were fed, we could get away without doing the rest.

I couldn't believe how easily I'd managed to take everything in my stride. I felt immense guilt when I thought about poor Alex, but my family's future had hung in the balance, and my priority had got to be Emily.

I wasn't sure if my behaviour was normal or if I was completely mad.

"Everything all right?" Frank asked as I walked into the house.

"It all seems fine."

He acknowledged my nod with a tilt of his head. We'd developed our own form of communication.

"The sty could do with a clean soon. It's a mess," I said.

"Maybe I could help you in a couple of days when I'm feeling a bit better."

"We'll see. Let's get you right first before we set you to work again." I smiled.

"I could help you, Mummy," Emily said. "I'm better now."

"Thanks, Em, but those pigs would eat you for breakfast." I meant that literally, but she laughed.

"I'm feeling much better today, lass." Frank said. "I'll be up to starting Em's lessons again tomorrow."

"Yay!"

"There were another couple of phone calls for Alex while you were out, lass."

My stomach flipped. "Oh yes?"

Frank nodded. "I told them he doesn't work here anymore."

"I see. What did they say?"

"Nothing. They seemed fine."

"I'll be glad when all this settles down," I whispered. "Okay, I'm off to the clinic to check on Steph. Then I'll be back to make a start on dinner. Any requests?"

"Cauliflower cheese," Emily said.

Maybe this was a normal request in most households, but it wasn't in ours. Emily hated cauliflower cheese. It had been, however, Alex's favourite. A fact that hadn't gone unnoticed by Frank.

"Are you sure, Em? Did you mean mac and cheese?" he asked.

"No, cauliflower cheese."

"Very strange." He raised his eyebrows and turned down the corners of his mouth, nodding.

"Very well, cauliflower cheese it is." I didn't think she'd actually eat it.

Over in the clinic, Stephanie was writing out a receipt for a client.

"Oh hi, Mrs Taylor. How's Fifi?" I bent to make a fuss of the bulldog at her feet. She didn't suit her name at all.

"She's fine—she just needed her jabs."

"That's good. And how's Mr Taylor?"

"Not so good—you don't have a jab for lazyitis, do you? No? I'll just have to put up with him." She laughed.

"If I could find a cure for that, I'd be a multi-millionaire." I also laughed.

"I wish somebody would. Anyway, bye girls. Have a lovely Christmas."

We watched as Mrs Taylor left with Fifi.

Steph pointed at them as they made their way across the car park, and stifled a laugh with her hand.

I turned to see what was so amusing.

Both Mrs Taylor and Fifi walked with their legs wide apart, as though they were wearing dirty nappies. Even their steps were in sync.

Everybody says it in jest but it's true. People do eventually start looking like their pets. I couldn't help the eruption of laughter that followed.

"Do you remember that woman in Manchester?" I said between fits of laughter.

"Oh my God, yes. I'll never forget her." Steph wiped her eyes.

"I couldn't make eye contact with any of you." My voice came out in a high pitched squeal.

"She was the spit of her Afghan hound. The frizzy strawberry blonde hair, the big nose and terrific eyelashes," Steph said, now almost lying on the desk holding her stomach.

We stayed that way for at least five minutes, both laughing uncontrollably. It felt so good to laugh. I couldn't remember the last time I had really laughed.

"Is that it for the day?" I asked, once we'd calmed down and caught our breath.

"Yeah, unless you can think of anything else that needs doing."

"No—divert the phone and you may as well call it a day," I said. "Are you out tonight?"

"Not sure yet. I'm waiting for Steve to ring."

"Well, Emily requested cauliflower cheese for tea."

"That's funny. I thought she hated cauliflower?"

"She does normally. I'll do something else too in case she changes her mind."

"Don't do anything for me. I had a sandwich not long ago."

"Okay, I'll cash up and then I'll be over."

"Was that Sally-Ann on the phone earlier?"

"Yeah, she's coming in to see me in the morning—she's looking for a job," I said, as I looked up from the receipt book, keen to gauge Steph's reaction.

"What job were you thinking of giving her?" she asked, her eyebrows furrowed.

"Well, it depends. I need someone to help around the farm initially and then the clinic. However, if the meeting with Dave and Michael goes okay tomorrow, I won't have to worry about the farm for much longer."

"That would be good for you, Vic. You've got too much going on at the moment. If there is anything more I could do to help you would ask, wouldn't you?"

"Of course I would, but I'm just grateful to you for running this place. I didn't realise how much Jonathan actually did before."

"You must miss him a lot."

"It's got easier. I was angry with him for a long time. Now I just feel sad when I think about him. The anger has gone."

"It wasn't his fault. He'd never have left you and Em by choice."

"I know that, but it was easier for me to cope with the anger at the time than the all-consuming sadness."

"Yeah, we humans are designed with amazing coping strategies built in."

I nodded. "Anyway, get going or else I'll be here all night."

"Outta here, boss." She laughed as she scurried out the door.

Emily ate the cauliflower cheese and asked for seconds. It terrified me when I thought of her getting certain traits off the Proteum donor, but on the whole, if this was as bad as it got from Alex, we couldn't complain.

The next morning I was running as soon as my feet hit the bedroom floor. I needed to check and feed the animals, check the butchery block and make sure everything was spic and span, and double-check the sty.

Michael was coming for a look around, and I worried he'd be able to tell what had gone on there at first glance. I'd already pulled the empty bin from the sty yesterday and hosed everything down.

Sally-Ann was due at the clinic at nine. Steph had been stressing about it. I wanted to scream at her that Sally-Ann was the least of my problems, but I bit my tongue.

"Toast okay, Em?" I asked as she came downstairs. Her eyes were barely open.

She nodded.

"I'll be back to make your lunch, but if you want anything else, you'll have to make do with cereal."

"Okay, Mummy."

"Frank, can I get you anything? There's tea in the pot."

"No thanks, lass. I can manage."

"Sally-Ann is coming in at nine and then I'll be back over here mid-morning in time to meet Michael and Dave."

"That's fine."

"Kiss," I said to Emily, puckering my lips.

She wiped her mouth of toast crumbs before raising her face for a kiss.

Once the farm rounds were done, I headed over to the clinic. I hadn't seen anything incriminating but it didn't stop me being paranoid. I would be glad when today's inspections were done.

Stephanie jumped out of her skin as I walked in.

"Relax, it's only me."

"I don't know why I feel so terrible." Stephanie sat back down.

"Neither do I."

"I mean it's not as if they were married, or even in a committed relationship. It was their first date, for God's sake."

"I'm sure she'll be fine. She wouldn't come in if not."

The door opened and Sally-Ann popped her head in.

"Oh hi, come on in. You remember Stephanie?" I asked.

"Yes, of course. Hi, Steph." Sally-Ann held out her hand towards Steph.

Stephanie jumped up from the chair to shake it, bumping her legs on the desk and dropping her pen on the floor, obviously flustered. I almost laughed at her.

"Can I get you a coffee? Tea?" I asked, looking at Sally-Ann.

"Coffee, please. Black."

"I'll get it," Steph said. "You want one, Vic?"

"I'll have a juice, please. I'm thirsty this morning. Come through to the back, Sally, I'll show you around."

She followed me as I walked around the back of the reception desk and through the door beyond. "As you can see, it's tiny. We only have one examination room which doubles as our surgery."

I led her through the next door, where Steph was standing at the sink filling the kettle.

"A small kitchen and bathroom." I pointed to a further door to the left. The door to the side of the bathroom had a combination lock, and I entered the four digit pin. "This is the storeroom. And that door leads back through to reception."

Back in reception, I perched on the edge of the desk.

"Take a seat," I said, offering the swivel chair. "So what I'm looking for is a receptionist-admin person who might help with a few other bits and bobs around the farm."

"I've never worked on a farm before. Will that matter?"

"It's not rocket science, but it's not glamorous either. Hopefully, the farm won't even be an issue in the next few weeks, but I don't want to count my chickens, pardon the pun. How are you around animals?"

"I like dogs but I've never really ..." She shrugged. "I'm sorry, I could lie to you, but I don't have much experience around animals either." She looked forlorn.

"No worries. How are you at answering phone and making tea?"

"Excellent." She smiled.

"Typing?"

"So-so."

"There you go, then. When can you start?"

"Are you serious?" She jumped off the chair and snatched at my outstretched hand, her eyes brimming with tears

I nodded, smiling as Stephanie walked in with the drinks.

"Steph, meet our new receptionist."

"Congratulations and welcome aboard. You'll love it here—we're a friendly bunch," Steph said.

"Thank you," Sally-Ann smiled a warm and genuine smile that seemed to put Stephanie at ease.

The phone rang. I looked at Sally-Ann my eyebrows raised. The shock registered on her face and her jaw dropped open.

I smiled. "I'm only joking." I answered the phone. "Farm vets, Victoria speaking."

"Morning, Victoria speaking, Mike here. We're at your place." I could hear the amusement in his voice and I knew his eyes would be twinkling. My stomach did a little spin. I wasn't prepared for the way my body seemed to betray me where this man was concerned.

"No problem, I'll be over in a tick. Put the kettle on." Stephanie and Sally-Ann were having a conversation about the upcoming festive season.

"Sorry to butt in ladies, but I'm gonna have to shoot off. When would you be available to start, Sally-Ann?"

"Yesterday." she said. "And Sal's fine."

"Okay then, Sal. If Steph's not busy, maybe she can fill you in on a few things around here?"

"Fine by me," Steph said. "Will you be back by lunchtime? I have a few things I need to do."

"Yeah, easy. I'll be an hour, tops. See you both then."

David, Michael and Frank were sitting at the dining table. "Where's Em?" I asked.

"I'm here," she said, as she jumped out from behind the sofa.

"Gosh, Em, you frightened me."

"She's got the devil in her today," Frank said. "I've spent more time searching for her than anything else."

"Have you been giving your Grandad the runaround, miss?" I tickled her until she begged for me to stop. "Right then, I've got things to do so can you start your schoolwork for me?"

"Aw, I don't like schoolwork."

"Nonsense, you're being silly today. Tell you what, why don't you draw me a beautiful picture?"

"Tea okay for you, Vic?" Michael said from the kitchen.

"Please, unless you're ready to go?"

"No, you're fine. They've just poured a drink and Dad's got to go home in a few minutes. There's a guy coming round to give him a current market valuation of the farm."

"Oh?" I said, puzzled.

"Yeah, if we're going in together, we need to do it fifty-fifty, otherwise our Ronnie will accuse me of robbing her inheritance."

I laughed. I knew he was right. Ronnie, his sister, was a tight-fisted, money grabber. We'd never really hit it off. I suspected she'd had her eye on Jonathan before I came along and scuppered her plans.

"So it'll be just us for the grand tour," he continued.

"Dunno about grand but that's fine," I said, my stomach fluttering at the thought of being in the truck with him, alone. I didn't know if I could cope with another crazy sensation on top of the already teetering pile of guilt, paranoia and dread.

David left once he finished his tea. They'd all discussed a price for the farm and everyone seemed happy with the deal. Michael intended to take over next Monday. He'd pay a nominal rent until the subdivision was through and he'd buy all the stock and livestock at cost.

I thought they were getting a bloody good deal, but I wasn't complaining. It would be fantastic not to have the headache of the farm any more.

"Right then, you ready?" I asked.

Michael stood up and took the cups to the kitchen.

"Very house-trained," I teased.

"You didn't meet my wife, did you?"

"No. I take it she was a tough nut?"

"That's being mild."

"Okay, Em, be good for Grandad, I won't be long."

I glanced around the room—no sign of her.

"Emily?" I raised my eyes to the ceiling and exhaled loudly.

"Hang on a minute," I said to Michael. I could hear giggling coming from behind the sofa again. "Right, Emily. Come out. Now!"

There were a few bumps and thuds before Emily stomped out wearing a pair of men's shoes.

"Where did they come from?" I asked as the answer dawned on me.

"They're Alex's," she said.

I remembered taking them off him after he had fallen asleep.

"Take them off!" I snapped, adrenalin surging through my veins.

"Aww."

"Off!"

She slipped out of the shoes and handed me her drawing. A person with lots of curly brown hair and red scribbles all over the chest.

"What's this, Em?" I asked, horrified.

"You."

"Then what's all this red stuff?"

"Blood."

My heart leapt out of my chest. I glanced at Frank before placing the drawing in front of him on the table.

"I don't have time now, but we'll discuss this later. Now you be good for Grandad."

CHAPTER 35

I gave Michael the promised tour of the farm, pointing out the existing boundary plus where we intended the new boundary to be. We strolled around the henhouse and introduced him to the hens. These girls were the only things I'd miss about the farm—I'd grown quite fond of them.

The cattle had never really been my thing, and when Michael asked me a question about them I looked at him blankly and shrugged. "You'll have to ask Frank. I'm sorry."

Next stop, the pigsty. I thought I might scream as Michael looked around.

He seemed happy with everything. The pigs squealed to be fed again which made my stomach lurch.

"Are you okay? You look very pale?" Michael asked.

"I hate pigs."

"Do you? I love them."

I shuddered and headed over to the butchery. He and his dad were planning to set up a local home kill and butchery service.

He inspected all the tools and, considering the smile on his face, seemed impressed. "When was it last used?"

"Dunno." My mind flashed up the image of Alex flailing

around, one arm gone and the other grasping me before being pinned to the wall. My eyes rested on the hook. I froze, horrified to see blood and tissue still attached to it.

My hand grasped my locket. "I've gotta get out of here." I spun around and raced to the door.

"It does stink a bit," he said, amused, and followed me out. "Are you all right?"

"Fine." The cold air was exactly what I needed. "Okay, so if you're satisfied?" I said, looking down at my mum's locket, dangling from my fingers. The chain had snapped.

"Perfectly, thank you."

I tucked the locket into my pocket. "I've got to get back to the clinic to relieve Steph for lunch. Shall I drop you home?"

"I can walk if it's easier."

"It's no problem. I'll drop you."

We got back into the truck.

"So you're taking control on Monday?" I asked.

He nodded. "Yeah. You don't mind, do you?"

"What do you think? I can't bloody well wait."

"I thought so. You've got a lot going on."

"It should be okay now."

"And we'll be neighbours," he said.

"Yes," I said, not really knowing what he was getting at.

I pulled up outside his parent's house.

"Thanks, Victoria," he said. His gaze didn't leave my mouth, making me self-conscious. He stayed a half second too long and licked his lips before jumping from the truck.

My heart raced. What just happened? I wasn't ready for feeling like this. I definitely didn't expect it. Yet I felt lighter than I had in ages. I took a few deep breaths before driving back to the clinic.

Stephanie and Sally-Ann were laughing as I walked in.

"What's so funny?"

"I was telling Sal about Mrs Taylor and Fifi yesterday. Did Frank get hold of you?"

"Frank? What for?"

"Dunno, he rang a few minutes ago."

"Rang here?" I picked up the phone and dialled the house. "Shit, no answer."

"I'm going over there now," Steph said. "I need to pick up my handbag, so I'll check on them I'm sure it's nothing. He didn't seem upset or anything."

"Okay, call me if …" I was over-reacting.

"I will. Back soon," Steph gripped my shoulder, then left.

"Have you had a break, Sal?" My voice sounded normal again.

She nodded. "We had a cup of coffee and a biscuit."

"What do you want for lunch? I bet you didn't bring anything did you?"

"No, but I'm okay."

"Don't be silly. I'll make you a sandwich when Steph gets back," I said. "Have there been any customers this morning?"

"Somebody came in for some antihis—antihismins—something like that for his dog."

"Antihistamines?"

"Yeah, antihistamines."

"Any calls?"

"Just the one from your father-in-law."

I nodded. "How did you get on with Steph?"

"She's lovely. I can't believe she's going out with that sleazy Steve, though."

"Oh. She told you? You don't mind?"

"Mind? You must be joking. I only agreed to go out with him because he kept asking me. I felt sorry for him, and it'd been ages since I'd been out for dinner."

"Oh well, he's too old for you anyway. You need someone your own age."

"Like that Alex bloke."

"Yeah, like that." I began rummaging through the drawer as though I'd misplaced something.

"Steph said he's not here any more," Sal continued.

"Who? Oh, Alex. Yeah that's right." I itched to change the subject. "Did Steph show you how to record payments?"

"Yeah, briefly. She said she'd get me to do it when we had one to record."

"Good."

The phone rang. I nodded at Sally-Ann. "Okay, here you go."

She picked up the phone. "Farm vet's. This is Sally-Ann."

I continued nodding and smiling.

"No, it's Sally-Ann, she is, hold on please." She placed her hand over the receiver. "It's someone for you."

"Hello, Victoria speaking."

"Vic, Angela Anderson here. Have you seen the news?"

"No, why?"

"That young guy, the one you've got working for you, what's his name?"

"Alex?"

"What's his full name?"

"Alexander Snow, why?"

"Well there's an Alexander Finnegan on the news right now, he's the spit of him."

I reached for the remote and changed the channel from the continual local adverts. "What channel?"

"One."

A second later Alex's lovely face stared back at me.

"Oh my God. What's he done?" I said.

"Is it him?"

"Yes, shush a minute."

... and to recap. He is dangerous. Do not approach him. I repeat, do not approach him.

"What's he done, Angela?"

"He's only gone and killed his whole family in America. They've just had a tipoff that he's living around here."

"I've gotta go …" I left the phone dangling and ran from the clinic. I didn't bother with the truck and ran to the house.

I burst through the front door. "Hello?" I called.

Silence.

Hello, Frank? Emily?" Emily's giggles came from the snug. Still playing hide and seek no doubt.

"Frank?" I popped my head into the kitchen.

Stephanie sat half-on, half-off a dining chair. Her head lay on the table. Vacant eyes stared at nothing—a gaping wound in her neck.

She was dead.

CHAPTER 36

I couldn't move.

Could barely breathe.

Found it impossible to tear my eyes from the awful scene before me. A bump from the snug followed by more giggles compelled my feet forwards. I slowly shoved the door open and braced myself.

All my fears were realised.

Frank lay on the floor on his back. Emily straddled him. Striking him repeatedly with a large carving knife.

"Emily!" I screamed.

"Hi, Mummy." She giggled again. Her eyes flashed evil as she lunged for me, the blade barely missing my face.

I grabbed her by the arm and twisted her little hand until she dropped the knife. An inhuman sound escaped her.

"What have you done? What have you done, Em?"

"We were playing hide and seek."

She dug her nails into my hand and I twisted her wrist again.

"Arrgh, you're hurting me."

"What have you done, Em? What have you done?"

My legs gave out on me and I fell to the ground, dragging Emily with me.

"Mummy?" She suddenly seemed normal again. "Mummy, what's wrong?"

I managed to get to my feet and pulled her from the room and over to the stairs. I had no idea what to do.

"Upstairs, Em," I said, still holding both of her wrists until we got to her room. "Take your clothes off, Emily."

"What's this? Why is it red?" She clearly couldn't remember what she'd done.

"Take them off. Now!"

I shoved her towards the bed, and got a pair of trousers and a top from the pile of ironing on the top of the chest of drawers. "Get changed," I said. "I'll be back in a minute."

I closed her door and ran back to my bedroom where I found a pair of tights in my bedside drawer and raced back to Emily's room. I tied the tights to her door handle and then to the door handle of Steph's room next door before running back downstairs.

The knife lay where it had fallen, on the floor of the snug. I rubbed the handle with the sleeve of my sweatshirt. I had to get Emily's fingerprints off it. I would say that I'd murdered Steph and Frank if I had to, but I couldn't allow them to take Emily away, to spend the rest of her life locked up like a monster.

I had just picked up the phone to call the police when I heard sirens. I ran back upstairs to Emily, untied the tights and found her lying on the bed. I knelt at her side and wrapped my arms around her tightly.

"What happened, Mummy?"

"I don't know, my baby."

The sirens came to a stop on the driveway and the sound of police radios surrounded the house. The front door wasn't locked and after a few bangs, they crashed it open. I walked to the top of the stairs. The hallway heaved with uniformed officers.

"You're too late," I said. "They're dead."

They all stopped talking, probably stopped breathing, as they looked up at me.

"Where is he?" a tall, burly cop asked.

"Who?" I asked, puzzled.

"Alexander Finnegan. Where is he, miss?"

I'd forgotten all about Alex. Of course he was the reason they were here. "He's gone."

The cops went off in different directions. There were several shouts as they found the bodies. "Can you come down, miss?" the same officer asked.

"I'd rather not right now. My daughter is up here—she's not well. I just came home and found them all. She's the only one still alive." Which was the truth—of sorts.

An officer came through to the hallway. "Two dead and no sign of the suspect down here. We need to search upstairs but it looks like it's just the same as before." Several officers ran up the stairs and searched through all the rooms.

Emily began to scream when they opened her door, but I ran in behind them and pulled her to me.

CHAPTER 37

The police were like an army of ants crawling through the place. They paid no attention to Emily and me, giving me time to get my thoughts in order.

They were obviously in no doubt that Alex was responsible. Let's face it, who would believe a six-year-old girl could be a cold-blooded killer? I had only just left the clinic and had a watertight alibi, so I couldn't be a suspect.

Everybody knew that Alex had left under a cloud after attacking Frank. Sweet Alex, who we thought couldn't ever hurt a fly, had actually murdered his entire family. And now, in a round-about way, he had murdered mine.

It struck me that every single person I cared about was gone—except, of course, for Emily, and that was only a matter of time.

I glanced down at the pathetic and terrified little girl in my arms. There were no longer any signs of the monster I'd witnessed earlier. In fact, if it wasn't for the dead bodies about the place, I'd think I imagined the whole thing.

A commotion outside alerted me that Lyn had arrived. The police wouldn't allow her to enter the crime scene and advised her to take me to her house. A uniformed policewoman assisted me downstairs with Emily. My legs felt like jelly, and I struggled to stay upright.

At the sight of Lyn, the tears began to flow. She pulled me into her arms and I shook uncontrollably, teeth chattering as though freezing cold.

Once in Lyn's car, I noticed Emily's hands and fingernails were still covered in blood and quickly dragged her to me again. I insisted on us both having a bath as soon as we arrived at Lyn's house and I scrubbed my daughter, almost ripping her skin off.

Dazed, Emily took everything I did without comment or complaint. I wondered how much she actually remembered and how much she'd blocked out.

We stayed with Lyn, Dave and Michael for a few days. I wouldn't allow Emily out of my sight in case she went on another killing spree. I now knew what she was capable of, but the others didn't. I couldn't wait to get her back home.

I functioned through a kind of numbing haze. Focused on Emily. Other than that, I wouldn't let myself think, knowing as soon as I let myself grieve for Frank and Steph, my guard would be down, raising the risk of getting found out.

The police were more than certain Alex had carried out the murders, especially when they found a notepad under his mattress with all our names listed. Jonathan's had been scribbled out. They were convinced Alex had caused his accident. They said Emily and I were lucky, as our names had also been on the list.

Michael still intended to take over the running of the farm, and I needed him to, now more than ever. However, I needed to do one more thing before that would be possible. So on Saturday morning, I made my excuses and left Emily with Lyn while I cleaned the pigsty one last time.

The funerals were to take place next week. Lyn and Dave had been fantastic and organised everything for Frank. It was one less thing for me to worry about. He would be buried in the same plot as his wife.

Steph would be buried in Manchester, and her distraught parents had arranged everything. I hated the thought of seeing them, but I owed it to my dear friend to go.

CHAPTER 38

FOUR MONTHS LATER

I stroked Emily's forehead and she turned her face towards me, her eyes flickering open.

"Hi, Mummy," she whispered.

"Hello, my precious girl. How are you feeling?"

"Tired." Her voice no more than a squeak.

"I know, sweetie. It's okay. You go back to sleep."

"Don't go."

"I'm staying right here. Don't worry." I placed her hand back inside the bedclothes.

She smiled at me and my heart contracted.

It had only been four months.

Four months since Alex, four months since Frank and Steph, four months of nightmares and utterly wretched loneliness.

I had contemplated confessing all, but there would be nobody to care for my sick daughter if I had. I felt immense guilt, but figured I'd paid for my sins in a roundabout way. Once Emily died, who knows?

Emily had begun to feel sick a lot earlier this time. She'd hardly left her bed for the past two weeks, and was living on liquid meal replacements as she had no appetite. Doctor Davies said a feeding tube might be necessary soon, but I wanted to hold off on that as long as possible.

The change in her breathing indicated she slept once again.

I walked to the window and had to squint my eyes from the glare of the stark white snow that had fallen overnight.

A scraping sound, the sound of metal on concrete, had me puzzled and I stretched to see what was making the noise.

Michael shovelled snow away from the path at the front of the house.

I felt grateful for his concern and the way he always seemed to be one step ahead of me, always thinking of ways he could make my life easier without muscling in and making a nuisance of himself. I appreciated his friendship.

I heard the front door open and Sally-Ann appeared out on the path next to Michael, handing him a cup of coffee.

Michael removed his gloves, balanced them on the concrete lion ornament by the front door, and gratefully accepted the steaming mug.

Sally-Ann had been a great help, staying with me since the funerals. I hadn't a clue what I'd do without these two special people in my life.

"Mummy?"

Her voice was so quiet I thought I must have imagined it, until Emily added, "I need some more special medicine. Please, Mummy."

My heart missed a beat. I'd resigned myself to the fact that I would lose my daughter very soon, but I hadn't realised how difficult it would be, knowing I could actually fix her for a while longer.

I'd thought of very little else lately.

Sally-Ann's tinkling laughter caught my attention and I glanced out at her once more before answering.

"I'll try, sweetie. I'll try."

EPILOGUE

THREE MONTHS LATER

Michael breezed into the kitchen, arms laden with goodies which he placed on the bench top.

"Two bottles of bubbly for you, fillet steak for me and a huge bar of chocolate for the invalid … where is she, by the way?" he asked, glancing round.

"Upstairs in her room. She should be down shortly," I said.

"Good, and is she feeling any better?"

"I think so. She said she's looking forward to everyone coming," I said. "I, on the other hand, am not. Having a barbecue wasn't one of your best suggestions, Michael."

"Why not? You're not having second thoughts, are you?" His eyebrows furrowed.

"It's been ages since I entertained and I feel jittery at the thought of everyone here."

"Nonsense, it's only Mum and Dad and the Andersons—hardly everyone. We'll save that for next time." He smirked.

I flicked the tea towel at him and laughed.

"Okay, Mum said she's bringing potato salad and a dessert. Is there anything you want me to be getting on with?"

"The music. I don't have much of a selection."

Michael smiled, held up one finger and with his other hand, rummaged in his jeans pocket, and produced an iPod.

"Is there anything you haven't thought of?" I laughed again.

"I don't think so. I'm determined we'll have a great time." He reached for my hand and pulled me towards him, expertly wedging me between him and the kitchen units.

I looked up into his lovely eyes and he bent in towards me, our noses touching.

"Are you okay?" he asked softly.

"I am now," I said, before he kissed me deeply.

The sound of someone running down the stairs made us spring apart and I turned rapidly back to the stove top, my face on fire.

We'd been seeing each other for a few weeks but we'd decided to keep it to ourselves for the time being.

"Here she is," Michael said. "How are you feeling, love?"

"Better, thanks."

"You still look peaky. Are you sure you're up to this?" I said.

"Yeah. It's just a cold," Sally-Ann replied. "I'll be fine."

"Okay, well don't feel you need to be here if you'd rather go back to bed," I said.

"Don't worry, I won't."

I turned my back on them and began peeling potatoes.

Sal had just signed up at the University of Glasgow for a five year Veterinary course, which I insisted on paying for. It was no skin off my nose—Frank had left me very well off, and let's face it, I didn't have anything else to spend the money on.

I worried about her going, but knew it would be the making of her. She would leave in September and be away term time.

Emily had passed away in her sleep on Monday the twelfth of May. It came as a huge relief. I couldn't bear watching her suffer for one moment longer. Plus, the temptation to fix her one last time had haunted me twenty-four-seven. Several times I had to stop myself eyeing Sally-Ann up.

It would have been so easy. But I hadn't seriously considered it, not really.

I still felt immense guilt for the deaths of my family. Jonathan had been out of my hands, but Frank and Steph would be here now had we not tried to play God.

I could talk myself into believing they all deserved it, Shane, Hector, Alex, and even Frank—but I couldn't justify Steph. She'd been totally innocent.

Michael cleared his throat, making me jump.

"Before everyone gets here, I want to make a toast," he said as he popped the cork on the sparkling wine and poured three glasses.

I turned to face him, wiping my hands on a towel.

"Okay, now we all know it's been a terrible year."

I glanced away, unsure where he intended to go with this.

"I realise how difficult planning for tonight has been for you, Vicki, and I know I bullied you into it."

I laughed and nodded, as tears filled my eyes.

"But I want to tell you how proud I am that you're taking this step."

"Hear! Hear!" Sally-Ann said.

I smiled and raised my glass towards him. Our eyes locked. Then he turned to face the far wall and the cluster of photo frames that adorned it.

"To loved ones, past and present," Mike said.

"To loved ones," Sally-Ann and I both repeated.

As we raised our glasses and drank, my eyes lingered on each image for a few seconds.

Jonathan, Frank, Steph and my beautiful Emily."

The End

ALSO BY NETTA NEWBOUND

Amanda Flynn's life is falling apart. Her spineless cheating husband has taken her beloved children. Her paedophile father, who went to prison vowing revenge, has been abruptly released. And now someone in the shadows is watching her every move.

When one by one her father and his cohorts turn up dead, Amanda finds herself at the centre of several murder investigations—with no alibi and a diagnosis of Multiple Personality Disorder. Abandoned, scared and fighting to clear her name as more and more damning evidence comes to light, Amanda begins to doubt her own sanity.

Could she really be a brutal killer?

A gripping psychological thriller not to be missed...

An Edge of your Seat Psychological Thriller Novel

For Melissa May, happily married to Gavin for the best part of thirty years, life couldn't get much better. Her world is ripped apart when she discovers Gavin is HIV positive. The shock of his duplicity and irresponsible behaviour re-awakens a psychiatric condition Melissa has battled since childhood. Fuelled by rage and a heightened sense of right and wrong, Melissa takes matters into her own hands.

Homicide detective Adam Stanley is investigating what appear to be several random murders. When evidence comes to light, linking the victims, the case seems cut and dried and an arrest is made. However, despite all the damning evidence, including a detailed confession, Adam is certain the killer is still out there. Now all he has to do is prove it.

An Edge of your Seat Psychological Thriller Novel

Detective Inspector Adam Stanley returns to face his most challenging case yet. Someone is randomly killing ordinary Pinevale citizens. Each time DI Stanley gets close to the killer, the killer turns up dead—the next victim in someone's crazy game.

Meanwhile, his girlfriend's brother, Andrew, currently on remand for murder, escapes and kidnaps his own 11-year-old daughter. However, tragedy strikes, leaving the girl in grave danger.

Suffering a potentially fatal blow himself, how can DI Stanley possibly save anyone?

A Compelling Psychological Thriller Novel.

In this fast-moving suspense novel, Detective Adam Stanley searches for Miles Muldoon, a hardworking, career-minded businessman, and Pinevale's latest serial killer.

Evidence puts Muldoon at each scene giving the police a prima facie case against him.

But as the body count rises, and their suspect begins taunting them, this seemingly simple case develops into something far more personal when Muldoon turns his attention to Adam and his family.

Ghost Writer is a 24,000 word novella.

Bestselling thriller author Natalie Cooper has a crippling case of writer's block. With her deadline looming, she finds the only way she can write is by ditching her laptop and reverting back to pen and paper. But the story which flows from the pen is not just another work of fiction.

Unbeknown to her, a gang of powerful and deadly criminals will stop at nothing to prevent the book being written.

Will Natalie manage to finish the story and expose the truth before it's too late? Or could the only final chapter she faces be her own?

A Gripping and Incredibly Moving Psychological Suspense Novel

When Geraldine MacIntyre's marriage falls apart, she returns to her childhood home expecting her mother to welcome her with open arms. Instead, she finds all is not as it should be with her parents.

James Dunn, a successful private investigator and crime writer, is also back in his hometown, to help solve a recent spate of vicious rapes. He is thrilled to discover his ex-classmate, and love of his life, Geraldine, is back, minus the hubby, and sets out to get the girl. However, he isn't the only interested bachelor in the quaint, country village. Has he left it too late?

Embellished Deception is a thrilling, heart-wrenching and thought provoking story of love, loss and deceit.

An Edge of your Seat Psychological Thriller Novel

Geraldine and baby Grace arrive in Nottingham to begin their new life with author James Dunn.

Lee Barnes, James' best friend and neighbour, is awaiting the imminent release of his wife, Lydia, who has served six years for infanticide. But he's not as prepared as he thought. In a last ditch effort to make things as perfect as possible his already troubled life takes a nose dive.

Geraldine and James combine their wits to investigate several historical, unsolved murders for James' latest book. James is impressed by her keen eye and instincts. However, because of her inability to keep her mouth shut, Geri, once again, finds herself the target of a crazed and vengeful killer.

A Gripping Psychological Suspense Novel.

Geri and James return in their most explosive adventure to date.

When next door neighbour, Lydia, gives birth to her second healthy baby boy, James and Geri pray their friend can finally be happy and at peace. But, little do they know Lydia's troubles are far from over.

Meanwhile, Geri is researching several historic, unsolved murders for James' new book. She discovers one of the prime suspects now resides in Spring Pines Retirement Village, the scene of not one, but two recent killings.

Although the police reject the theory, Geri is convinced the cold case they're researching is linked to the recent murders. But how? Will she regret delving so deeply into the past?

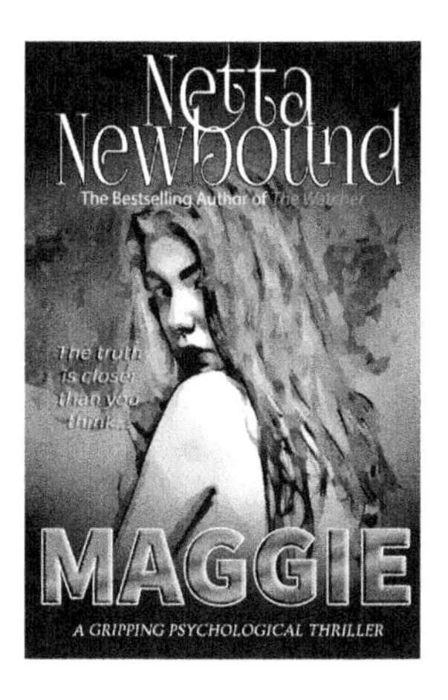

Do you love **gripping psychological thrillers** full of twists and turns? If so you'll love **best-selling** author Netta Newbound's stunning new *Maggie*.

When sixteen-year-old Maggie Simms' mum loses her battle with cancer, the only family she has left is her **abusive stepfather**, Kenny.

Horrified to discover he intends to continue his nightly abuse, Maggie is **driven to put a stop to him once and for all**.

However, she **finds her troubles are only just beginning** when several of her closest allies are killed.

Although nothing seems to be linking the deaths, Maggie believes she is jinxed.

Why are the people she cares about being targeted?

And who is really behind the murders?

Sometimes the truth is closer than you think.

THE BEST-SELLING SERIAL KILLER THRILLER THAT EVERYONE IS TALKING ABOUT

Life couldn't get much better for Hannah. She accepts her dream job in Manchester, and easily makes friends with her new neighbours.

When she becomes romantically involved with her boss, she can't believe her luck. But things are about to take a grisly turn.

As her colleagues and neighbours are killed off one by one, Hannah's idyllic life starts to fall apart. But when her mother becomes the next victim, the connection to Hannah is all too real.

Who is watching her every move?

Will the police discover the real killer in time?

Hannah is about to learn that appearances can be deceptive.

An Edge of your Seat Psychological Thriller Novella

All her life twenty-two-year-old Ruby Fitzroy's annoyingly over protective mother has believed the worst will befall one of her two daughters. Sick and tired of living in fear, Ruby arranges a date without her mother's knowledge.

On first impressions, charming and sensitive Cody Strong seems perfect. When they visit his home overlooking the Welsh coast, she meets his delightful father Steve and brother Kyle. But it isn't long before she discovers all is not as it seems.

After a shocking turn of events, Ruby's world is blown apart. Terrified and desperate, she prepares to face her darkest hour yet.

Will she ever escape this nightmare?

ACKNOWLEDGMENTS

As always, I need to mention Paul, my long suffering husband. Your support means the world to me.

To my wonderful critique partners Susan, Marco, Jay, Sandra & Serena—you're the best.

To Mel, Ross, and all my friends and fellow authors—thanks so much for letting me bend your ear.

The wonderful ARC group – you're awesome.

To all the team at Junction Publishing - you are amazing!

And finally. To my wonderful family, especially Joshua, David, AJ, and Marley, my lovely grandsons, who give me immense joy. I am truly blessed.

ABOUT THE AUTHOR

My name's Netta Newbound. I write thrillers in many different styles — some grittier than others. The Cold Case Files have a slightly lighter tone. I also write a series set in London, which features one of my favourite characters, Detective Adam Stanley. My standalone books, The Watcher, Maggie, My Sister's Daughter and An Impossible Dilemma, are not for the faint hearted, and it seems you either love them or hate them—I'd love to know what you think.

If you would like to be informed when my new books are released, visit my website: www.nettanewbound.com and sign up for the newsletter.

This is a PRIVATE list and I promise you I will only send emails when a new book is released or a book goes on sale.

If you would like to get in touch, you can contact me via Facebook or Twitter. I'd love to hear from you and try to respond to everyone.